ONE WITH THE Waves

a novel

Vezna Andrews

SANTA
MONICA
PRESS
TEEN

Published by:
Santa Monica Press LLC
P.O. Box 850
Solana Beach, CA 92075
1-800-784-9553
www.santamonicapress.com
books@santamonicapress.com

Printed in the United States

Santa Monica Press books are available at special quantity discounts when purchased in bulk by corporations, organizations, or groups. Please call our Special Sales department at 1-800-784-9553.

ISBN-13 978-1-59580-122-7
Ebook ISBN-13 978-1-59580-769-4

Publisher's Cataloging-in-Publication data

Names: Andrews, Vezna, author.
Title: One with the waves / by Vezna Andrews.
Description: Solana Beach, CA: Santa Monica Press, 2023.
Identifiers: ISBN: 978-1-59580-122-7 (print) | 978-1-59580-769-4 (ebook)
Subjects: LCSH Surfing--Fiction. | Family life--Fiction. | California--History--20th century--Fiction. | Bildungsroman. | BISAC YOUNG ADULT FICTION / Sports & Recreation / Water Sports | YOUNG ADULT FICTION / Coming of Age | YOUNG ADULT FICTION / Historical / United States / 20th Century
Classification: LCC PS3601.N552775 O64 2023 | DDC 813.6--dc23

Cover and interior design and production by Future Studio
Title design by Tony Gold
Cover photo: ©Keolafirsov/Dreamstime.com

For Jack

&

For my father, Janusz,
and all of us you left too soon

"Surfing frees everything up. It's just the best soul fix. Life should be stress-free, and that's what surfing is all about. It's something you do in your sleep, with your eyes closed; it's something you'll constantly embrace and be passionate about, and whatever it takes, you're gonna do it, because nothing else in the world can give you that kind of self-esteem."

—**Rell Kapolioka'ehukai Sunn,**
Surfer magazine, 1995

"The inner self is a great place. It's closer than most people think and it is nearly perfect. When a person can find the way to access this wonderful state at will, there is no worry about being caught inside again. Surfing has an endless supply of lessons to teach us. Surf realization is about believing those lessons can, and should, be applied to life."

—**Gerry Lopez,** *Surf Is Where You Find It*

"Really, I'm sure I was a seal in another world because I'm so fond of the water."

—**Princess Ka'iulani,** *The Sun*, October 24, 1897

ONE

March 1983

It was black outside the oval windows. Then there were bright lights, and a dark void loomed beneath me. *That must be the ocean,* I thought, swallowing into the tense pit of my stomach. As the plane began to lower in the haze, the lights crossed, forming stars, and then came into focus, becoming an expansive grid, a glowing graph of a large city. It seemed as big as the one I'd just left. But as the plane angled for landing, the expanse of blackness seemed to go on to infinity. *It is the ocean!*

My mind flooded with images from a month ago. When it turned black outside the hospital window, Dad urged me and Mom to go home and get some sleep. Under the fluorescent lights, his skin looked greenish. It hurt to look at his diminished body, all skin and bones. When I said goodbye, he smiled at me, his brown eyes full of affection and desperation at the same time. With a jolt that pierced my heart, I felt the devotion he'd had for me ever since I was a baby. I could still feel him looking at me like that now, a month later. Panic gripped my insides with a realization: *It was the last time I saw him.*

Up until he died, I was in denial, thinking he'd get well. It seemed like he'd been sick for a long time, though he was only diagnosed a little over two years ago, after New Year's. Now it seemed like it had all happened so fast. Too fast. I closed my eyes, my sweatshirt hood covering my face from the aisle, and tried to rest, leaning uncomfortably against the window of the airplane.

Home. *I'm leaving the only home I've ever known.* Out of a corner window of the loft on a clear day, there was a speck of blue in the distance—the Hudson River. The Hudson was so polluted that no one was allowed to swim in it. If they did, they'd get probably get very sick. Dad told me about a police diver that dove into the Hudson. He wore a full diving suit and face mask, covering his whole body. His suit hit a snag on something, which tore a hole, and he died mysteriously a week later.

The Hudson flowed out to a bay, eventually. It was a two-hour subway ride to Coney Island, where the beach was far from ideal, littered with trash and used needles. I knew that whales, dolphins, and seals lived in the Atlantic, though I never saw them. *What will it be like living by the ocean? Will I see a whale?* The only whales I'd seen were fake, at the Museum of Natural History; a sperm whale battling a giant squid, and a blue whale the length of a city block. I'd walked under it with Dad.

Since I was born, Dad had taken care of me, my constant companion when I was little; tall and sturdy, with a brown scruffy beard and a sense of calm. Sheltered in his arms, I was his Little Bear. He called me Misiu (pronounced "mee-shoe"), a Polish word meaning "little bear" or "sweetie," used to express affection for those dear to you. I called him Dad or Misiek (pronounced "mee-shehk") meaning "bear" or "big teddy bear of a guy." I used to pretend his study was a bear cave. I'd put a big sheet over his desk and pillows inside it to form cave walls. We'd play this game until I fell asleep at his feet, snug in the cave while he worked at his desk.

When I was born, Dad quit his teaching job at Fordham University to stay home with me, so Mom could keep her job. It was Dad who changed my diaper, gave me baths, and fed me. It was Dad who took me to preschool, and Dad who picked me up every day. It was Dad's shoulder I cried on, and because I didn't have a brother or sister, it was Dad who played with me. I always confided in Dad. We were really close. All through middle school nothing changed between us, until the end of eighth grade when he got diagnosed and then I started high school.

Each night Dad was in the hospital, I'd lean out the window from the top of the building we lived in. Through the murky gray I strained to see the stars, but the haze from the city lights screened them out. The dirty air, a thick, glowing mist, hovered everywhere. Tall buildings with illuminated windows made up the city blocks, the streets, their lines, a continual grid in the dark. The tallest one, the Empire State Building, loomed over all, its antenna piercing the smog. Down in the street, an empty bus, lit from inside, flew by, leaving plastic bags and other trash in its wake. I'd felt like that out-of-service bus, flying through the city on automatic, not stopping, empty but for a light. A hope.

I remember sitting alone on the cold radiator, twelve stories high, unable to sleep. Dad told me they never built thirteen stories in the city due to superstition. It was an unlucky number. Thirteen *was* the worst year. I was thirteen when we found out Dad had cancer. An ambulance screamed over car horns honking in the street. I gripped the window ledge, my fingers going numb. *Is Dad up?* I hoped he wasn't in too much pain, but I knew that was why they were giving him morphine. I wished he was home, so we could talk.

My heart grew heavy at the thought of cement covering the entire island. It smothered all nature. *What was it like when it was all green?* I wondered. *Before the Dutch colonized the Hudson, when only the Native Americans lived here, what wild animals roamed free?* Now rats roamed the subways underground, and dirty pigeons huddled in the streets. Dad called them "rat-birds."

I shuddered. That night, I thought I'd see Dad after school the next day, like always.

Now I sat alone on the plane. I couldn't sleep the whole flight, agonizing in my seat. The constant mechanical hum droned on, as thoughts about what California would be like gnawed at me. I searched out the airplane window for the moon in the sky, but couldn't find it. In my mind, I heard Dad say, "Where's that moon I love?" And when he saw it, he'd say, "Ah, there it is." Then he'd look into my eyes and say, "I love you more than the moon, Misiu."

Hot tears streamed down my cheek. I wiped them off with my hand and re-covered my face with my sweatshirt hood, trying again to rest against the airplane window. I closed my eyes. I pictured the entire island of Manhattan covered in gray cement. As I finally drifted to sleep, the pavement cracked open and water gurgled out. The broken concrete spread its fingers as green sprouted up in places. Soon there was no gray; it was all green and blue. Water formed tributaries along banks of grasses, feeding into rivers that led to the ocean.

A loud bang from the belly of the plane rang out over its roar. The flight attendant announced on the loudspeaker that we were making our final descent. I gripped the armrest as the plane dropped, descending over the airfield.

When we finally landed and taxied to the gate, I had to wait until everyone else got off because I was a minor flying alone. *What a joke.* I'd been taking the subway in New York

City by myself since I was eight. When the flight attendant gave the okay, I walked off the empty plane and through the tunnel ramp. I spotted my aunt's husband, Charlie, who we called Uncle Charlie, talking to another flight attendant. When he saw me, he jumped up and down, wide-eyed and smiling, waving excitedly.

"Hey there, Ellie Bo-Belly!" he called out. I was surprised to hear him call me that; he hadn't since I was a kid. Now he was jumping from one foot to the other. I couldn't help but crack a smile, he looked so silly. His auburn hair was cut very short, and his ears stuck out.

"Hi, Uncle Charlie."

He sized me up. "Geez, you've grown a lot!" He went in for a hug and, to my surprise, picked me up and tried to swing me around, like he did when I was little.

"Ahh!" I yelped as he swung me in a half circle. It was awkward.

He put me down. "California, here she comes! Uh-oh, watch out, she's gonna be surfin' and skatin' and gettin' into trouble—just like I did."

He aimed the last part at the flight attendant, a pretty woman with dark brown skin, her hair in a braided style, who raised her eyebrows and asked me, "You sure this is your uncle? He acts like a kid!" She turned to him. "Okay, now, I need to see some I.D."

"Here ya go. You can see for yourself, I'm an old man." He gave me a big wink. Uncle Charlie wasn't really old; he was only forty, two years older than my mom. I studied his freckled, suntanned face, following the lines etched under his cheeks, along the side of his long nose, to the brightest blue eyes I'd ever known. From the corners of his eyes, laugh lines radiated out. He had the ruddy complexion of a once-pale redhead who'd spent a lot of time outdoors.

The flight attendant took his driver's license. "Charles MacGreggor?" she read aloud.

"Yes, ma'am. But you can call me Charlie."

She examined the license for a slow minute, then handed him a pen. "Sign here please, Charlie." He scribbled his name on the form, then he turned to me.

"Is this all you got?" He took my knapsack off my back.

"No, I've got a suitcase."

"It'll be in baggage, downstairs," the flight attendant said. "Safe travels, girl."

"Thanks," I said as we walked away. "Bye."

As we stepped onto an escalator going down, I asked, "Where's Aunt Jen?"

"Oh, I imagine she's waiting up for you at home. She's usually in bed by now, so she can be up to surf at sunup. I usually am, too, but today I was workin' late at the station, so I figured I'd swing by and pick you up, Ellie Bo-Belly!"

"You don't need to call me that. I'm not a kid anymore."

"Oh, but I do! Wait, are you embarrassed? I'm sorry, maybe you'd prefer a new nickname." He put his hand up to his mouth, mocking shock.

"Just Ellie's fine."

"Just Ellie? Nope, not happenin', Ellie Bo-Belly." He winked at me with a cheeky grin.

I had to take off my sweatshirt when we walked outside the airport—I was sweating. *How weird. Back home it was hailing snow pellets.* Striving to keep up with my uncle's gait, I stumbled. I tried to focus on my surroundings, but all the colors blurred into one another. The headlights from a stream of buses and cars going by as we crossed over to the parking lot were too bright. I looked down, resting my eyes on the dark pavement below.

We stopped abruptly at an old, bright-yellow Volkswagen bus with a white top. Uncle Charlie skipped ahead, his thin figure disappearing behind the back of the van. He peered around the open door, eyes wide, and stuck his tongue out and blew a raspberry. It sounded like a fart. I couldn't help but let out a chuckle, even though I could barely stand.

He loaded my bags into the VW bus, and off we went. "Be home in a jiffy," he assured me.

My weary body sunk into the seat, but I was too wired to succumb to sleep. Ironically, "The Girl from New York City" by the Beach Boys began to play on the eight-track player car stereo. As we drove in the dark, I could just make out the silhouettes of big palm trees lining the streets, which seemed odd in the middle of a city. Then the ocean appeared, an ink-blue horizon with a black sky above. The half-moon shone a bright half-circle, its reflection dancing on the dark blue sea. As Charlie swung a left, I rolled the window down and took in a deep breath of fresh ocean air, soaking in the sight of the moon aglow.

Charlie took another left, this time down a side street and then parked in front of a white fence. I could make out a small house among the shapes of trees and bushes.

"Here we are," he said cheerfully. He hopped out and ran around to open my door before I could. He held out his hand to help me down.

"I'm okay." I stepped down without his help.

"Okey dokey, Ellie Bo-Belly." Uncle Charlie went to the back of the van to get my bags.

Between the treetops was an open expanse of mid-night-blue sky with shining brilliant stars. No murky gray blocking them from sight. Reeling, I soaked up the sight of them as they beamed their light down upon me. Dad always said that our ancestors lived up in the stars. That bottomless pit of raw aching in my insides suddenly surfaced. I held my breath, desperate to know if Dad was up there now. *Dad, can you see me?*

Charlie swung past me, skipped up some stairs, and opened the gate. I followed him, focusing on the stone path beneath me. A thump startled me; he'd kicked the front door open with his foot.

Inside, the warm glow of lamps illuminated the little house, and the delicious smell of something sweet baking filled the living room. Aunt Jen greeted me, beaming a big smile. "There you are!" Her olive eyes were shining, her face suntanned and radiant. With open arms, she rushed toward me and gave me a big hug. Her brown hair cascaded in an unruly mass, soft curls brushing against my face. I softened in her embrace.

"Welcome to our home . . . well, it's yours, too, now. Welcome to your seaside home, Ellie." Her voice was steady, her words sincere. Her tone instantly grounded me.

"Yeah, welcome to the beach shack," Charlie butted in. "Watch out, it might fall over if the wind's too strong."

"Thanks," I murmured. I stepped back as a big dog that looked like a wolf pushed into me, sniffing excitedly. My body stiffened. Its wagging tail batted my leg as it circled me.

"This is Zuzu," Aunt Jen said. "She's friendly, she's just trying to say hi."

Uncle Charlie patted the dog's back. "Zuzu, calm down, girly girl." She continued to move in circles, rubbing against him each time she turned. "Oh, I missed you, too," he gushed, scratching the dogs chin.

"Oh, so you missed the dog but not me, eh?" Jen replied, giving Charlie a comical look.

He shot her a smile, a twinkle erupting in his bright eyes. "Yeah, but I missed my sweetheart even more!" He lunged forward and embraced Aunt Jen, lifting her feet off the ground and planting a big kiss on her lips. Zuzu twirled around them, her tail moving to and fro. Even after Uncle Charlie put Jen down, they stayed connected. There was an electricity between them.

My aunt turned to me, squeezing out of his arms. "He was away for three days in a row at the engine house," she explained.

"Yeah, this old geezer kind of missed this one here," Charlie added, motioning towards her with his thumb.

Jen crossed her arms. "Oh, just a little, compared to Zuzu." She turned to me. "But we've missed *you*, Ellie. It's been too long." She sat on the couch, her tender eyes searching mine. She patted the seat next to her. "Come sit down with me. How long has it been?"

I collapsed onto the sofa. "I think I was eight, last time I was here," I said softly.

"That long ago? Ah, yes, it was for the wedding. You were such a pretty flower girl—so cute. But I've seen you since then, when I visited. It's Charlie who hasn't seen you—"

"How old are you now?" Uncle Charlie interrupted.

"Fifteen. I'll be sixteen this summer."

"Fifteen! That's when I really got into surfing."

He and Jen looked at each other, then they both looked at me.

"Are you hungry?" asked my aunt. "Would you like some apple pie? I've just baked it."

My stomach was tied in knots. "No thanks." I looked around the room. The house was little, but cozy. There was a fireplace in the living room area, and a small table. The walls were painted a pale yellow, and were covered in pictures and paintings. I could see a row of tall, oblong objects in the hallway. As I focused on them, I saw that they were stacks of surfboards.

"Your room is down the hall, by the boards," Jen said. "Would you like to see?"

"Sure."

"You must be tired." Her voice was soothing. "That was a long way to travel, all the way across the country."

"Yeah," I answered faintly. *Now I'm here, in another part of the world, and I'm not just visiting—I'm going to live here. Do they really want me here, or are they just being nice?*

"Come on, I'll show you your room," my uncle beckoned with enthusiasm.

We walked down the hall and turned right, through a doorway. It was a spacious corner room, painted a pretty blue with two large windows framed by soft white curtains. Beach landscape paintings adorned the walls. A bedside lamp shone amber light onto an antique bedframe covered in a floral quilt. My grandma's crocheted blanket lay folded at its foot. Mismatched rugs were thrown over the wooden floor, painted a gray-green.

Uncle Charlie sat my bags on a bench by the corner. "Hey where's your surfboard?" he asked as he mimed looking around for something.

"I don't have one."

"Huh? Yeah you do." Grinning at me, he pointed to the hallway. "I've got one just for you! That is . . . if you want it."

"And I've got one for you after you get tired of that banana," Jen added.

"It isn't a *banana*," Charlie protested. "Just because it's yellow doesn't mean it—well, it may kind a look like a banana, but . . ." He cracked a smile. It was obvious that they were crazy about each other. Last time I'd been here, seven years ago, they'd gotten married. They seemed to be just as happy now as they were then. It had been a long time since I'd felt part of a happy home.

My stomach rumbled. "Maybe I will try some pie."

"Good!" said Jen. "It's still warm. It tastes really good with ice cream."

"Mmm . . . I like the sound of that," Charlie said with a fond look and a wink at Jen. "I'll put some wood on the fire."

Uncle Charlie made a fire, and I was glad of that. It was much warmer in California, but here by the ocean there was a chill in the air. My eyes followed the flickering as I savored each bite of pie and vanilla ice cream. I relaxed into the warmth, and when the heaviness of exhaustion overcame me, I excused myself to bed.

Aunt Jen knocked and popped her head in the door. "I had this urge to tuck you in, like I did when you were little, but I guess you're too old for that now."

"Yeah," I said. *That would be awkward.* I couldn't remember the last time my mom had tucked me in. Dad had always done that when I was little.

"Well, good night, Ellie. Sleep well."

"Thanks, good night."

She hesitated at the door. "I'm so sorry about your dad, honey," she said softly. "We're both so sorry." Her voice sounded pained. I was grateful for the dark so we couldn't see each other's faces. "Please know that Charlie and I are here for you if you want to talk about anything."

I tensed. "'Kay. Thanks." I did not want to talk.

"Love you," she added before she shut the door.

I let loose a breath. Alone in my new room, snug in bed with a new life before me, I still felt that space of emptiness inside me. It seemed like it would always be there.

Memories flooded in from the month before. I remembered how I thought I'd be able visit Dad again. It had rained all day that day. After school, I stopped at the school entrance with everyone else, transfixed by the downpour. Outside, a freshman boy tried to open an umbrella, but the wind blew it the wrong way. I braced myself, and then, clutching my red umbrella, I ran out into the storm. The wind blew it up and I tried to pull it back down, but one side had broken. I grasped its edge and kept running the three blocks to the subway, fighting the wind.

Drenched, I fled down the dark, dank steps that smelled of urine. On the subway platform, a homeless man sat on the bench talking to himself. I veered away toward the end of the platform. I dared not get too close to the edge. The electric rail had terrified me ever since I was little. I knew that if someone fell on the tracks, if they didn't get hit by the train, they'd die instantly if they touched the third rail—by a powerful electric shock. There were news stories of strangers pushing people onto the tracks. You had to have your guard up at all times.

A group of rats was searching for food on the tracks, among the garbage. As one crawled over a bottle, a flash of its bald pink tail gave me the heebie-jeebies. I knew when I saw rats that it would be a long wait till the next train, but a waft of hot wind ruffled my hair. The rats began scurrying away.

I stared deep into the subway tunnel, where it was pitch-black. A distant rumbling grew louder, and then the train thundered in as the conductor blared the horn. The brakes screeched in a high pitch, piercing my ears. I covered them with my hands to muffle the noise.

I sat down in the empty last car, facing an ad: *Virginia Slims . . . You've come a long way, baby*. A poster of a lady frozen in a smile, wearing a fur coat, holding up a cigarette. My body tensed. It was disgusting that people killed animals for fashion, and that they were going extinct because of it. A swell of rage rose in me—Dad had lung cancer. The doctors said smoking could have caused it. My gut churned at the thought that there were ads to sell things that killed you. The tobacco companies were making money, while my dad was suffering from it. I wished the graffiti that covered the subway walls would spatter over the ad.

The fluorescent lights in the empty train car were too bright. I shut my eyes and saw Dad, greenish and sick under the hospital light as I walked away. The train car rattled, bashing left and right. My fists began to sweat as I stiffened against it, trying not to worry about Dad. Metallic howls echoed through the tunnel. My heart raced, beating against my chest as if desperately trying to tell me something.

With each stop, more and more people filled the car until a mass of dark coats closed in on me, suffocating me. I pushed through to the doors as the train came screeching into my station. Just as they opened, I leapt out and ran up three flights of stairs.

The wind had eased a little. Opening my umbrella, it cast a pink hue over my hands. My soaking wet sneakers—once white, now a dirty gray—splashed water with each step. Clumped by the street gutter, trash was damming up a murky river. I leaped across it onto the sidewalk. The rain drummed onto my umbrella, muffling the honking of car horns. Pulling it down against the top of my head, I hid from the businesspeople rushing by.

When I got home, I was surprised to see Mom sitting at the table by the door. She glanced up from the teacup trembling in her hand, her expression tight with strain, eyes swelling with tears. A horrible feeling hit the pit of my stomach.

Mom stood up, clicked towards me in her high heels, and hugged me too tight. *Something isn't right*, I thought, trying to breathe.

"Aren't we going to see Dad now?" I gasped. But she didn't let go. "Mom!"

I finally broke free. She diverted her gaze to the floor. This wasn't like her; she didn't hug me often. She hated to be called Mom; she preferred Julia.

She stood, wobbly in her heels, and looked at me as if all of a sudden, she'd remembered something. "We can't." My heart pounded and I became lightheaded. Mom reached out for me. I stepped in closer, and she gripped my arms so hard they ached. With bloodshot eyes, she peered at me from behind her platinum bangs and spoke listlessly. "He's gone."

The dreaded thought whirled through me. *It can't be true!* Then it hit me. *Dad is gone. He isn't ever coming home.*

If Mom hadn't grabbed me and held me so tight, I would've fallen. Everything got blurry as a wave of nausea overtook me. I threw up all over Mom's black sweater dress. I continued to retch, but there was nothing left in me. My brain flooded with regret. *We shouldn't have left the hospital last night. Maybe we could have done something. Maybe he wouldn't have died if we were there.* But Dad always insisted we go home to get some sleep. I gasped, trying not to taste my puke. My throat burned.

I found out later that he hadn't died that night. It was the next morning while I was at school, after another blood transfusion. Mom was there with him when it happened.

My whole body grew tense. In my new bed in California, I had an overwhelming sensation that I was sinking into a deep, never-ending hole, stuck in a giant sticky web of darkness. The painful memories, like shards of glass, cut deep into me and pressed inward. It was hard to breathe. I had to get out of my head. I bolted up and rummaged through my suitcase for my Walkman, my Christmas gift that year from Mom and Dad. I'd immediately given it back to Dad so he could listen to music in the hospital. When I'd visit, I'd squeeze in next to him in the bed and we'd listen to music together, sharing the headphones.

I put on the headphones and searched the radio. I landed on 106.7 KROQ as the DJ blurted out, "Now for U2's new single for 1983, 'New Year's Day' from their just released album *War.*"

My heart dropped. Dad and I had listened to this song when it first aired in January, on my Walkman in the hospital. He'd been happy. He'd said the song was about the release of Lech Walesa, the leader of the Polish Solidarity movement, from prison. At the time, the lyrics made me happy, too. *Dad will be with us again*, I'd thought. *He'll be back home soon.* The bassline under a haunting piano melody led to the urgent wailings of both Bono and the guitar—building into an anthem of longing. *I thought I'd be with you again, Dad.* My tears flowed like a river.

I forced away the memories. In my mind's eye, I saw that dark blue horizon from the van ride here, after leaving the airport. The bright half-moon's reflection on the shiny black surface of the sea made light patterns that moved, as if dancing.

TWO

Where the Sun Shines Brighter

It's so quiet!

That was my first thought when I woke up, my eyelids fluttering against the sunlight as it gushed through the open window. The tiniest bird I'd ever seen was hovering right outside. I jumped out of bed and leaned on the ledge to get a closer look. To my delight, we were almost face to face—me and a real live hummingbird. I'd never seen one before. His bright-orange throat and rust-red and emerald-green body glittered in the sun. He stayed suspended in air a few feet away, his wings beating so fast they blurred.

"Good morning," I said out loud. With a metallic whir, he darted in a zig-zag up above me, next to a vine of hot-pink flowers. I breathed in the fresh sea air. *I'm at the beach!*

I tiptoed out of my room, walked down the hall, and made my way out of the house through the front door. The slice of ocean below me was a vibrant cobalt-blue. As I ran down the street toward it, the slice grew larger, and the hue lighter.

I crossed an empty avenue, walked down the next street to an alley, and then passed more houses until I reached a paved pathway edged with flowers. The morning sun reflected off the ocean's surface like glass in patches, glistening like a jewel. As I wandered onto the cool sand and up to the water's edge, the expanse of ocean surrounded me. The continual roar of the sea filled my ears, the surf crashing down in drumrolls. The pale-blue sky was reflected in the water below, with nearly no difference between the two. It was as if I'd come to the edge of the earth, and in front of me was only air and sea.

Little white birds were poking at the wet sand with their beaks where the water receded. When the water came in, they scurried away from it. My toe touched the water. *Freezing!* Small black dots were scattered over the horizon. As I got closer, I could make out that the dots were people sitting out there on surfboards. One figure jumped up and rode a neon-red board across my field of vision. From the horizon line, a dolphin leapt straight into the air. I gasped. Another surfaced and did a similar leap, arcing and flipping up its tail before diving under. They continued to frolic, side by side. It looked like they were very close to the surfers, who just watched as they went by.

I stood mesmerized, in awe of the wild dolphins, desperately wanting to be out there close to them. What world was this, that dolphins and surfers shared? I wanted to be a part of it. I never could have imagined that such a place existed: the polar opposite of my life in New York City. Up until now. The magical, almost angelic energy of the dolphins playing in the surf was palpable. *They're real. Right here. So close.* What secrets of the sea could I learn from them? I wanted to swim out. But the water was so icy cold.

I watched as the figures stood up and rode wave after wave. One of the surfers rode a wave all the way to shore, and then started walking toward me. A familiar voice called out: "Hey, Ellie!" The morning sun illuminated her face with orange light.

"It's you, Aunt Jen!"

She wore a glossy black wetsuit. Her hair was drenched, matted to her head, and she carried a shiny, colorful shortboard.

"Have you got your surf stoke already?"

"Huh?"

"You itchin' to get out there and surf?"

"Yeah. Did you see the dolphins?"

She nodded. "Uh-huh, a mom and her baby."

"Were you close to them?"

"Yup, they came close. I think the little one was curious. Maybe she heard you were here." She squinted as she faced the sun. "Now that's the first smile I've seen since you came. It suits you!"

I scanned the horizon line for fins, but now there were no dolphins in sight.

"I have a serious question to ask you," she announced, her face grave. "What's your favorite muffin?"

I couldn't help but crack a smile. "Ah . . . I don't know."

"Blueberry? Banana nut?"

I shrugged.

"Well, we're just going to have to find out. I've got some blueberries, bananas, carrots, apples, and nuts."

Together, we headed back up to the house. As we passed people's gardens, I soaked in all the bright colors. The bottom of Jen's shortboard reflected our surroundings, with stencils of tropical flowers and leaves in neon green, yellow, and pink on top of what resembled graph paper. After crossing Manhattan Avenue, my eyes feasted on the biggest, brightest red flower I had ever seen. It looked electric in the sun.

"What kind of flower is that?" I asked.

"Hibiscus. Each flower only blooms for one day. Seems that one bloomed just for you." She beamed at me. It struck me that the colors here were so much brighter. The sun seemed stronger in California, too. In New York City, it was like a gray filter covered the sky. But here, there was no filter, just full-force sunshine.

When Jen and I got home, she made yummy banana-nut muffins for breakfast. Mom certainly never baked; the kitchen was for making coffee.

Aunt Jen and Uncle Charlie stayed with me all day for a few days, taking me with them everywhere. If Jen had to go out, Charlie was by my side. When Charlie left to go to work at the station, Jen was there. I was used to having lots of time alone over the past two years, so this was a change. But I liked it. They got along well, for the most part. Occasionally they argued over silly things, like Charlie not cleaning up the kitchen and leaving things around the house. Then Charlie would tell Jen she was nagging, which made her mad. It made me realize how long it'd been since I'd had this kind of regular family life back home. Before Dad got sick.

At night, as I lay in bed, memories flooded in of the long, indistinct days after Dad's death a month ago. Mom didn't change out of her gray bathrobe. Staring at the wall, she sat motionless at the table, the only piece of furniture in the front of the loft. She blended into the white walls—her platinum hair, her pasty skin. The sunlight streaming in chiseled her high cheekbones.

"Can you get me something at the bodega?" she asked, still facing the wall. I had a prickly feeling all down my spine that settled in my stomach. I felt bad that I'd thrown up all over her cashmere dress. It hung in the sun by the back window, still smelling of vomit.

"Sure," I said, hoping this might mend things. She scribbled what she wanted on a piece of paper. Her bobbed hair, usually perfect, looked like a rat's nest. I took the note, put on my dirty sneakers, grabbed my Walkman, and headed out.

When I was little, when I was sent out for eggs or milk on the weekends, it made me feel grown-up. I'd liked contributing, and liked the responsibility. Now I felt like I had to, or else something bad would happen. Something even worse than Dad dying, if that were possible.

I pressed play on my Walkman. Side B of the Clash's new album rang out with "Ghetto Defendant." As I stepped into the sunlight, my brow furrowed. *How can the sun be shining and the sky be this blue, when everything is so messed up?* I hid from the bright-blue sky, my shoulders hunched as I braced myself against the chill. My legs were moving on their own, walking the block and a half to the bodega.

I had to ask the man behind the counter for the bottle of Stolichnaya vodka locked behind a plexiglass cabinet, and the pack of cigarettes. He never asked for ID. I guessed I could pass for eighteen, but he didn't seem to care if I was underage or not. The twenty-dollar bill did the talking. I didn't want to get her cigarettes, but I sensed it was the lesser of two evils—though I didn't know exactly what the worse thing was. On my way back, I drifted close to the buildings, under their shadows. I had the creeping sense that something was lurking around the corner.

That night, Mom slept in my bed, which was strange because I wasn't used to being so close to her. I couldn't relax. Hoping for the relief of sleep, my eyes followed the cracks in the ceiling. Tears welled up as I traced the path the cracks formed, remembering the last time Dad and I went hiking along the Adirondack trail.

Two and a half years ago, that hike had begun like many others, with anticipation of an adventure. The wide expanse of forest seemed infinite, in direct contrast to the grid of city blocks I was used to. Dad had stopped at a tree, picked some leaves off, munched on one, and given one to me. "Tastes like root beer," he'd said, and it did. He'd told me it was called sassafras. As we focused on securing footing on rocks and tree roots, we talked about anything and everything.

Lying in my bed, I began to shake uncontrollably, and my crying woke up Mom. She turned to me and rubbed my back. I let her, though I didn't feel any better from it.

"I won't ever be able to talk to Dad again," I choked out between sobs.

Mom sat up, cursed under her breath, and then exploded: "You know *I* can't talk to him either! He was supposed to be with me forever. He wasn't supposed to do this to me! It's all gone to shit! What am I'm supposed to do now? I can't go on like this."

"What do you mean?"

"I can't do this. I can't . . . I can't fucking take it anymore. *I want to kill myself!*" She screamed out in rage, slamming her fists onto the bed. I stiffened, my stomach gripping into itself. Her words echoed in my mind, darkening the already gray, bleak room. She turned towards me. "What do we do now, Ellie?" Her breath reeked of vodka. In the dark, I searched for her eyes, but vacant, lifeless black holes had replaced them.

"I don't know." A chill ran down my spine. *Is Mom going to commit suicide?* She was starting to scare me. She *was* depressed, but we both were. She hadn't been going to work and she was drinking vodka like water, but she wasn't *that* unstable, was she? I watched her intently as she lay down and fell back asleep. I couldn't sleep until the dawn's blue haze lightened the room.

The next day, I tried to make her go to work. I made her coffee and brought it to her, but she didn't respond. She wouldn't get out of bed. She hadn't made me go to school, but after a week of being with her like this, I almost wanted to go back. But I didn't. I couldn't. I couldn't stand to see the faces of everyone that'd been feeling sorry for me all year, now stricken with the bad news. Especially my best friend, Sayen. The past few months, I'd made myself a stranger to her outside of school. I told her it was because I was visiting Dad every day after school, which was true, but I did have some time after I visited him on weekends. I spent that time alone, reading and listening to records.

The next day, Mom was gone when I woke up. She was gone all day, which was a shock. I hid from daylight under my sweatshirt hood, walking around aimlessly in the cold loft. The cracks in the walls formed the outlines of shadows of what used to be: Me and Dad cooking for Mom while listening to records. All of us dancing after dinner. Dad reading me books at bedtime until I told him I was much too old for that, then sharing our dreams of the future.

But our future was blacked out, like the dirt on the walls—a layer of sheer black, making the walls and everything gray. The biting air settled in my bones and wouldn't let me rest. *It can't get any colder. I'm already wearing a down vest!* We weren't supposed to live here; factories and warehouses made up the other floors, so the heat went off at night.

I wound up at the stereo cabinet and flipped through Mom and Dad's extensive record collection. I put on one of their favorites; Elvis Costello. When "Alison" played, I froze, gripped with the memory of waking up in the middle of the night from a nightmare, just after Dad's diagnosis. I'd walked through the loft in my nightgown during one of their all-night dinner parties, through clouds of pot smoke, past people drinking and snorting cocaine at the dinner table—to my parents clinging to each other, slow dancing to "Alison" in the dark.

That afternoon, the steam in the radiators spurted on, and

I fell asleep on the floor. When I awoke, Mom was sitting in the dark in the corner, whimpering while "Alison" played on the turntable.

"Mom, are you okay?" I got up and went to her. She was wrapped up in a ball, gripping herself tightly. It was like she didn't see me standing in front of her. I took the needle off the record. "Mom," I repeated, kneeling down in front of her. The city lights mixed with moonlight to reveal agony in her expression. Her eyes screamed out in pain.

"Listen," Mom began. "I'm just . . . I feel like there's a hole where my heart used to be."

It was exactly what I felt but hadn't been able to put into words. I looked away so she couldn't see the hot tears streaming down my face. This time, I struggled to not make a sound. That would make it worse; maybe Mom would have a fit and threaten suicide again, so I didn't dare. She turned my head back towards her, forcing me to face her red-rimmed eyes, the whites lit up.

"I know this isn't what Dad would've wanted for you," she said. "I spoke to Aunt Jen. She wants us to come live with her and Charlie for a while—"

"In California?" I interrupted, shrugging off her touch and raising my voice. It was so cold, I could see my breath. In my mind's eye was a vacation postcard of people in bathing suits on a sunny beach. It was such a harsh contrast to the bleak, dark room.

"Yeah . . . California." Mom tried to sound excited, but she fell flat. "Aunt Jen thinks it's just what you need. I wouldn't be able to go until the summer, but we think it will be good for you to go now."

I turned to her. "Without you? I couldn't leave you!" My response was from my gut. "What does Aunt Jen know about anything?"

"I agree, my sister is no expert on anything. But I can't leave the gallery now. I need to find a replacement director first."

I bolted up, raising my voice. "How is that what's best? That's stupid!" *Tearing us apart, too? Leaving our home?*

"I can join you in a few months. We need a change of environment, Elle—"

"Don't call me Elle!"

"Why not?"

"I'm not French. I don't like it." I started pacing.

"But you are my girl," she said.

I leaned against the wall. "I know what it means, but it's not my name. Grandma's name was Eleanor." I was named after her mother, Eleanor Clein, whom I had dearly loved.

"Okay. Sorry, Ellie."

I collapsed, slumping down next to her. "What about school?"

"We don't have the tuition money for spring semester."

"What?"

"I spoke to the principal. You'll be able to take some time off and then finish sophomore year after spring break, at public school in California."

"Why didn't you tell me?"

"I thought we'd figure it out here, but now that Aunt Jen is offering for us to stay *there* . . ."

"What about my friends? I can't just leave."

She cut me off with forced enthusiasm. "Oh, Sayen and the rest will be happy for you. Come on. The beach! It will be fun."

"I'm not *a kid,* Mom." I had repeatedly ignored her requests to call her by her name, Julia. Now suddenly that it was just us, she didn't complain.

"You were eight the last time we visited them," she said.

"We don't have any family left here."

Hardly any of my dad's relatives had survived World War Two in Poland—my grandma was lucky to have escaped with Dad. She'd died when I was five.

I knew Mom had missed Aunt Jen ever since she'd moved away to California years ago, before I was born. They were the best of friends when Jen had lived in New York. They used to have long talks on the phone when I was little. She came to see us sometimes, but I hadn't visited her in California in seven years.

"They've offered for us to move into their back rooms," Mom said.

"But what about *our* home, here?"

"I thought I'd rent the loft out for a while, just in case."

Hearing Mom say that was a relief. That meant it wasn't final; we could come back if we decided to.

"Mom, what's happening to you?" I asked carefully.

"What do you mean?"

"Is that the real reason you're sending me away? You can't go to work and you aren't eating. You can't stand to look at me. Is it because I remind you of Dad? Is that why you hate me?"

"Stop it!" She threw her hands up to cover her ears. "I'm not well. I can't handle this. I almost lost my job. I'm sending you to Jen because I care about you. I can't take care of you right now. I can barely take care of myself. I'm scaring myself with . . . with the thoughts I'm having. I'm scaring my sister. So, I'm going to try a program at the hospital when you leave. And I need to keep my job here for a while, so they'll give me a referral to a gallery in Los Angeles. Then I'll join you."

I was surprised she'd agreed to do a program at a hospital. *But who will help me?* I didn't say it out loud; I was afraid of making her more upset. Instead I asked, "Which hospital?"

"It doesn't matter which—"

"Is it Bellevue, Mom?" I realized I didn't want to hear the answer. Bellevue was the psychiatric hospital.

"Yes, but it's just for two weeks."

My heart sank.

THREE

Longing to Surf

Every day, as soon as I woke up, I ran down to the beach to watch for dolphins. In my mind I'd say, *Come say hi to me, my friends!* And magically, they'd always come. They leapt and waded just outside of the surfer's lineup. I felt as if they were speaking to me: *Come into the water and play with us—we can't come to shore.*

I longed to learn to surf so I could be out there with them. I'd asked my aunt to teach me, and she'd said, "Sure." But she hadn't.

When I asked her again, she said, "As soon as Mother Ocean lets us." She meant we had to wait for a good day, when the ocean was calm and the waves were small beginner waves. Right now, the winter surf was strong. Aunt Jen told me, "The biggest storms we've ever seen have come this year, these past few months. They wiped out piers and flooded the strand, destroying homes up the coast. Hundreds of sea lions and seal pups washed ashore."

"Oh no! What happened to them?"

"The ones that survived were taken to the marine mammal rescue. People died, too." Jen stopped herself, realizing she'd mentioned people dying in front of me, and quickly changed the subject. "Come summer, there'll be smaller surf. And the water? Much warmer."

Each evening, I walked down to the beach to watch the sun set. That big orange disk would lower into the blue-green horizon line, become a half-circle, then be gone. It left clouds in fluorescent colors: coral and peach, an occasional fiery red streak across the fading blue. Charlie would join me if it was one of his days home from the fire station. He and Jen liked to stay near me. I was glad that Charlie talked enough for the both of us, because I didn't feel like talking much. Dad had understood me without my having to speak. He knew I was quiet, and tended to be shy, so he often voiced what I was thinking.

Without Dad, even breathing was hard. I only inhaled halfway, afraid of what I might feel in my heart if I took a deep breath. I wasn't sure I wanted to participate fully in life now, without him. I wasn't as far gone as Mom. I mean, I didn't want to kill myself. But I was a shadow of my formal self.

The whole time Dad was sick, me and Mom were together, but now we were two thousand miles apart. It helped to call her on the phone at the hospital. When Dad was sick, Mom was always talking about how things were going to go back to normal when he got better. It was never even mentioned that he might die; it wasn't a possibility in her mind, and I could see now how I'd held onto that. Now I had nothing to cling to but memories, and they hurt more than comforted. They arrived like dreams—I couldn't control them. They flooded in, and in an instant, I was no longer stable on my feet and had to sit down. Now that I was around laid-back people like my aunt and Charlie, I became aware that I was constantly on edge or in a state of shock. If the dog appeared, batting her tail, I jumped. Thankfully, the memories mostly came when I tried to sleep.

After watching a beautiful sunset over the ocean one night,

I lay in bed, remembering the books on California I'd gotten from the library in New York. I'd stared at them, feeling nothing, empty. Everything had been taken from me, and now *this* was before me. A sailboat out on the ocean, seagulls suspended in mid-flight against bright pinks and oranges of a watercolor sky. It seemed like such a fake paradise, nothing like the life I knew. In the city, sunsets only lit up the tops of tall buildings. The sun set somewhere far away to the west, on the other side of the continent.

Coming up from the subway after my last day of high school, the tops of buildings glowed peach from the sunset. Its beauty made my heart ache for Dad. The March cold was harsh, piercing through my jacket, my face and hands blown raw. Bracing myself against the gusts, I tried to imagine the sun setting on the beaches of California.

My feet had been moving fast, automatically, while my mind wandered. Inside my jacket pocket, I held the cold metal key. I was shocked to see two people sitting in my doorway. It stunk like burning plastic. They were smoking crack. Adrenaline pumping through me, I kept walking past my door, pretending I didn't live there. I went down the block and around the corner to the phone booth. I fumbled in my jeans pocket for a dime and called home.

Please answer! I could see my breath in the dull light of the booth. It was already dark and the streets were emptying. No answer. *She must still be at the gallery.* I hung up. If Dad were here, he'd be home, up in his study, and he'd come down and scare those people away. I could call Mom at the gallery, but it wouldn't do any good because it was so far away, in SoHo. I would need to take the subway again, and I'd have to wait a long time for a train to come now that rush hour was over.

I rambled through the empty maze of streets, going in circles. When I finally came back to my building, I was relieved to see they were gone. I quickly unlocked the door, ran down the hall, and pressed the button for the elevator. I jumped in and unlocked the top floor with my key. After the elevator door closed, I sighed, slumping against it.

When the door opened, I unlocked the gate to our floor, stepped out, and locked it behind me. I went to the kitchen and opened the refrigerator out of habit, though there was nothing in it but condiments—remnants from our earlier family life. Dad was the one who cooked, and Mom had stopped buying food. Hospital bills were stacked up on the counter. Dad's advance for his next book had been drained. Mom wasn't attending parties and openings as frequently as she usually did, and she'd been selling less art. She still got her paycheck, but without her commission it was barely enough.

In a box in my dad's study, I found a photograph from our last visit to California. In it, I was jumping in mid-air on the beach, a big smile on my face as Mom and Dad stood beside me. My braids had flown up over my ears, and I was wearing a flower lei Aunt Jen had made for me. I couldn't remember the last time I'd smiled.

I put the Polaroid in my suitcase. *This is really happening.* I was being torn away from the only home I'd known and all my friends at high school. Sayen was the hardest one to leave. We'd been friends since middle school. As if she'd known this, earlier that day she'd hugged me and given me a goodbye card; it was a drawing in colored pencil of a rainbow over the ocean, with handwriting that read: *Have fun in California. I will miss you.*

My hands trembled as I packed, but I knew I had to give things a try in California. For Mom.

I forced the memories of New York out of my mind. I grabbed my Walkman and tuned in to KROQ. The DJ, Rodney on the ROQ, announced, "And now for X, the band with 'Some Other Time' from their second studio album produced by Ray Manzarek of the Doors." It was a cool punk band I'd never heard before. Butterflies fluttered in my stomach as the female singer harmonized with a man during the chorus about the world ending tomorrow, echoing my thoughts about school starting soon.

But for now, I got to have lazy days, soaking in my new surroundings. If this had been a vacation, it would've been different. I would've been able to enjoy all the sunshine. Instead, I felt like I was in someone else's shiny new life that I didn't belong in. I wasn't supposed to be here. I was supposed to be all the way across the country, in high school with my friends, happy . . . joking with Dad about how much his chemo sucked but we'd gotten through it.

But instead I was here, in a foreign place, with a hole where my heart should be. *Dad, it's me, Misiu. I'm here in California. I really miss you.*

One morning, I headed out with Charlie to check the surf. He stopped dead in his tracks. Below, blue-green stripes of swell were sweeping across the expanse of ocean, surging towards us.

"Corduroy," he said.

"Huh?"

"Corduroy, the lines of swell, of waves comin' in."

"I thought you were talking about corduroy, like pants."

"Huh . . . yeah, it looks like that, the grooved texture, looks like corduroy. Guess that's why we call it that."

Light from the sun reflected off bands of wave crests, darker lines at the hollow where they broke. The rows of incoming waves resembled cords on ribbed silky cloth.

The waves continuously soared towards me, erupting in violent outbursts and reaching out to me across the sand. Gliding, gushing, flooding, receding, and starting over again. Taking it all in made me feel stable. The hum of the breaking waves unraveled my stomach knots as I breathed in the fresh sea air. I let myself fully breathe it in.

"Got to get out there," Charlie announced with building enthusiasm. "Looks good . . . solid!" He was hopping from one foot to the other, like a boy playing the hot potato game. "Surf's up! Surf's up! Woo-hoo!"

"Can I try?" I asked.

He chuckled. "You wanna go out in overhead waves your first time? Some of those sets are double overhead!" He stared me down with his piercing blue eyes. Then lines appeared at their corners as his face broke into a smile. "Wait till this storm's over, Ellie Bo-Belly. You need a small day."

I was curious to know why he and Jen got so excited about flinging themselves into ocean storms. Jones Beach, the one I'd known back East, was like a lake compared to this. But most mornings, if they felt like it was good enough and not too windy, they'd always go surf. I learned that in Southern California, the wind usually came up around ten in the morning, creating a rippled ocean all afternoon. Uncle Charlie called it "afternoon chop."

I looked forward to the days Charlie was home from the fire station, hoping he would go surf so I could watch. He rode a ten-foot Hap Jacobs single fin, which he called a "log."

Before heading out on his longboard he'd take requests from me to do a headstand, my favorite; or "the cockroach," where he put his legs and arms up in the air and squirmed them about, miming a bug on its back. That one cracked me up every time. He had a unique surfing style. It was often plain silly. While riding a wave, he would do a creeping walk down to the front of his board and "hang ten," his skinny frame in silhouette. Then he'd pop the tail out of the wave, which would spin the board around, and walk back, spinning the board around again. He called this "the helicopter." It was like a cartoon of Bugs Bunny on a high-wire. Jen teased him, saying "You're stuck in the sixties." He'd stick his tongue out to his chin and go cross-eyed. Then he'd say, "Yup."

Everybody loved Charlie, and everyone knew him. He made folks laugh with his antics, and his jolly "Hey, how ya doin'!" was always the beginning of an upbeat conversation. I got to know just about everybody in the beach parking lot because of him. They were mostly Jen's and Charlie's ages. No women except Jen, and occasionally her friend Sally when she wasn't on tour.

Sally was a professional surfer. Jen told me Sally was good friends with Rell Sunn, the famous Hawaiian surfer, water woman, and lifeguard. They'd become fast friends doing contests together, and they traveled the world, surfing every ocean. When the surf was giant, Sally would show up in her hot-pink-and-yellow Victory wetsuit and her new thruster, a shortboard shaped by Don Kadowaki and covered with her sponsors' logos, and competently maneuver herself on epic waves with expert skill. Jen kept up with her, riding one of Don's thrusters, too—a six-foot-three-inch tri fin.

Don rode the best waves each day with a smooth style and such grace. Charlie said, "He used to shape boards for

Dewey Weber, one of the all-time greats, but now he does his own. He shapes for all the pros." In his neon-orange wetsuit, Eddie Diaz did this new awesome thing—he could fly on his board into the air a little, and then land back onto the wave in the middle of his routine. He painted surfboards for Don and other surfboard shapers. Then there was Charlie's good friend, who people called "The Duke"—a combination of his first name, Dougan, and his last name, Seok, together. But Jen said, "He looks like Duke Kahanamoku, the legendary Hawaiian surfer, with his good looks and aloha spirit." He always had penny candy for me, Lemonheads, Bottle Caps, or his new favorite, Runts. The Duke always surfed by my uncle's side, trading off waves and splitting peaks on his "pig" board.

There was also an older guy people called "The Mayor" because he'd been a permanent parking lot fixture ever since anyone could remember. Charlie called him "Ol' Man." Jen called The Mayor by this last name—Wilkies—so that's what I called him. Charlie's friends had various nicknames for my uncle; one day I heard a guy call him "Shaggy" from the *Scooby-Doo* cartoon. I thought that was funny. *If only Zuzu looked like Scooby*, I mused.

Uncle Charlie's friend, Nate, who had long dreadlocks, showed up now and then in his beat-up beige microbus. He was fun to watch on his ten-foot, single-fin Bing board. He'd do tricks like Charlie, like take off fin first. In quirky movements, he'd kick his leg back and forward from the knee while walking down the nose. If Charlie was Bugs Bunny, then Nate was Daffy Duck.

Sometimes I saw high school boys who looked my age or older surfing in the afternoon. I assumed it was after school, or after work. One of them I'd seen a few times. Fresh out of the ocean, his wet hair shined black like his wetsuit, his broad shoulders outlined by a black-and-white checkered surfboard.

One day, as he passed me on the beach, our eyes met. His eyes were such a beautiful green, like sea glass. "Hi," he said, startling me.

A stranger wouldn't say hi in the city. I wouldn't even dare to make eye contact. I'd gotten in the habit of always looking down, and not focusing on anyone but rather looking past them. I'd learned not to challenge someone with direct eye contact when on the subway. It could start a fight.

But the way this boy looked at me was the complete opposite of a look from a stranger on the streets in New York City. It was like he knew me, like I was a good friend he'd known for years. His green eyes were framed by dark eyebrows, his prominent nose and face a dark tan from the sun or his heritage or both. He looked older than me, with his broad chest and strong arms.

I was curious about him, but my heart was in my throat. "Hi," I stammered hurriedly, not wanting to seem unfriendly. *Maybe he thinks I'm someone else?* I wondered if he went to the high school I'd be starting at soon, and if so, if we'd be in the same class. But he looked older; maybe he was a senior or in college. The thought of starting at a new school soon gave me goosebumps.

Jen said Mom was out of the hospital, so I called her at home. "Are you okay?" I asked. "You're back home for good?"

"Yes, I'm home, darling. But it's not the same without you. I miss you."

The way she said "darling" always rubbed me the wrong way, but I ignored it. I was just so glad she was out of the hospital. "Miss you too, Mom. When will you come out here?"

"Not until June. But it will be summer before you know it."

"That seems like so far away," I said. "I start school here soon."

"It will be nice for you to meet other high school kids," she said.

"Yeah, I guess." I didn't want to think about showing up at a new school so late in the year. I changed the subject. "I hope I get to start surfing out here soon."

"Oh, I don't know," she cautioned. "I'm sure Jen will take you as soon as it's safe. If it's cold, maybe it's best to wait till summer."

"I could get a wetsuit and surf now. Can I get one?"

"Well, they're expensive, and the move is costing a lot. We'll have to save up for one. We'll see how things stand when I get a job out there."

I didn't ask when that would be, though I wanted to. It seemed like it would be a very long time. I got quiet instead. I hadn't thought about needing a wetsuit. I was so eager to get out there and surf that I'd convinced myself I wouldn't mind freezing, but I knew that was foolish. The water was so cold, and most everybody wore one. I'd tried to swim out one day in my bathing suit, but the numbing whitewater was so cold that I couldn't breathe when it engulfed me. The icy water hit my face over and over, making it burn. Later my head hurt, and the chill stayed with me all day.

"You got an ice cream headache!" Charlie told me with a smile.

"A what?"

"Ice cream headache," he repeated. "When your head hurts so much from the cold water, you get a headache . . . like when you've eaten ice cream too fast."

"That's what you call it?" I asked.

"Uh-huh." He shook his head. Then he blew a raspberry. "Oh, excuse me!" he said with a big grin. He liked to tease me, and I knew he only teased people he liked.

It seemed like the wild dolphins were teasing me, too. They magically appeared and sprang out of the water in leaps and bounds any time I went down to the beach to watch the surfers. I desperately wanted to be out there in the water with them, but it was nice to just experience the beach, nature, and wildlife, as opposed to the city I was used to. Flocks of seagulls huddled into the sand to rest, ducking from the howling wind. I walked around them, so as not to disturb them. The roar of the ocean, its song, was telling me that I wasn't alone. Life all around me was constantly changing minute to minute, as each wave washed ashore.

The two red-and-white-striped smokestacks of the Scattergood steam plant stood tall at the north end of the beach. The Standard Oil refinery was just beyond it. But here—the beach was untouched. I could dig up sand crabs at the water's edge, like I used to do when I was little. Small snowy plovers and sanderlings, the ones my aunt called "peep birds," pecked at the shore. They were so cute, darting about, running from the incoming surf. Taller ones with skinny legs, called willets, fished along the shore with their long beaks. Occasionally, I could see what they were after: silvery schools of anchovies in the water's shallows. Pelicans soared along the waves, seeming to almost ride wind like the surfers rode water. Sometimes, from high up in the air, they dive-bombed for fish. Terns, which looked like seagulls but had black caps on their heads, gathered here to rest. Seals and sea lions sometimes surfaced, popping their heads up out of the water. They looked like cute dogs, with their big brown eyes.

Zuzu, a big German shepherd, looked scary to me at first, like a police dog or a wolf. I was unfamiliar with dogs, having never had or known one. When I was little I'd asked if I could have a dog. Dad had said, "The city is no place for a dog," and I knew better than to ask my mom, since she hated dogs. One time, when she went to a client's home to install some art, their tiny dog bit her ankle. She wasn't able to wear high heels for two weeks. So, I never had a dog.

"You know that book about Ferdinand and the bull?" Uncle Charlie asked me one day when we were out walking Zuzu.

"Yeah." I remembered it. The bull liked to sit and smell the flowers.

"Well, that's Zuzu," he explained. "She was all skin and bones when I rescued her because she'd gone on a hunger strike with her previous owners. They tried to train her too young. She wasn't meant to do Shitzen training."

"What's that?" I asked.

"Police-dog training. It wasn't her nature. When I got her, I cooked for her every day, trying to get her to eat. Now she's a happy girl, huh?" He patted her back and Zuzu batted her tail, which I learned meant she was happy. Whenever Charlie asked her if she wanted to go on a walk, she stood right by his side, looking up at him with shining eyes, her pink tongue out and her tail going crazy.

Uncle Charlie handed me her leash. "She'll walk right next to your left leg. Just give her a little slack, and say 'heel.' When you want to let her be free to sniff and stop and do what she pleases, you say 'okay.'"

When I first tried walking Zuzu, she pulled me this way and that. "I don't want to make her do something she doesn't want to," I said.

"Oh, dogs *love* to be given direction," Charlie replied. "It makes them feel secure. Dogs are pack animals. They're loyal to the pack leader, and you're the leader now."

I tried again, and was surprised how easily it came. "Heel," I said, and instantly Zuzu was at my side, trotting along, looking up at me for more cues. After a few blocks, she seemed to be smiling, her tongue out, licking the salty air. She was walking right by my side, keeping pace with me. It was something we were doing together. We were a team.

Over the next few weeks, my fear of Zuzu faded. At night, I would pet her by the fire, leaning against her. She was my big, furry pillow. With her black nose and brown eyes outlined in black fur, she reminded me of a bear. *She's just a big teddy bear*, I realized. When I went to my room to sleep, I left the door open, and soon Zuzu would be lying at the foot of my bed. When I got up in the morning, she popped her head up to look at me, ears pointed, ready to go for a walk.

Each day, I explored the neighborhood with Zuzu. It was the complete opposite of New York City's factory buildings, lined in pavement. All the houses here were small one-story cottages in pretty colors with gardens in the front and back, full of tropical flowers, plants, and trees. I learned from Jen the names of all the flowers. It was late March, and already the peach blossoms were blooming. Bright-pink buds, a little fuzzy like pussy willow, opened into tear-shaped petals that looked like they were made of paper. In the sun, they erupted out of branches, their magenta hues ablaze against the cobalt sky.

Jen's garden, just outside my bedroom window, was magical. No one would imagine that such a place existed between the back of the house and the garage by the alley. Pink jasmine bloomed in clusters, cascading down the green-covered walls, emitting a heady scent. I breathed it all in. It didn't attack my senses like my mom's perfume; that was fake, artificial, too much to take in. This was pure nature. Jen's garden was a sanctuary. It was how I'd imagined *The Secret Garden* when Dad read it to me when I was little, but this was real. I'd even tasted it. Jen gave me a flower you could eat; honeysuckle. And there were roses of every color. When one was particularly perfect, I'd sink my nose into its center, my cheek against the soft petals, breathing it in. Each one smelled so different. I loved the scent of the light-purple ones most. They were kind of lemony. When my legs brushed the lavender plants, they released an herbal, woodsy aroma. Next to them was sage, which were "native to California," Jen said. They soaked up the sun and emitted a fresh, earthy spice I couldn't get enough of.

One day, after a walk with Zuzu, I sat in one of the cozy wicker chairs in the center of the garden by the fountain. It was hard to believe that all this green was always here in California, even now, in winter. The winter here was like spring. *There isn't a single tree within ten blocks of our loft back home*, I reflected. Cement seemed to cover the entire island. But inside our loft, Dad had kept a tree in a giant pot. It grew from a few feet above me to well over Dad's head. It touched the ceiling at fourteen feet, its canopy of leaves filling the skylight. He'd water it every Sunday while we listened to records. When Dad was in the hospital my mom took over watering the tree, but soon the leaves paled and some fell. It started to not look so good. A month after Dad died, so did his tree.

Suddenly I realized: *Dad and the tree had something like symbiosis*. I'd learned about it in science class. Two different species living together, plant and human, needed each other.

But what about me? I'm still here. Dad and I were always together, as long as I could remember. Either he was physically next to me or he was in my head; the stuff we'd talk about was always on my mind. Once a week, we'd walk up to the New York Public Library near Times Square. Dad had an open notebook by his desk where I'd write stuff down that I wanted to look up, and we'd bring it with us. It was our list. I remember writing "hawks" and "falcons" in the notebook a few years ago. When we found out that their nests were called scrapes, we thought it was funny, because they made nests in the skyscrapers. We also learned that hawks mate for life. "Just like you and Mom," I'd said. He had brushed the top of my head, smiling in agreement. Remembering that moment, I felt comforted at first, but then it hurt more than it was worth.

"You sure look peaceful sitting there," Jen said, startling me from my daydreaming. She giggled, spotting Zuzu asleep at my feet. "You two make quite the pair."

"Oh, hi," I said. "It's so nice here."

"Glad *someone* besides me appreciates it. Charlie calls it 'the jungle.' But he doesn't really mind it so long as he doesn't have to do any work back here, and it's satisfying to take care of my own garden instead of other people's all the time."

She sat down in the chair next to me and sighed. A few birds were chirping in the tree. One landed on the fountain, drank, and then cleaned its feathers. Jen turned to me and asked delicately, "How are you doing? You okay?"

I didn't answer, and I was relieved when she continued. "It must be hard being out here without your friends and your mom . . . but she'll be here soon."

"Yeah," I said, looking down at Zuzu.

"And when high school starts, you'll be sure to make new friends."

I sighed. I didn't want to think about school.

"I want you to know, you can depend on your Auntie Jen.

I'm here for you." I met her soft eyes. They shone with sincer-ity, and her voice was heartfelt. "Anything you need, anything you want to talk about . . . or if you don't want to talk. I'm here for you."

"Thanks." I smiled at her. She was really nice, but I didn't feel like talking.

While out walking Zuzu the next day, I couldn't help but think about starting school the next week. I didn't know anyone, and it would be odd being the new girl showing up so late in the year. I clenched my fists, tightening my grip on Zuzu's leash. My stomach growled; the sea air had made me hungry. I burst into a run back to the cottage to find Uncle Charlie in the kitchen, making sandwiches.

He made the best sandwiches. He'd slice up everything from the fridge, which was always full, and pile on springy white things called sprouts, which I learned were just that—sprouts of seeds. It was the exact opposite of coming home to an empty fridge back home.

"Would you like a pickle?" Charlie asked me.

Without warning, I burst into tears. Pickles were a thing with me and Dad. In middle school, he would pack them in my school lunch almost every day because he knew they were my favorite.

Charlie looked up at me, surprised. After a moment, he walked over and gave me a hug. "Okay, okay, no pickles. Don't cry, Ellie." He patted my back. When I kept crying, he said, "I promise not to ask you if you want a pickle *ever* again! No more pickles, okay?" He took the jar over to the trash, unscrewed the lid, and turned it over, emptying it. "They're not allowed in this house anymore. See?"

This made me laugh, which was hard while crying. "But I like pickles," I sniffled.

Poor Uncle Charlie looked so confused.

"It's just . . . Dad . . ." I started to explain, but choked up again.

Charlie's bright blue eyes pierced through my tears. "I'm real sorry about your dad. That's gotta hurt more than anything."

I nodded.

After lunch, I sat in the garden. I closed my eyes so I could hear the roar of the ocean better. Zuzu lay at my feet and snoozed. I breathed it all in—the fresh smell of the earth, the sea in the air, its hum in my ears. My heart swelled in my chest and I was struck with a piercing glimmer of Dad. I talked to him in my mind. *Dad, are you watching me? Can you hear me? Is this really my life now? I wish you were here. I know I'm going to learn to surf. You just watch. I will!*

FOUR

El Niño Storms

The night before my first day at Mira Costa High School, a prickly feeling spread down my spine. I'd seen the school while driving by with Aunt Jen. It was a cluster of one-story buildings painted a creamy white.

"That's the school?" I asked.

"Uh-huh," Jen nodded.

"Why isn't it a big building?" Jen told me it was because the hallways were outside. *That's so strange*, I thought, my palms sweating. *But where are the wire fences and metal gates?* Back home, all the school buildings were tall, with bars protecting the windows. My high school was surrounded by a fifteen-foot wire fence. If there wasn't a fence, suspicious people or the homeless would loiter on the school grounds, like they did outside in the streets.

The next morning, Jen said, "You need to get outside in the fresh air, it'll do you some good before school." We took Zuzu and walked along the Strand, a paved path right next to the beach. When Zuzu stopped to smell every patch of dirt, flowers, or another dog's pee, we looked out at the ocean. Jen sized up what the conditions were that day. She called it "surf checks."

"Big and messy," she said.

I squinted against the wind. The stormy sea looked dangerous, but I blurted out, "I could try and surf it, right?"

"No way!" she huffed. "No shape, it's all over the place. Charlie calls it 'Victory at Sea.'" She chuckled, beaming at me. "Well, let's get you to school."

I tensed at the thought, but I knew I had to go.

Aunt Jen drove me in her pickup truck, a faded green 1968 International. It felt odd not taking the subway to school. The butterflies in my stomach were going crazy by the time we got there. Jen went into the office with me. The lady there offered to show me to the classroom.

Jen gave me a big hug. "I'll pick you up right when school gets out."

"Okay," I said. "Can we surf after school?"

"The surf's not good today." My chest sank a bit. She must've seen my disappointment. "Soon, I promise."

At first, it was torture being introduced to my sophomore homeroom class as the new student. Everyone was staring at me. After that everyone ignored me, which I was okay with because I just wanted to blend in and disappear. But soon, I realized I stuck out like a sore thumb.

Kids dressed differently here. They were wearing bright colors, shorts, and miniskirts, versus the long pants and sweaters we wore back East. The teachers dressed more casually here. Instead of the suits they wore at my school in New York, here teachers wore bright blouses or sundresses. The popular girls' clothes looked new, and their hair looked poofy and big, like they hot-rollered and teased it and blew it dry and then used lots of hair spray to help it defy gravity. In my old school, everyone generally wore dark colors, and nothing looked new. I was still dressed like that—jeans, navy sweater, dirty sneakers.

When my homeroom class left to go to math, we passed another class walking towards us. "Who's that?" one girl spat out, pointing at me.

"Grody," another girl said, and snickered. They both laughed, their feathered blonde hairdos shaking. I looked down at the floor and slid against the wall past them and into the classroom. I slouched into my seat, letting my long, dark hair fall in front of my eyes, trying to hide the tears that were welling up. I picked up a pencil and drew a picture of a wave in my spiral notebook to comfort myself. At my old school, we'd all been friends since middle school. Before classes began, we'd gather around together, chatting. When Sayen had found out Dad was in the hospital, she'd put her arm around me during class and whispered, "I'm sorry, Ellie. I'm sure it's gonna be all right." It'd been hard to leave my old friends.

The next day at school was more of the same, and the next. No one sat next to me at lunch, so I brought a book from my aunt and uncle's house to keep me company: *Surfing Guide to Southern California*. The cafeteria had two big double doors that were always open, leading to an outdoor eating area. Kids could eat inside or at the tables outside. I'd never eaten outside at my old school. When kids passed by me in the outdoor halls, they ignored me or they snickered.

After school one day that week, I called my mom on the phone." Aunt Jen is like a weather person on TV," I told her. "She knows everything about the wind and tide and what makes the waves good for surfing."

"Well, she's been there for fourteen years now," Mom replied, seeming preoccupied. She was back at the gallery and busy.

I went on anyway. "I'm not real sure I get it, but Jen says it's a mix of the right wind, swell, and tide. Today she said the wind was out of the west, and there was a south swell. She pointed out to me that, every fifteen minutes or so, there were some big waves. They usually came in threes, called sets. Oh, and the tide is important, too. We took Zuzu for a walk around high tide, and she pointed out how some people were having trouble catching waves. We bumped into some friends of hers, and they were talking about how it was better earlier."

"Uh-huh. I need to go. How's school?"

"It's okay," I lied.

"Oh good. Let's talk later, okay?"

"Okay," I sighed, relieved to change the subject. "I can't wait for you to come out."

"Yes, we're going to have a fun summer," she said in a rush. "Bye now!" The phone went dead.

"Bye," I replied, but I wasn't sure why. She'd already hung up. *She's not here with me.* The thought rubbed a sore spot in me. I stared at the avocado-green receiver before I hung it back on its hook on the kitchen wall. *I hope she's okay.*

I thought about how Mom and Jen were sisters, but they couldn't be more different. They looked different, acted different. Mom had a "new wave" hairstyle that she died platinum blonde. But Aunt Jen's was natural, wavy, and brown. My mom wore perfect outfits put together head to toe, usually black, always high heels, always red lipstick and makeup. Aunt Jen never wore makeup, and she only wore t-shirts and jean shorts, never black. She hardly ever wore shoes. My mom could be uptight about things, but Jen didn't seem to be uptight about anything. They had both grown up in New York City. *Was it California and surfing that changed Jen? Or was she just always different? Did Mom used to be like Jen, and it was the city and her job that changed her?*

Aunt Jen was beginning to feel like the older sister I never had.

Saturday morning was chilly, so I slipped on a sweatshirt. I walked Zuzu down to the Strand and went up through the surfers' parking lot. There was Wilkies, sitting in the front seat of his old, faded-blue car, a Volkswagen Squareback. He was always there. Like Charlie had said, "Ol' Man Wilkies" was the unofficial mayor of the parking lot. Some people called him Alice Cooper after the heavy metal rocker, because he somewhat resembled him with his long, greasy hair and scrawny build. I couldn't tell exactly how old he was, but likely old enough to be Charlie's dad, or older. He had a permanent tan and hardly ever wore a shirt, only surf trunks. Wilkies had a steady, laid-back disposition. When he spoke, he did so in a calm, slow manner and in a low, flat tone.

He glanced up at me from his newspaper. "Hi."

"Hi," I responded.

He stepped out of his car. "Zuzu's looking good. How old is she now?" He started to pet her.

"I think she's seven."

"Huh." He peered at me from under his clear green visor. Long, greasy locks fell out from underneath the white elastic strap. "How old are you?

"Fifteen."

"Huh," he said. "She must be happy to have a friend like you to take her on walks."

"I guess so," I replied.

"Listen, I heard about your dad, and I'm real sorry," he said. "You must miss him a lot. It's hard to lose a parent at any age, but it's got to be even harder, you being so young."

I nodded and looked down at the pavement. The thought of him stung, like poking at an open wound.

"Is your mom coming soon?" he asked.

"Yeah, soon," I said, even though I knew it wouldn't be till June. My eyes fixated on an orange surfboard on top of his car.

"Good, it'll be good to have her here," he said. Following my line of sight, he added, "Want to see my new board?"

"Sure." I was relieved to change the subject because I was fighting back tears.

He pulled the board off of the surf racks and held it up for me. He ran his calloused, knotted fingers across it like it was the most precious thing to him.

"Yup, another one of Don's boards," he said slowly. "This one's a beauty."

It was shiny and smooth, and its hue faded from an amber to a bright orange. It came to a purposeful point at the top, emphasized by an outline in aqua-green stripe.

"It's very nice," I said.

"And it works really well, which is the best thing. It's one of those new thrusters. Have you gone surfing with your aunt and uncle yet?"

"No. I want to, though."

"Well, I'm sure they'll be happy to take you out just as soon as the swell eases up. You arrived with the biggest waves we've seen here in twenty years. It's been a series of freak storms. El Niños. You know, it's taken down a bunch of piers and some buildings."

"I didn't know about the buildings."

"Oh yeah! And it swept all the way up to the Strand, tearing it up. Giant boulders from the Breakwater were hurled into the parking lot. Boats sunk in the harbor." He turned and gazed out at the ocean. "And guess who surfed one of the biggest days out here?"

"Who?" I asked.

"Your aunt. Yeah, and Sally, too. All the pros flew in to surf it, and the local pros like Benny . . . Mike Benavidez. And there's Sally and Jen riding triple overhead waves."

"Wow," I said. "I want to surf."

"Well, the summer should be good for that, and the water will be warmer, too."

"Yeah," I said as Zuzu was pulling me away. "Okay, see you around."

"Yeah, see you around," he replied, waving.

When Jen burst into the house after surfing, she seemed energized. She quickly showered and set to baking the next batch of muffins.

"Wilkies said you surfed one of the biggest days here," I said. "During one of the storms."

"Yeah, the wave faces were twenty-five feet plus. There were only two pros out at Breakwall, and they had to take a boat into the lineup. Then Benny, a local pro, was brave enough to paddle out. It took him half an hour to get out. He started out just north of the Breakwall and ended up all the way up at Eighth Street."

"Wow."

"Anyway, that day, guys were afraid to surf, it was so big. But after seeing Benny make it out, Sally paddled out, too. I watched Sally get the biggest wave I've ever seen a woman on, so I jumped in, too. I tried to paddle out but couldn't make it. I kept trying and on my third time, I was lucky enough to make it out."

"Did you get one?"

"Yeah, I got one. That's all I needed, I was one and done. It hit me after, how crazy that was. But Sally got three good ones that day. That's a lot for a day like that. There were a lot of pros out there trying to get the best waves."

As Jen mixed the bowl's contents, the scent of cinnamon and nutmeg filled up the little cottage. I asked if I could help. She gave me some carrots and a cheese grater, and I shredded them into the bowl. We added raisins after the flour mixture. When they were done, we ate them, warm out of the oven.

"You know, these would be even better with cream cheese frosting," she exclaimed between bites.

"Frosting sounds good."

Aunt Jen popped up out of her chair. "You know, I think I can!" She went to the counter, grabbed a lemon from the bowl, opened the fridge, and took out some cream cheese. She proceeded to mix them in a bowl, but it looked like it was hard to do.

"It's hard, 'cause the cream cheese is cold," she said.

I got up to help.

"Want to try it?" Jen held up a spoon she'd dipped in the mixture.

"Sure," I said.

She spread a bit on a muffin and handed it to me. My expression must've shown how sour it tasted because Jen broke out in laughter. "Sorry," she said between giggles. "That must've been sour."

I started to laugh, too.

"Some sugar?"

"Yeah," I said. She took some maple syrup out of the fridge, poured it in the bowl and mixed it again. She put it on my muffin. I took a bite. It was delicious.

"That tastes like grandma's carrot cake," I said, forgetting at first that it was Jen's mom, too.

"Wow, you're right. It does, it tastes just like it." Jen looked out the window, lost in thought. Her eyes welled up with tears. "I miss her," she said softly.

"Me too," I replied. But I missed Dad even more.

"How are you holding up, honey?" she asked me.

"I'm okay," I answered, but I knew it was a lie.

"It's okay to miss him," she reassured me, brushing a hair back behind my ear. "You know, it's okay to be angry, too. It's okay to feel, whatever it is. You can talk to me about it, you know."

"Yeah," I said, but I didn't feel like talking about it. It was too much. I was afraid if I talked about it, I would fall apart and I wouldn't be able to control myself. Starting to talk about it would be like taking out a piece of a dam, causing a waterfall as big as Niagara to flood everything. Or like El Niño, storming in and taking down piers. And I didn't want to be like Mom and not be able to deal with it. The thought of that happening scared me.

FIVE

Stoked

I could hardly sleep that night. Thoughts flooded my mind of finally being out there with the dolphins tomorrow for my first surf lesson. I'd wanted to learn to surf for weeks now, but every day, Aunt Jen had said it was too big and not safe for me. Then, at dinner last night, she'd asked, "Would you like to go surfing tomorrow?"

"Would I!" My heart pounded so fast, I sprang out of my chair, "Yes, yes, yes!"

I'd tried to call Mom, but I couldn't get through. "There must be an opening at the gallery tonight," I'd explained to my aunt and uncle before they had a chance to ask.

I lay tense in bed, consumed with thoughts. I was a good swimmer, but I'd only swam in lakes or the calm Atlantic Ocean. This was the Pacific. Here the ocean seemed more wild and untamed than back East.

I gripped my blanket. The moonlight shone bright on Zuzu at the foot of the bed. I sat up and crawled near her, brushing my face against her fur. I could see the moon through the tree branches from this spot. It was almost full. In my mind I heard Dad say, "I love you more than the moon, Misiu."

A gust of ocean breeze wafted in, making the curtains flutter. I breathed it in. Fresh sea air. Was this really the same moon

I used to look for, from the top of the building in New York City that I'd lived in? It was so noisy there, even in the middle of the night. *How quiet it is here.* The glare of the city lights created a haze of pollution so thick, I couldn't see the stars. I could see stars here. Between tree branches, they beamed brightly.

Deep in my gut, I yearned for Dad. I focused on a star until a ring of colored light surrounded it and it appeared to be moving, like a candle flickering. I reached for my Walkman, hoping Rodney on the ROQ was on. Late at night, it usually was. I was in luck. Blondie's "Dreaming" was playing. Mom resembled her so much that people even asked for her autograph sometimes, thinking she was Debbie Harry. It happened once when we were out celebrating Mom's birthday with Dad, their friend Peter, and a big group of friends at the Odeon in Tribeca. When my parents looked at each other from across the table, sparks flew from the fire of their locked gaze. That was before Dad was diagnosed.

I awoke to the sound of the tea kettle. It was still dark out. Suddenly it hit me: *I'm going to surf today!* I jumped out of bed and hurried into the kitchen.

Jen was pouring water from the kettle when she saw me. "Hey, good morning!"

"Good morning," I said, blinking under the kitchen light.

"Would you like some hot chocolate?" she asked.

"Um . . . I'll try some tea," I decided.

"Oh, okay then." She studied me and giggled. I wondered why. *Maybe she's just so happy we're finally going surfing, like I am.*

"I'll make you one nice and strong like mine," she said.

"Thanks, I'll get ready." I ran back into the room and quickly changed into my bathing suit. When I came back out,

Jen was sitting at the kitchen table, sipping her tea with her wetsuit half up and her bathing suit top on. A mug sat steaming in front of the chair opposite her, and over the chair hung something black. I walked up to it and felt it—it was rubbery and thick.

"Is this—"

"Uh-huh," she replied, grinning. "Uncle Charlie picked it up for you."

"A wetsuit? A wetsuit!" I jumped up and down.

"We figured if you're determined to do dawn patrol with me, you shouldn't freeze."

"Oh, thank you!" I tripped over the dog as I reached out to hug her. "Oh, sorry Zuzu!" She bolted and wagged her tail wildly, pacing back and forth while we hugged.

I began to pull on my new wetsuit, bit by bit. Carefully. I sighed. It was laborious, but I was determined to do it.

"It's okay to give it a little tug, you won't break it." Jen chuckled.

I worked it and worked it, and finally, I got it up over my legs and belly. I felt constricted. "It feels tight."

"That means it fits you right. It's got to be snug so no water can get through. It looks good." My aunt helped me get the wetsuit up all the way, zipping the back. I sat down slowly. I wasn't sure it would stretch with me, it hugged me so tight. I sipped the warm, milky tea with honey.

"You like the tea?" she asked.

"Yeah, I do. It's kind of spicy. It smells good."

"It's Earl Grey," she said.

"It kind of smells like jasmine flowers," I said.

"It's got bergamot in it," Jen said. "Oil from a kind of orange."

"Mmm." That was fitting for my aunt, to drink something

fragrant from a fruit tree.

Uncle Charlie popped his head in the door. "Did I hear an Ellie Bo-Belly monster? I did!"

I felt something wet in my ear. I shrieked.

"Did you just stick your finger in my ear?" I'd forgotten he did that when I was little.

"Maybe," he said, grinning.

"Eww! You licked it first?" I bolted up, and he dashed behind the kitchen counter.

"He's had way too much coffee already, watch out!" Jen stood up, beaming.

Charlie stepped towards her, gave her a big kiss, and announced; "Okay, I'm off. Have fun!"

"Bye, Uncle Charlie," I said. "Thanks for the wetsuit!"

"You're welcome. It's from the shipping container at the Dive 'n' Surf shop sale. Sorry they didn't have any bright colors that people like now."

"Oh, I like black," I said.

"Me too," said Jen.

He winked at us through the open door. "Have fun, surfer girls!" He shut the door behind him, heading out to spend the next three days at the fire station. I knew he would've rather surfed with us.

"That fits you really well, Ellie, even though it is a boy's suit. They don't make wetsuits for girls. Mine's a men's small . . . I'll get your board."

I followed her out the back door to the garden. She picked up a big yellow surfboard leaning against the shed. "This is Charlie's Greg Noll board he got at his shop here twenty years ago," she said. "He's called 'Da Bull.' He rode the biggest wave anyone has ever caught at Makaha, a forty-footer."

"That's giant," I said.

"Yeah, and we're talking forty-foot Hawaiian, so it was probably double that."

I held open the gate for her. Zuzu watched us go from behind the fence with sad-puppy eyes.

"Bye, Zuzu, be back soon!" Jen said.

"Aww, bye Zuzu!" I called out. As we walked down the hill I asked, "Did Greg Noll surf here?"

"Yup. He started surfing in the forties with the famed Manhattan Beach Surf Club at the pier."

"When did Charlie start?"

"Oh, can't you tell? He's stuck in the sixties."

The sky was getting lighter every second. That patch of blue grew bigger as we advanced closer. The expanse of sea became encompassing, an infinity of ocean before us.

At the Strand, Jen stopped to study the surf. "Perfect little peaks . . . and glassy!" She winked at me. "Ready to catch some waves?"

"Yeah!" I sure was! My heart was thumping. "Can I carry the board from here?"

"Sure. Since it's hard to fit it under your arm, you can carry it like this." She swung it up over her head, balancing it with her arms on either side. Then she put it on my head. It was heavy and hard to get a grip on, because it was so thick. Holding myself straight, I let the weight of it rest against the top of my head while both arms worked to steady the board. When we reached the sand, Jen regarded me. "Are you sure you don't want me to carry it?"

"Nope." My arms were weak, but I was determined to carry it. I grappled with it all the way to the water's edge.

"Let me help you put the board down." Jen lifted it off my head and sat it down between us. "Did you ever skateboard?" she asked.

"No."

"Okay, let's try something. Let yourself fall forward and just before you fall, catch yourself, like this." She demonstrated. Leaning forward, she stuck a foot out just in time. I did it too, though it seemed silly.

"Okay, now let's do it again." We did it a few times more. Aunt Jen chuckled. "That's it, then, you're goofy!"

I furrowed my brow.

"I'm regular, and you're goofy," she explained.

"Huh?"

"Goofy foot! See, I put my *left* foot forward and you put out your *right*. It's the way we stand on the board." She showed me. "Most people stand like me, we call it regular. *You're* goofy foot."

"Is Uncle Charlie goofy?" I asked.

"Nope, he's regular. But he sure is goofy, though, isn't he?"

"Yeah," I agreed. We laughed together. If anyone was goofy, it was Uncle Charlie.

Jen sat down next to the board and showed me all the different parts and names. The front was called the nose, and the back was the tail. The sides were rails, the top was the deck, and the bottom had no special name, though it was sometimes referred to as "rocker," meaning the overall curve of the board. At the board's tail, on the bottom, was the fin.

Aunt Jen lay on the top of the board and showed me what position to be in, with her toes at the tail and her hands by her armpits. Then she jumped up into surfer position. We practiced this together a bunch of times. She called it the pop-up. She lay in the sand, and I lay on the board. When Jen called out, "Pop-up!" we both jumped to our feet, pulling our legs right up under us. Jen said I was a natural at pop-ups.

I stood up in surfer stance, my right foot forward, arms

out. Then she shook the board from under me, rocking it back and forth, while she explained how you want to keep your knees bent to keep your balance. Both heels had to be down so your feet had a good grip, or you'd fall off.

"Okay, let's go out," she said. "We'll only go in waist-high, and I'll push you into some waves, okay?"

I nodded, and she picked up the board. As we stepped into the water, the chill froze my feet, but my body was covered in a protective layer like a seal's. The sea, a clear blue-gray, seemed to glisten on its own; the sun hadn't come up bright yet. The waves were green as they formed; when they broke, the white-water glowed like iridescent moonstone, with highlights in pastel colors of a rainbow. A pink streak that had marked the sky was fading as it turned bluer by the moment.

"Ah, it's so beautiful," Jen stopped and sighed.

"Yeah," I agreed. I took a deep breath. I was struck by how lucky I was to be here, far away from the city, on the other end of the continent, at the edge of the world.

Aunt Jen held the board between us as we walked into the water, waist-high. "See, the nose is facing out to sea," she explained. "Perpendicular to the line of waves coming in. That's how I want to hold it, otherwise those waves'll knock me down."

I nodded.

"Watch," she continued. "I'll hold it the wrong way." She turned the board so it was parallel with the shoreline. A wave came in, breaking into a fury of foam, smacking the board into her. In pretend surprise, she opened her mouth, as it knocked her down with its force. She came up drenched and smiling. I giggled.

"Funny, huh?" she said. "Not so funny when the board smacks you in the head."

My aunt put the board down on the surface of the water between us, nose out to sea, as we continued to walk out. When whitewater gushed towards us, she pressed down on the tail of the board to lift the nose up and over it.

"Here, try this," she said. "Jump up as you hold down on the tail." She patted the deck at the tail of the board. At the next burst of whitewater, I pushed my hand down next to hers, and jumped up. We went over it easily.

"Let's go in a little deeper," she said. "Hop on!" I jumped up to lay on top of the board. "Scoot up a bit," she said. I pulled myself forward. She pushed the board over another bump of crumbling foam and turned the board around so I was facing the beach.

"Okay, I'm going to push you into one. Remember your pop-up?"

"Uh-huh," I replied, peering behind us at the incoming wave. It looked ominous from here. I fought a rising panic as it grew.

"Not this one, it's too big," she said, to my relief. "We'll wait for a good one." The wave crashed behind us, thunderous and booming. Jen wrestled the board as I floated on it, over the hump of soup. We waited like this, letting a few more waves break and pass by.

"You ready?" Jen said. "This one's for you."

My heart hammered in my chest as I got into position with my hands at my sides by my armpits, my toes tucked at the tail of the board. I held my head up, facing forward, bracing myself. With a sudden jolt, I was thrust forward. A thrill shot through me as the ocean seemed to make a clear path before me. Aunt Jen was shouting, "Pop up! Pop up!"

Before I knew it, I was standing up on the board, gliding forward with the momentum of the wave. Moving fast.

My heart leapt. Almost to shore, I grew unsteady and jumped off into the water before I fell. As I got up, Jen was cheering, "Woo-hoo!" Arms high up in the air, she clapped and shouted, "Wow! Ellie! That was great! Woo-hoo!" She was grinning from ear to ear. I was, too.

I wanted to do it again right away. The board had washed up on the shore. When I grabbed it, it seemed less heavy as I walked back out towards my aunt. She held her hand up in the air to me, we did a high five. "You stood up on your first wave!"

"Let's do it again," I said.

"Okay, hop on."

With the next wave, I popped up onto my feet again, and flew. I soared. I caught wave after wave that morning. With each one, a rush of adrenaline and an overwhelming exhilaration burst through me. When I lost my balance, I wasn't afraid because I was falling in water. I counted, and by the end, I'd ridden sixteen waves.

When I became exhausted and numb from the cold, we decided to head home for breakfast. The sun shone bright as we walked barefoot up the hill. I was thankful that my aunt was carrying the board now. My legs were burning; they were hard to lift up, but somehow I kept walking. At the sound of the gate clicking behind us, Zuzu rushed out to greet us, her tail wagging with unrestrained energy.

"Hi Zuzu-bean!" Jen called out.

"Zuzu, guess what? I caught like sixteen waves!" I patted her as she nudged her head into me.

"You sure did! You're a natural!" Jen turned on the outdoor shower. I rinsed off and headed to my room to change.

My first thought was, *I want to call Dad and tell him.* Then I realized that I couldn't. Because he was dead. Panic surged through me. I crumpled on the bed, bursting into tears. *I'll never talk to him again—he's really gone!* I buried my head in my towel, grief twisting in my gut. I didn't want Jen to hear me, but it was too late. She was knocking on the door.

"Ellie . . . are you all right?"

I couldn't fight it. It was too overpowering. *No, I'm not all right.* I felt like I'd *never* be all right. My throat welled up. I couldn't speak. Jen slowly opened the door. She sat down next to me on the bed and put her towel around me.

"Are you okay?" she asked softly. I attempted to talk, but the lump in my throat prevented me. "It's okay, let it out, let it all out." She leaned into my back, one hand resting between my shoulder blades. I wailed in anguish. The dam had burst and I couldn't stop. In my mind, I saw the breaking waves from that morning, powerful, roaring as they exploded.

"It's just that," I began, "I wanted to tell Dad about today." I choked on a sob.

"I know, I know . . . it's hard. I know you miss him . . . I want to talk to my mom sometimes, too. It's hard." She gently rubbed my back. "You know, you can call your mom and tell her about today."

"But it's not the same with Mom," I said.

"Give her a chance. She'd love to hear about your first time surfing, I'm sure."

I quieted. "Okay, I'll call her."

"Good." Jen smiled.

I dried my face, changed into clothes, and called Mom. "Mom, I stood up on like sixteen waves!"

"What? You went surfing already?"

"Yup."

"Oh, darling, I can't believe it! Isn't the water cold?" She seemed agitated.

"Uncle Charlie got me a wetsuit."

"Oh!" she gasped. "That was nice of him." She sounded sarcastic, but I ignored it.

"Yeah."

"But is it *safe*? Are there sharks?"

"No, I haven't seen any." I was annoyed that she focused on the worst that could happen, when clearly, this was one of the best experiences I'd ever had.

"This calls for a celebration!" Jen declared. "I'm fixing some banana pancakes." She was getting all the ingredients together.

"Is that Jennifer?" Mom asked. "Can I talk to her?"

I handed my aunt the phone. "She wants to talk to you."

"Oh." Jen took the phone. "Hi . . . yes, she did—amazing! Charlie picked her up one . . . oh yeah, it's too cold for just a bathing suit." She poured some flour into a bowl, and cracked an egg in.

"Oh, no worries . . . she's safe, no sharks." She turned and winked at me as she held the phone to her ear with her shoulder. She was busy stirring the batter in the bowl. "Okay, bye, Julia! Love you!"

I hadn't realized how hungry I was until that first bite of banana pancakes topped with butter and maple syrup. "Mmm, this is so good. Thanks."

"Sure thing." Jen took a bite. "Mmm, sure is!"

After breakfast, full of yummy food, I relaxed into the comfortable sofa, warm and cozy in the little cottage. But there was more, something new. I felt satisfied, but also satisfied with myself. *I did it. I surfed waves.*

When Charlie came home a few days later, he said I was surf-stoked, and I was. I couldn't wait to get back in the water.

When Jen described the surf lesson, Charlie seemed

tickled pink. "Sixteen waves, huh? That could be the standing first-time record!" He grinned as he glanced at Jen, his bright-blue eyes twinkling that special way they did when he looked at her. He turned back to me. "Hey wait, aren't you gonna be sixteen soon?"

"Yeah, in July."

"Sweet sixteen!" hooted Charlie.

"We'll have to do something special on your birthday," said Jen.

"Yeah, like double those sixteen waves!" said Charlie.

That night, when I shut my eyes to sleep, I saw the ocean horizon, vibrating. Like after you've looked into the sun and the impression stays with you when you close your eyes. Incoming lines of waves came towards me, over and over again. Soothed by the sea's lullaby in my mind's eye, I drifted off to sleep.

SIX

Getting Worked

Every morning I awoke before the sun rose, in anticipation of another surf lesson with my aunt. I joined her for a cup of warm, fragrant Earl Grey tea with milk and honey at the kitchen table, and then maneuvered myself into my still-wet wetsuit from the day before. Not an easy task. Cold, damp, a struggle to get into, but it was all worth it. My aunt and I walked barefoot down the hill to the beach. She told me that I would soon grow surfer feet, like hers, meaning I wouldn't be sensitive to every pebble. I wanted to have surfer feet, and proudly walked barefoot.

I could never do this back home in the city. Once I got yelled at by the teacher for taking my shoes off in the middle-school playground: "You'll get diseases! Rats and trash and dog poop cover these streets! Put your shoes back on right now!" *How different it is here.*

Above the cobalt sea, a streak of peach cloud crossed the sky. Aunt Jen carried her board under her arm, down the hill. It was difficult for me to carry the Banana board; it was so wide, it couldn't fit easily under my arm, and it was long and heavy. But I insisted on doing it every time, balancing the board on the flat part on top of my head, or sometimes I dragged it behind me in the sand, pulling it by the nose to the water's edge.

I hoped the conditions were okay for me to surf. I couldn't tell if they were, unless the waves looked like giant walls. I watched Jen as she squinted and studied the water. On days when she said the surf was too big and not good for a beginner, I would put the board down and watch. It was almost just as good to watch surfing as it was to surf.

I sat on the beach and scanned the bunches of dark figures out there, trying to identify who was who. It was impossible to do unless I saw them ride a wave. Eddie was easy to spot in his neon-orange wetsuit. He took off, flying down the line, then hit the top of the wave so fast that his whole board came come out of the water and then re-entered the face of the wave. Don, in his black wetsuit with fluorescent green arms, smoothly dropped into a huge wave and did a "bottom turn," meaning he turned hard at the bottom of the wave, went vertical to the top, and pivoted "off the lip," or he went "off the top," meaning he carved a turn at the top of the wave. He did this five or six times in a row, continuously re-entering the force of the wave, his long black hair whipping in the wind. Sometimes, he would end up on top of the lip and appear to float back down. This was called a "floater." I was mesmerized. *I want to be that good.* I made a promise to myself that I'd be out there even on the biggest days, with the best of them, soon.

When the conditions were okay, I went out by myself in shoulder-high water, surfing "the inside." I fought with all my might to stay standing, getting smacked in the face by hard, icy cold water over and over again. Jen had taught me to "turtle" whitewash that was too big to paddle over. As a torrential mass of water surged towards me, I flipped over, grasping the board tightly. Upside down, the board on top of me and pressed against my cheek, I held my breath while the wave passed over me. When I flipped back around, I could breathe. When a wave broke further outside, I'd let the whitewash push me towards shore and I'd pop up to my feet and try to ride for as long as possible before falling. Sometimes I'd make it all the way to the beach, the nose of the board skimming the wet sand.

I wanted to make it outside to the lineup, where the other surfers caught waves and where the dolphins were. Here, it was too shallow for the dolphins. But there were much bigger sets out there, and many days of them. Now I could appreciate the small day my aunt had chosen for my first lesson.

Frustrated and eager to paddle out, I decided to try it one day. Bursts of cold spray spurted at me as I walked in, waist-deep. I turtled the whirl of overhead whitewash and paddled as hard and as fast as I could. I dug my hands deep, making cups with them like a seal's flippers, letting no water through my fingers, pushing hard against the incoming gush. But I was weak. I didn't have the muscle development other surfers had from years of doing it. I wasn't going anywhere; I was moving backwards toward shore.

Another wave came crashing down on me. I tried to turtle my board, but I was too late. Its force ripped my grasping hands from the board and violently flung me, spinning me and hurling me down to its murky depths. I wasn't ready for this. In a state of shock, in the freezing cold, unable to see anything, I became disoriented. *Which way is up?* I needed to breathe. The weight of the Pacific held me down for a long time. I didn't think I could hold my breath any longer, but I was being forced to. Arms and legs flailing, somehow, I made progress and finally surfaced, gasping for breath. I looked around for my board. It was traveling on the water's surface towards the beach. I tried to run after it, but my legs were heavy in the soup. I swam, getting stuck in large clumps of seaweed. I threw a patch out of my way, wading in the thick.

"Kook!" shouted a man as he shook his head in disgust. "Hang onto your board!"

"I-I'm trying to," I gasped.

"It could hit someone," he scolded. "Grommet!" he added, before he paddled past me on his way out to the lineup. I wasn't sure if he was annoyed because I was a girl, or just because I was learning. But I didn't let that stop me. I caught up with my board in the shallows. It was tangled in seaweed, getting tossed around by the whitewater. I picked it up by the nose and faced the incoming waves. I was determined to make it out. I tried again but became utterly exhausted. I had to accept that it was too hard for me to make it out that day.

When I spoke to Charlie about it later, he said he was proud of me that I tried to paddle out. But he gave me some advice. "Next time, don't fight it—relax," he said. "If you panic, you lose energy. It makes it harder to hold your breath. Fighting it only drains you of the strength you need for the next set. My lifeguard friends'll tell ya. When people panic in the water, they die. Panic is the worst thing you can do."

Charlie saved lives every day, so he knew what he was talking about. He had the lines etched in his suntanned face to prove it—lines of wisdom. He handled his board with precision. He could weave in and out of people on the inside, avoiding them expertly. He'd surfed ever since he was a kid.

"You can practice holding your breath," Jen advised. "Then you won't be scared when you get held under."

I decided to do just that in the bathtub every night. I held my breath, counting. I wanted to be able to relax in that situation next time. I wanted to be fearless.

Jen had learned to surf late, at nineteen, when she moved

out to California. A natural athlete—unlike my mom—Jen took to it right away. She'd been surfing for fourteen years. I watched in awe as Jen dropped in on overhead sets and flew down the line, going off the top again and again along the curving curl. She worked the wave to the very end, kicked out, and landed perfectly on top of her board. She made it look so easy. She dove big sets, making it under and through to the other side. She made it out on the biggest days, with all the other guys. She didn't let being female stop her, and I wasn't about to, either.

"Most people are done when they get worked," Charlie went on. "They're done trying to surf, even grown men! Kudos to you for pushing on, Ellie."

"It's part of it," Jen said. "Getting held under, it's part of surfing. May as well get used to it and go with the flow. You can't fight Mother Ocean."

"What does 'grommet' mean?" I asked.

"Did someone call you that?" said Charlie, the corner of his mouth curving up into a smile.

"Yeah."

"Grommet's like kid surfer," he said.

"I'm not a kid."

"It can just mean younger surfer. People say 'grom' for short."

"It's not a bad thing," Charlie added. He pushed his base-ball cap back to scratch his forehead, giving my aunt an impish look.

"What about 'kook?'"

Charlie's face twisted into a frown. "Who called you *that?*" he seethed.

"Um, an old guy." I shrugged.

"No one should *ever* call you that, it's not right," he

explained in a serious tone. He stood up, took off his baseball cap, and slapped it onto the table. "You show me who that was, and I'll give 'em a piece of my mind!"

"I guess it's not a good thing," I gulped.

"Don't listen to no grumpy old man," Jen said, shaking her head.

"A kook is someone who doesn't know what they're doing in the water," Charlie continued, pacing back and forth. "But you're learning and you're a grom! So that's just inappropriate."

Jen sighed. "Sometimes guys aren't so nice in the water." Her eyes, full of empathy, met mine. "But don't let that get to you."

I wasn't hurt by what the old man had said. I was curious about what words meant in surfing, and what was considered proper behavior and what wasn't. I knew it wasn't good to get in someone's way while they were on a wave, so I was careful to avoid it. Jen tied a leash to the board, which I strapped around my left ankle before paddling out, so it wouldn't fly away from me.

I got pummeled—or "worked"—many, many times. But I was learning to not fight it, to relax. Soon I was making it outside, beyond the "impact zone" where the waves broke, far out where the surfers waited and watched for waves, where I had seen the dolphins come that first day.

I sat next to Jen in the lineup, scanning the horizon for a glimmer of swell.

She coached me. "Okay, here's a left. Point your nose a little to the left when you take off. Paddle that way, paddle hard! You got it!"

Wilkies shouted, "Go, Ellie!"

Soon other people shouted "Go, Ellie!" too.

Eddie shouted, "Go grom!"

"Hey, it's a *girl* grom!" the Duke shouted out, laughing. "But what should we call her?"

"Her name's Ellie," Jen called back.

"Ellie—that's not suitable," he said. "We'll see . . ."

Other guys shook their heads, obviously annoyed. Some guys didn't want me in the water, they made that obvious. I ignored them. I was used to ignoring people on the subways and city streets. As for the ones that supported me, mostly friends of my aunt and uncles, I ate it up.

I hoped that Mom would get a job here, and that she'd like living here. I was beginning to, because of surfing.

It was hard to go to school after surfing. It was hard to say goodbye to Zuzu—she didn't understand why I had to leave her. Aunt Jen would drive me. Most of the kids rode bikes or drove themselves to high school, but I hadn't even thought about getting a driver's license in New York City. No one drove there.

I'd be bored sitting by myself at lunch, but then I'd think about surfing earlier and feel charged with energy to face whatever came my way. Now it was late April, I was relieved there were only a couple months of school left before summer break.

One day a girl came up to me at lunch, squinting her pale blue eyes. "Are you in my class?"

"Yeah, I think so." I recognized her. She had long, orange hair while most of the other girls were blonde.

"I'm Caitlyn," she said. Her smile was framed by freckles, which stood out from her chalky complexion.

"Hi, I'm Ellie."

She sat down next to me. "Are you new here?"

"Yeah."

"Where are you from?"

I didn't like that it was obvious I wasn't from here, so I said, "I live on Twenty-Eighth Street."

"Oh . . ." She glanced behind her. Some other sophomore girls from my homeroom were heading over to our table. She turned back to me. "But like, where did you go to high school before?"

"New York City."

"Wow, that's really far away." Her eyes opened wide.

"You're from New York?" interrupted one of the blonde girls, Brooke. She was standing behind Caitlyn, a pink sweater tied perfectly over her shoulders, the collar of her white polo shirt popped up.

"Duh," commented another girl. "You don't look like you're from here."

Suddenly, I was surrounded by girls in the middle of what had started as a private conversation between me and Caitlyn. Bonnie, one of the most popular girls, said, "She looks like she lives at Hobo Bridge." All the girls laughed. Bonnie's outfit looked brand new; her bright-green sweater vest and pinstripe blouse looked like they had come from an expensive store.

Inside, I jolted back at her harsh words, but I didn't show it. I stared down at the sandwich my aunt had made for me, hoping to disappear. My eyes focused on my dirty sneakers. They looked worn out. My face grew hot.

"She lives on Twenty-Eighth Street," said Caitlyn.

"Maybe she's in a foster home?" They all snickered. I held my breath.

"Looks like she wears hand-me-downs from an older brother," said another girl.

I wanted to scream back at them that I lived with my aunt and uncle, but I didn't because suddenly I was ashamed that I was living here without parents. I clenched my fists against the stomach knots that were forming.

"Pathetic," spat Bonnie before walking away abruptly. The rest of them followed.

"I'm starved," Caitlyn said, opening up her lunch bag. Another girl showed up at the table, sat down next to Caitlyn, and smiled at me, oblivious to what had just happened.

I wasn't hungry anymore. My stomach had turned over, but I managed a faint smile back at her. The "foster home" comment touched a nerve. I didn't belong here.

"What's Hobo Bridge?" I asked Caitlyn.

She hesitated before answering. "It's a place on the railroad tracks under Sepulveda Boulevard," she said softly.

After Caitlyn started talking to me, some other girls did, too. The group of popular girls made it clear that they didn't like me, but I wasn't too bothered since I could sit next to Caitlyn and her friends at lunch. But I looked forward to school ending more than anything so I could concentrate on surfing more.

SEVEN

Nai'a Aumakua

One morning I paddled out, turtling my yellow Banana board a few times as I went. I sat there watching the horizon, fixated on the lines of waves rolling in.

"Dolphins!" a guy near me exclaimed.

I scanned the ocean's surface, my heart beating fast. I'd been waiting for this moment. Fins appeared about thirty feet away, and then—dolphins surfaced. A pod of three headed south, gracefully leaping and diving in arcs, up and under. They'd cross in front of me soon.

All of a sudden, one changed direction. Instead of continuing on its course straight, it angled, heading straight for me. As it got closer, I saw what a big animal it was. I tensed, gripping the rails of the board. It surfaced two feet in front of me, its soulful eye meeting mine. Etched in its gray skin were scars, and there were nicks in its fin. Most of the dark marks looked like scratches, but some of them were deeper, bigger. One was in the shape of a crescent moon. The dolphin leapt in front of me, a massive body, its tail flicking the water in its wake and splashing my face. I screamed. My heart was pounding. It came up so close, I could've touched it. Then it was gone.

"Aunt Jen!" I called out, but she was surfing too far down the beach to hear me. She hadn't seen, so I told her about it later, how it had come to say hello to me. It hurt that I couldn't tell Dad about the dolphin. I thought about its crescent moon scar, and how Dad would always look for the moon at night.

When I told Mom about the dolphins, she said she was scared I'd get hurt because they were wild animals, and she was worried I'd get bitten by a shark. I told her that Jen said when the dolphins came around, people were safe, because the dolphins would chase away the sharks. Mom didn't believe it, but I did. The dolphins had a gentle, playful, intelligent energy that was unlike any other animal.

What do the dolphins mean to the native people here? Dad and I would've talked about it. Then it hit me—we would've gone to the library to look it up.

The next day after school, I headed to the library, taking the Strand all the way to downtown. It felt odd to walk down the beach to the library—a sharp contrast to my trek to the main library in New York City. *I'm so lucky to be here.* The ocean, sparkling blue, was to my right. I looked for dolphin fins out there. When I got to Fifteenth Street, I walked three blocks up the hill to the library, a small building near city hall that was very small compared to New York City's tall buildings.

The librarian helped me find what I was looking for. One native tribe from Malibu, just north of us, were the Chumash, which meant "seashell people." I found a creation story of theirs called "The Rainbow Bridge." It said that the first people lived on an island off this coast called Limuw, now Santa Cruz Island. They were happy, but soon there were too many of them on too small of an island. Hutash, their creator, made a tall bridge out of a rainbow, and told them to cross over it to the mainland, where there would be plenty of room for them. But some people looked down while they were crossing the bridge, got dizzy from the fog, lost their balance, and fell. As they fell, they cried out to Hutash for help, so she turned them into dolphins.

I liked the idea that dolphins were once human. They seemed really smart, more than people realized. I looked up more about them in other books. I learned that the ancient Hawaiians believed the spirit of a person who'd died could enter into a sea animal, becoming an *aumakua*, or "helper." I imagined someone in peril out in the ocean, and the spirit of a loved one in the form of a dolphin, or *nai'a*, appearing and helping them to shore. I wondered if Dad could become an *aumakua* if I was about to drown. I believed that the dolphins would help me if I needed it, and I was beginning to adopt the Hawaiian and Chumash belief that they were our ancestors, our family.

In a marine biology book, I found out that dolphins used sonar to tell where things were in the ocean. They sent out a sound signal that bounced back to them, so they could "see" things near and far. It was called *echolocation*.

Now I knew that dolphins had great hearing, I made up my very own dolphin call. Each day when I'd made it outside, I'd rub the rail of my board near the nose, and sure enough, the dolphins would come and say hello. My heart skipped a beat at the sight them.

One morning at school, after I'd been surfing, when I bent down to pick up a piece of paper that had fallen off my desk, water dripped out my nose onto the floor. It continued to drip when I sat up, drops falling onto my notebook.

"Eww, gross!" scolded a girl who sat in my row, a snobby blonde named April. She grimaced as I covered my nose with my hand in embarrassment. April made sure the word spread around about it quickly. At lunch, she marched over to the popular girls' table. They kept looking at me, pointing and laughing. Then Bonnie and Brooke barged over to my table with April. Caitlyn was sitting opposite me, so she didn't see them coming.

Bonnie nudged April towards me. "Umm . . . like, what came out of your nose today?" April prodded. "Are you sick?"

"Like, if you have some kind of hobo flu, you shouldn't be at school spreading grody germs," snapped Bonnie.

"Guess they don't give out tissues in foster homes," added Brooke in a snarky tone. Bonnie laughed.

Caitlyn gaped at me, wide-eyed in alarm. I stared down at my peanut butter and jelly sandwich, dread prickling through my body.

"So gross," Bonnie scoffed at me, then turned and walked away. Brooke and April followed.

"Are you sick?" asked Caitlyn in a panicky voice.

"No," I said, but I felt sick to my stomach.

Later, I told Charlie what had happened. He said, "Your nose drained. It happens all the time after surfing. Especially if you got held under."

I didn't tell him the mean things the girls had said. I didn't tell anyone about that. But after hearing what Charlie said, I felt proud when my nose drained after my morning surf sessions. It was my own private acknowledgement that I was charging waves, that I wasn't afraid of getting worked. But I brought tissues to school in my backpack the next day. I didn't want those girls teasing me about it again. They did anyway. Every time they saw me, they touched their noses and said, "Grody," or "Gross me out." I stiffened, pretending they didn't get to me. I tried to ignore them and think about surfing.

Before I knew it, I was learning how to turn my board while surfing. Aunt Jen said this was the next step; to be able to go left or right, and to know which way to go. Sitting out there, facing the horizon, I'd ask her, "What's this?" when a wave was approaching.

She'd reply, "It's a right," or "It's a left." Sometimes she'd say, "Don't go—it's walled." I couldn't really get it. Lots of waves weren't easy to tell, but one day I finally figured it out. We'd walked down to the water's edge. Jen was excited because there were perfect little peaks. She pointed out a left to me.

"See how it slopes down at an angle this way from the peak?" She made a triangle with her hands, her fingers touching each other. "Whichever way it slopes down at an angle is the way it's going."

We were facing the ocean from the beach, and the wave sloped to our right. But from the outside, if you paddled to catch it, it would be a left. That was the perspective from which you called it.

Outside, I sat further out than Jen, because with a longboard you had to. My board was nine feet, and Jen's was only six feet, three inches. I needed to be further outside to start paddling and catch the wave sooner. If I sat in with Jen, the wave would be too big once it got to me. This was called "taking off late," and was dangerous. The power of the wave beginning to break could send you and your board flying. I had already learned this the hard way. Free-falling was sort of fun, but scary if you didn't know what you might hit. I got hit by my board a few times; it hurt, and left bruises.

By May, the weather was starting to warm up. Sitting alone at an outdoor table at lunch one day, I took off my sweater. Bonnie, Brooke, and April walked up to me.

"Looks like she's getting into fights at foster care," Bonnie said, scowling at a big purple bruise on my arm. April laughed. I wanted to reply that it was from falling on a close-out and hitting the rail of my surfboard, but all I could do was freeze. I looked down at my brown paper lunch bag, my gut twisting in panic.

"Aww, too bad . . . she's gonna have to move to a new home in Gardena and she won't go to school here anymore," Brooke said sarcastically.

"We'll miss you so much, grody girl," spat out April. Before I could summon up the courage to reply, they spun around and left. I sat there, drained of energy, my stomach in knots. I didn't eat lunch until my appetite kicked in while walking home from school, in anticipation of jumping into the water as soon as I could grab my board.

One morning, Jen paddled up to me as we waited for waves during a lull. "Okay, so now that you know your rights and lefts, I'll explain etiquette."

"Etiquette?" I was confused. "You mean like table manners?"

"Yeah, but it's more about being fair and safe than polite. It's crucial, otherwise you can get hurt." She sat to my left as we faced the horizon. "If a left comes now, I have the right of way because I'm deeper," she said.

I squinted into the morning sun as I turned to look at her. "So, if we turn around and paddle for the wave, you're at the higher part of the triangle?"

"Yes, and you're more towards the corner as it slopes down."

I nodded.

She continued, "I could *let* you have the wave if I want,

but if I catch it, you should let me have it. If you go anyway, it's called 'snaking.'"

I was amused. "Like you call that person a snake?"

"Yeah, and it can be very dangerous, especially if the waves are big and timing is crucial. People get into fights."

"So, if it's a right, I have the right of way?" I asked.

"Yes, exactly."

"But what if I want you to go with me?"

"Then you can tell me to go. That's called a party wave."

"I wanna do a party wave," I requested.

"Okay," she said. The next wave was coming in, and Jen said it was a left. "Paddle, we'll go together!" She stood up and I did, too. I was laughing the whole way. After I fell, Jen crossed in front of me, and rode the wave all the way in. I hopped onto my belly to catch the whitewater in, giggling as it lurched me into the sand.

"That was so much fun!" I cried out.

"Yeah, nice to party with you!" Jen gave me a high five.

I was careful to follow the etiquette stuff that Jen taught me. I didn't want to be a "snake." Now that I knew the rules, I got mad when guys snaked me. Lots of times they did, thinking I couldn't catch a wave because I was a girl. I wanted to prove them wrong.

While looking through the pile of surfing magazines my aunt and uncle had in the living room, I came across an awe-inspiring picture of someone surfing in Hawaii.

"Gerry Lopez," Charlie said over my shoulder upon entering the room. "Gettin' tubed. Mr. Pipeline."

"Is Hawaii where surfing started?" I turned in my seat to face him.

"Yeah, sure did—the Polynesians brought it to Hawaii. Queens surfed, girls surfed just as much as guys. In fact, Hawaiian queens had their own breaks no one else was allowed to surf. I bet if you cut off the queen, you'd be in trouble." Wide-eyed, he mimed cutting his throat with his finger, backing into the kitchen. Then he turned away, towards the counter.

"Really?" I asked. "Guys here cut me off all the time."

"Wha—?" he faltered, the coffee pot in hand, turning back towards me.

"Yeah," I said. "And some guys stare at me in a mean way."

He slumped back against the counter, his face in shock, then concern. "That's called stink-eye."

"Stink-eye? It sure does stink." I blinked, recalling the unfairness of being made to feel unwelcome in the place I now cherished most.

"Yeah, well, they stink if they're being mean to a grom, and you're my niece!" he seethed, slamming the coffee pot down. "Let me know who next time, and I'll give 'em a piece of my mind."

Guys didn't dare do that when I was out surfing with Charlie. But they did with Jen sometimes, especially if they didn't know us. Jen told me that most guys thought surfing was a boys' club, and girls weren't welcome. She said guys "vibed" her all the time, meaning they gave out bad vibes and stink-eye. Guys felt territorial, and not just if it was their local spot to surf. Even if it wasn't, they felt surfing was a man's sport. Jen said guys had tried to run her over before. They made it clear to her that they didn't want her out there. But she ignored them. Often guys got mad when she surfed better than them; they were jealous and felt threatened.

"All except my surf buddies and dear old Charlie," she said. Other than them, "No guy wants to be out next to a woman who is surfing better than him."

There were hardly any pictures of women surfers in the magazines. Two years ago, the May 1981 cover of *Surfer* was the exception; Margo Oberg was on the cover. Aunt Jen said she was the first woman pro, and that she'd won five world championships. But that was the only cover with a female surfer on it in twenty years. There were plenty of photos of scantily clad women in the magazines for no reason, or because they were in the bikini contests held during the surf contests. The message was clear: stick to looking good and watching from the beach. I wanted to puke.

I sat on my board in the dewy morning mist the next Monday, listening to the sound of foghorns. The milky white-gray mist enveloped me. Aunt Jen called it "May Gray." She said soon it would turn to "June Gloom." I couldn't see the shore, or ten feet to my left or right. I liked practicing my pop-ups in the privacy of the fog. It felt like I was surfing in my own mystical world. I didn't want to get out of the water, and I dreaded going to school. The popular girls kept on about my nose draining, calling me "grody" and joking that I was in foster care. I didn't want to give them the satisfaction that they'd gotten to me. I just wanted them to leave me alone. *At least Caitlyn's my friend, and I have surfing. Dad would've been proud of me.* Suddenly the weight of him being gone seemed too much to bear. My heart raw, I floated out there, abandoned, surrounded by fog.

Then, from out of the mist, a dolphin flew across my field of vision. I screamed. It dove under, and I slipped off my board and went under, too. Opening my eyes underwater, all I could see were murky shapes, like filtered sun through a tree branch laden with leaves. There was an alluring high-pitched call, then some clicks and buzzes. I surfaced to breathe, followed my leash to my board and held on, my legs dangling. At the sound of the water surging, I turned to see more dolphins diving down, spray flying into the air. The dolphins circled me. My heart was racing. There were more than before; I counted seven of them, diving down and coming up in arcs. Their movements were so joyful, it was uplifting. They all had different nicks in their fins, and scars in their skin. I tried to make out a crescent moon scar, but they were moving too fast. Then they stopped and just floated in a circle around me. *Can the dolphins sense my pain, my loss, and have empathy for me?*

Then they were gone. I was shaking.

School wasn't so bad that day because the amazing experience with the dolphins stayed with me. On my walk home, I thought about Mom coming soon. She was so New York, how would she ever fit in here? The butterflies fluttering among colorful flowers and the birds chirping lifted my spirits. It was totally different than the subway ride home I was used to. *She's sure to appreciate all this beauty*, I thought. I hoped.

EIGHT

Heels

The day Mom was to arrive, it had been June Gloom all morning. A layer of fog covered the sun, making it overcast and a bit chilly. I loved weather like this, though most people didn't. They complained, saying, "When's the sun going to come out?" But by noon, the sun would always burst through.

I was relieved school was over, now that it was summer. It'd been like a thorn in my side that I couldn't surf all day. Now I could.

When I went with Uncle Charlie to pick up Mom, the sun had overtaken the sky. In the yellow VW bus, Charlie circled the airport a few times, happily singing "California Dreamin'" along with the Mamas and the Papas on his eight-track player.

I saw her walk out. She had cut her platinum blonde hair shorter, in layers. It was longer on top and spiky around her forehead. She wore black all the way down to her toes. It was a striking contrast to her pale white skin and red lips. In her high-heeled boots, she was lugging a black suitcase that was bigger than her.

"Mom!" I waved my arms out the window.

Uncle Charlie pulled over and jumped out. "Is there a snowstorm coming I don't know about?"

Mom scowled. "It's raining cats and dogs in New York!"

"This ain't New York! You've been here before, you should know that." He opened his eyes wide, stuck out his tongue, and made a fart sound at her.

She smirked. "Charming, Charlie. I see you haven't changed a bit."

I couldn't help but giggle as I hopped out of the van.

"Come here, Elle, so I can squeeze you!"

"Ellie, Mom!" I corrected her.

"Ellie, yes, come here!"

I walked over. She squeezed me too tight. Her perfume was strong, and as she released me, her breath smelled of alcohol. I tensed.

She took off her black jacket. "Oh, it's so hot here!"

I squinted up at her. "Yeah, sunny California, Mom." The sun was blaring down on us.

Charlie took the same route home he'd taken that first night when I'd arrived. Tall palm trees lined the streets. The next song on the eight-track player started, and Mom shouted, "What is this sappy music?"

"It's the California sound—you're on the West Coast now!" Charlie said.

"It's fucking crap!" Mom spat out, ejecting the cartridge.

Charlie glanced back at me with a look that said he found Mom amusing and he was about to laugh. I shook my head and put on a grave face, which he saw in the rearview mirror. He made a sharp left, the vast expanse of ocean stretched out to our right.

Mom put her hand up to shield her eyes. "It's so bright!"

"Guess the June Gloom is over for the day," Charlie replied. "Hey, look at that left off the jetty!" I focused on the wave. A surfer had stood up and was going down the line. As we passed by, he continued on the wave.

"He's still riding it!" I exclaimed. "And all the way to the next tower!"

"Tah-wee!" Charlie howled.

Mom didn't flinch. She was looking straight ahead.

"You missed it," I said. She didn't respond, seeming preoccupied.

"That one'll take him past the tower, all the way to shore," said Charlie.

Mom was fumbling in her purse. "I know I put them in here." She sounded irritated. When she finally found her sunglasses and put them on, we were pulling up to the front of the house.

As Charlie parked the van, he declared in a happy-go-lucky voice: "Home sweet home!"

Mom tilted her head to peer out from behind her sunglasses. "Is the house really that bright a green, or is it my glasses?"

"Huh? Oh yeah, like key lime pie!" Charlie grinned.

Mom frowned. "That green is garish."

Charlie went around the van to grab Mom's bag from the back and chuckled. "Maybe you'd prefer it black?" He heaved her suitcase down and then, in exaggeration, struggled to carry it. "Whoa! Whaddaya have in here? Gold bars?"

Mom smirked. "I wish. Lots of shoes."

"*Gold* shoes? Seriously?"

"Some gold heels, yes."

He swung both of his arms up, like he was fed up. "Who needs shoes?" he said, raising his eyebrows. "You're at the beach!" He lifted a foot up in the air to show that he was barefoot; he'd driven to the airport that way. He lugged the suitcase up the steps and to the front door.

Mom walked up the steps and stopped, looking at the house. "Not black, but maybe if it were a gray . . ." When she stepped forward, her heel missed the pavestone and sunk into the sandy dirt, causing her to almost fall. Luckily, I was nearby, so I caught her arm and steadied her. She gasped, cursing.

Charlie saw this and chuckled. "You might want to take those city shoes off."

The front door flew open. Aunt Jen was there, beaming her sister a big smile. "Julie!" She stepped up to Mom and gave her a big hug.

"Julia," my mom corrected her.

"Sorry, Julia. So good to see you, sis!"

"Th-thanks, Jen," Mom stammered. "Good to see you, too."

Jen gestured toward the living room. "Come on in. There's tea, and cookies I just made."

"You made cookies while we picked up Mom?"

"Yeah, just some peanut butter ones." She acted like it was nothing to whip up cookies in no time.

"Uh, I'm on a diet," Mom said.

Charlie seemed more at ease now he was in his own home. "Can I get you a beer?"

"Not beer," Mom huffed. "Do you have anything stronger? That was a rough flight."

"Oh, shoot, Sis," said Jen. "Take a load off and get comfy."

"Yeah," Charlie piped in. "You can take those shoes off and hang loose." He chuckled and started looking for something for Mom in the cabinet. "Hmm . . . I'm don't think we have anything . . . Wait, we may have some tequila in the garage."

"Anything!" Mom blurted out.

"Comin' right up, Heels." It was that moment when Uncle Charlie gave Mom the nickname "Heels." Ever since that day, I never heard him call her anything else.

The heat of the summer was unbearable for my mom. She got headaches every evening from the hot afternoon sun. She said they were migraines. She always wore black sunglasses, even in the house.

Mom had gotten a job at a gallery in West Hollywood that didn't start until noon. When she was home, she stayed in her bedroom. On her days off she slept late, even past noon. She wore a sleep mask in bed so the bright California sun wouldn't wake her up. Aunt Jen said maybe it was the Santa Ana winds that caused her headaches—hot, dust-filled winds from the inland desert. But I didn't think so. I would pass by Mom's room next to the garage after my morning surf. After I ate breakfast, I would pass by her room again on my way out to walk Zuzu. I didn't hear a sound. When I returned home, I was again disappointed when Mom wasn't up yet. She'd covered her windows with black fabric to block out the sun. "I have trouble falling asleep," she told Aunt Jen.

One day after we'd had an early dinner, Mom was sitting at the table in her sunglasses, holding her head in her hands. She had finally showed up just before we ate. "I had to take a sleeping pill," she explained, "and then I couldn't wake up."

"I'm sorry you couldn't sleep, Sis. How's your new job going?"

"It's okay so far," she sighed. "What a commute, though!" Mom accentuated this with both hands outstretched. "I'm not used to all this driving."

Jen listened sympathetically. I was annoyed but tried not to show it. Jen said Mom was having a hard time adjusting to California, but I could see it wasn't about California. It was about life without Dad. I'd always thought Mom was so strong.

She seemed to be; she always had an opinion, and expressed it openly. Usually it was a criticism of sorts, after which she would stomp off in her high heels. She couldn't wear her heels in the garden, as they would sink into the dirt, so she kept them in her room Charlie had built next to the garage.

All of her heels were lined up in a row, running the length of an entire wall of the garage: black, gold, red, white, and clear pumps, strappy sandals, and boots. That way, she could put them on and get into the little car she'd leased and go straight to work. She didn't have to step foot in the garden—no pointy stilettos sinking into the earth, getting dirty.

Her car was a bright, glossy red Porsche 944 sports car—she said it was called "Guards Red." The Los Angeles gallery owner was paying for the lease on the new 1983 model. It reminded me of a Barbie race car I'd wanted one Christmas when I was little, but never got. Mom said plastic toys were awful, and didn't go with the minimalist aesthetic she was going for with the industrial loft we'd called home. I learned early on that toys scattered on the rug were not tolerated. At friends' houses, I got to play with their barbies, until dolls were replaced by books as I grew older.

Most days since she'd arrived, Mom was busy working at the gallery in West Hollywood. So I spent the days with my aunt and uncle and Zuzu, just like before. We always invited Mom to come along, but she never did. In the mornings, we'd invite her to come to the beach while we surfed. But it was colder than she thought here, and she needed her sleep because her nights were late and she had things to do.

Mom promised she'd take me to the museum as soon as she had a day off. The problem was, the only day off she had was Monday, a day when most museums were closed. Also, she always woke up late, and was tired or had a headache. By the time she woke up I was already in the water, and I didn't want to get out except to eat.

One day, I came in the house famished after surfing all morning. Mom was at the kitchen counter, a large glass of water in front of her. She was leaning her head in her hands.

"Are you okay?" I asked her.

"It's just a headache." She took some pills out of a bottle and swigged them down with her big glass. She grimaced after swallowing and let out a sigh. "I'll be all right in a few minutes. Want to go to the art museum today?"

"Sure." I could hardly believe it, that we were actually going to go somewhere together. "I'll get dressed right away."

I ran to my room to change, then back to the kitchen to grab a sandwich. Mom's glass was still there on the counter, half empty. As I quickly made my sandwich next to it, I caught a whiff of it. It was not water. I picked it up and smelled it. It was definitely vodka. *Why is she drinking if she has a headache? Also, why is she drinking vodka in the morning? How much did she drink?*

I tried to push the thoughts out of my mind. I went through the garden to her room and knocked on her door. "Mom, I'm all ready to go. Do you want a sandwich?"

There was no answer.

I opened the door. She was lying in bed, asleep. "Mom? Are you okay?" I walked up to her tentatively. "Mom? I'm all ready to go." She looked like she was dead. A chill crept up my spine. I gently shook her shoulder. "Mom?" She didn't move. I stood there for what must've been five minutes, hoping for her to wake up. "Mom?" My chest tightened. "Mom! Are you okay?"

She stirred and mumbled something I couldn't make out. I stiffened, clenching my fists.

"Mom, are we going to go?"

"Sorry," she said with her eyes still closed. "Just let me sleep, my headache's gotten worse."

I gave up and left, slamming the door shut behind me. *I don't want to go if Mom's drunk anyway.* We'd go another day. After I ate my sandwich, I took Zuzu for a walk and then paddled back out for more waves.

We never did make it to the art museum that summer.

NINE

Calamity Jane

With the July sun came warmth. Those June Gloom mornings, when the mist and fog surrounded me, were over. The sun warmed up the water and heated up the sand, and my canopy of privacy was lifted.

Now that the sun lit up the playing field, I was overly conscious of people seeing my mistakes. The mornings were crisp, clear, and bright. There were no longer only a few scattered souls out there; the beaches were now flooded with people. Blankets covered the sand. Kids and teenagers hung out at the beach, usually showing up in groups. I stuck to surfing, and then I'd walk home. I was too self-conscious to even lay in the sun and read by myself.

I noticed my appearance changing in the mirror. My pale skin now had some color, richer and warmer from the sun. My brown hair had some highlights in it. I was starting to get stronger. My muscles were growing and firming up. I noticed it in my arms. Before, they were sticks. Now they were beginning to have some shape to them. It looked like my scrawny neck was getting thicker, too. I liked the changes. Except for my small breasts. I wished they were fuller . . . mine were like preteens buds just emerging. I also thought my butt was too big.

Come mid-July, the water warmed up so much that I could

surf in my swimsuit. The only one I had was a modest purple one-piece that was now a faded lavender. I felt like a little girl in it since all the local girls my age had bright-colored, open back swimsuits that cut all the way above their hips, creating a V-hip. Some wore tiny string bikinis—new ones that showed half of their butts and tied up above the hip, making their tan legs look longer. Even though my face and arms had some color, my legs were still white, since they'd been covered by a wetsuit for months. I was embarrassed by their paleness.

After a surf session one afternoon, I walked by a group of those girls as quickly as I could. I could tell they were staring me down, even with their big mirrored sunglasses on. I was overly conscious of my body, aware of my insignificant breasts and my larger-than-model-size butt. I hugged the big yellow surfboard to me, trying to hide. My faded purple one-piece had stretched because it was old. It was saggy, dripping with water. *I should've made sure I got all the wet sand out before I crossed the beach.* I tried not to limp, but I'd hurt my leg. My feet were screaming at me, on fire from the hot sand, but I pretended not to feel it. I wanted to develop surfer feet.

These girls didn't surf, though; they just liked to lay out and tan on their bright towels. Their tan skin glistened, lathered in baby oil. Their sunscreen smelled like those artificial piña colada air fresheners in New York City taxicabs.

After I passed them, the girls burst out laughing. I was sure they were laughing at me. I started running, spurred onward by the hot sand. *Ow, ow!*

"Ellie?" someone shouted. I turned around. It was one of the girls. She took her sunglasses off as she walked up to me.

"Yeah, hi, Caitlyn," I mumbled. She had on a bubble-gum-pink bikini that looked brand new.

"Oh my gosh, like . . . isn't the water so cold?"

"It's okay."

"It's freezing! You won't see me in that water until it warms up in, like, August. I'm just happy working on my tan."

"And I'm working on my surfing," I replied, leaning into my big board.

"Having a fun summer?"

"Yeah, how about you?"

"Totally!" She bent her knees with enthusiasm. She glanced back at the girls sitting on the towel. They just sat there, some facing away, some looking at us, but not in an inviting sort of way. I could tell Caitlyn was eager to wrap up our awkward conversation. "Kay, well, see you around!" She whipped around, turning back to them.

"Okay, nice to see you," I mumbled as I continued to limp across the sand, struggling with my board. My leash was dragging, but I trudged on.

At the Strand, I stopped to wrap the leash around the fin and tail of the board. I spotted the boy I'd seen when I'd first arrived here, with the checkered shortboard and beautiful green eyes. He was headed towards me. It was the first time I'd seen him without a wetsuit, just in swim trunks. The bareness of his golden-brown chiseled chest caught me by surprise. I quickly looked down and awkwardly tried not to show my limp.

"How was it out there?" he said with friendly enthusiasm as he approached me.

"Huh?" I looked up to make sure he was really talking to me. His gray-green eyes danced like sparkling gems when they met mine. His broad grin gave him an impish quality I hadn't noticed before.

"How were the waves?"

"Oh . . . good!" I said. The waves were good, it was just me that wasn't any good. I hoped he hadn't seen me eat it out there.

"Radical. It looks fun!" He threw his head back as he took in the surf, his grin spreading even wider.

"Yeah, um, it's beautiful out there," I said, taking in the sea air and exhaling.

"Sure is! Sun is shining, there's surf . . ." He stretched open his free arm to accentuate his exuberance. "What more can we ask for?"

"I don't know," I agreed, smiling. But deep down I knew: friends. The awkward encounter with Caitlyn had clearly showed me what I was lacking. She had friends and was hanging out with them, and it wasn't me. She hadn't invited me to join them.

I bit back my disappointment and responded to the kind boy in front of me with gratitude for his comradery. "Have fun."

"Thanks, see ya around!"

"Kay, see ya around." *Ughh, why did I have to repeat exactly what he said? What an idiot!* But I hoped I would see him soon. Running into him was the only thing that had kept me from crying after my awkward exchange with Caitlyn.

On my way through the parking lot, Wilkies stopped me.

"I saw you go for that set wave. You pearled it. You were a little too late."

I hung my head, my gaze fixed on the asphalt. "Yeah, that sucked . . . and I hurt my leg."

"You went for it, you charged!"

"Yeah." I sighed. I knew he was trying to make me feel better, but I was frustrated with myself. I walked on, heading home. I struggled to carry the big board, my arms aching. In the outdoor shower, clumps of sand came out the bottom of my bathing suit. Embarrassment flooded through me; Caitlyn and those girls probably saw lumps in the butt of my old one-piece, making me look even more like a kid. *Oh gosh, I hope that boy didn't notice!* Later I realized that I'd burnt my feet from the hot sand, too.

I got hurt a lot that summer. My newly exposed skin was black and blue with bruises. I bruised my rib, my leg, my arm. I sprained my finger and got a small cut above my eyebrow that only needed a butterfly bandage, no stitches. "Thank God you didn't poke your eye out," Mom said when she found out.

Wilkies started calling me "Calamity Jane." I cringed; it wasn't a cool surfer name. But I knew you couldn't choose your *own* nickname—it had to be given to you by someone else, and then it had to stick. I hoped this one wouldn't stick.

Uncle Charlie laughed when he heard it. Then he saw the expression on my face and quickly said, "It's not a bad thing. If you get hurt, it means you charge!"

"Hey, at least it's not 'Wiggles'!" Jen said.

Charlie chuckled. "Ha! Yeah, that's right, we used to call your aunt 'Wiggles.' When she went down the line on her twin fin, she did this thing where she moved her hips." He got up and shook his hips around.

"That looks like the hula!" Jen chimed in. "Oh, and who are you to talk, *Richie*?"

"Yeah, Wilkies sometimes calls me that. I don't know why." Charlie smiled sheepishly.

Jen laughed. "Because your ears stick out like Richie from *Happy Days*!"

"They do not!" Then, without touching them, he wiggled his ears.

Jen and I both burst out laughing.

One day, waking up from a nap after surfing, I heard voices in the living room. I opened my door but paused when I heard Aunt Jen say my name.

"Ellie had a hard time at high school here."

"What?" my mom screeched. "She told me school was fine! That's dreadful. Oh, I never should've listened to you and sent her here early!"

"What else could you have done? She couldn't live alone in the city while you were at the hospital . . . and you said you didn't have the money."

"That's true," said Mom.

"She'll start a new year here in the fall and everything will be okay."

"I hope so," sighed Mom. "If only her dad were here. He took care of her so well. He took care of *me*." Mom started to cry.

"It's okay," my aunt consoled her.

"I went to the AIDS benefit last night at the Roxy. Jen, everyone I know is scared to death. My best friend in New York . . . he's sick and he thinks he has it."

"Oh my God, I'm so sorry," my aunt said.

I walked into the room. "What? Peter's sick?"

"Yes, I'm going to see him next time I'm there," Mom said, wiping her eyes.

I'd known Peter my whole life, ever since I could remember. He'd gone to Columbia with my parents and was at every dinner party my parents threw. He was a kind person, a writer and a poet. I couldn't bear to think of him dying, too. Ignoring the hunger pains in my stomach, I decided to go back out surfing.

Surfing never felt like work to me, even with all that paddling. Getting hit by my board, free-falling from eight feet up above water, getting pummeled by a set . . . somehow these things made me feel better. Maybe it was because, after being thrown about like a rag doll, I managed to survive. Or, as Charlie called it, "getting tossed around in the washing machine."

That was nothing compared to how bad I felt inside. My heart was wrecked, and I was out here in a foreign place with no friends. My closest friend, my dad, was gone. It didn't help much that my mom was here, because I never saw her. She left late in the morning when I was still in the water, and she worked late nights. Mom didn't get what surfing meant to me, and she didn't seem interested in finding out. She never woke up early to see me surf. Charlie made me laugh, and he and my aunt were really nice to me—but they weren't my mom and dad.

For some reason, I could take the hard knocks. I wasn't scared of big waves. I just felt I had to do my best. When sizable sets came, I ignored my fear and, without hesitation, I went for it. I had a competitive streak; I wanted to be as good as the boys. I didn't like guys assuming I couldn't surf, or that I wouldn't go for big waves because I was a girl. They assumed that at first, which fueled me to prove them wrong.

The Pacific Ocean was frightening to some people, with good reason. People died here, even strong swimmers. After all, we needed to breathe air. I thought of it this way: The ocean was the world of dolphins, sharks, whales, and fish—all animals with fins. The land was the world of all animals with legs, feet, and paws—humans included. We could play in the zone between the shore and the surfer's lineup, but once our feet couldn't touch the ground, it was risky. On the edge separating worlds, we were between life and death.

That's why it was so exhilarating. My mind couldn't dwell

on thoughts of the past or future. I was forced to be in the present because my life depended on it. I had to be completely focused. When an incoming swell loomed on the horizon, I'd go for it in an instant. I'd paddle, dig deep, and at just the right moment I'd push myself up and jump my feet under me, gripping the board. At some point during each wave, I would fall. It was inevitable. Falling into water was a lot better than falling onto cement from a skateboard.

My aunt's friend Sally gave me a skateboard that summer. It was a Sims, Lester Kasai. The bottom said "Lester," printed in dayglow-green letters over a big blue paint splat. I made the mistake of trying it barefoot. I slid on the pavement and scraped up my foot. Charlie carefully picked out the pieces of gravel and bandaged it. He made me swear to wear sneakers next time.

"You need skate shoes," he declared when I showed him my dirty gray sneakers. The next day, he came home with new ones for me, Vans. They were #44s, navy with white soles. I didn't need any nudge to wear them; due to the bad scrape, I'd had to miss a few days surfing. And I needed to surf—I was addicted to it. After riding one amazing wave, I felt victorious. It made all the bruises worth it.

I was trying to *not* live up to the Calamity Jane nickname. Avoiding pearling was number one, which seemed practically unavoidable up to this point. Surfers pearled when they were too far forward on the board, making the nose go under and tail flip up and over—flinging them. Falling on the fin, or "skag," as Charlie called it, wasn't fun either. I got cut on the side of my torso when the fin sliced right through my wetsuit one morning. I was lucky I was wearing my wetsuit. Jen showed me how to fix it with special glue that looked like tar and smelled like chemicals. With practice, I learned to dodge my board when falling. I'd push the board away from me in the moment that I knew I was going to go "over the falls" or "eat it."

One day, I flew off my board while attempting to make a steep drop. Upon returning to the lineup, Charlie said, "Why don't you wait for a good one? You're trying to go on every wave."

I hadn't thought about that. I was trying so hard, so focused on *catching* waves, that it hadn't occurred to me there was another way.

"Wait for a good one," he repeated. "Most of them are closing out today."

"Closing out" meant that the wave would break all at once, straight across, forming a long wall. Surfers called these conditions "walled," which meant the waves had no shape. Walls could crush a surfer, because there was no surface to continue riding on. Imagine a skateboard ramp that ends in a sheer drop.

Stalking out the *good* waves became my new obsession. I watched and learned from Jen, Don, Eddie, Nate, the Duke, Wilkies, and Charlie. They moved around when surfing, never taking their eyes off of the horizon. They just knew where to be all the time; it seemed like the waves came right to them. It was like they had a sixth sense, telling them where the good waves were going to break. I wanted to be like them.

After a frustrating session of falling on many close-outs, which ended with me cutting my lip on my board, I walked by Ol' Man Wilkies leaning on the parking lot railing.

"Hey Ellie, you're bleeding!"

"I know." My hand was covered in blood after I touched my lip.

"Come here, I've got some ice," he said. "It'll stop the bleeding."

I went over to him. He got some ice out of a cooler in his car, wrapped it around a cloth and gave it to me. "Here, hold it to your lip. You can sit here." I held it with one arm, the other holding my board up as I sat on the edge of the open back of his car.

He peered at me, leaning closer. "You still have all your teeth?"

"I think so." I touched my teeth to make sure.

"You had to check, huh?" He chuckled. "Calamity Jane," he said, shaking his head.

He said it again. I didn't want to have a clumsy surf nickname. I sat there, awkwardly holding the ice to my lip, mad at myself for going on that last closeout.

He took the surfboard and set it down next to his car. "You know, ain't nothin' gonna fill up that hole."

"Huh?" I was confused. *Does he mean the cut on my lip?*

"That hole in your heart," he continued. "Only thing you can do is give it to God. I've been there before, so I can tell where you're at. I've been so down in the dumps, I almost killed myself. I couldn't stop drinking, so I lost everything. My wife, my job. I lost it all, and then with God's help, I pulled myself up by my bootstraps—haven't touched a drink since."

"Did your wife die?" I asked.

"No. She just left. It felt like a death, though. If it weren't for A.A., I'd probably be dead."

"A.A.?"

"Alcoholics Anonymous. Meetings for people with drinking problems."

"Oh . . . my mom should go there," I thought out loud.

"Huh," he grunted. "I suppose a lot of people should. But it's one of those places you have to get to yourself."

TEN

Sweet Sixteen

"What do you want for your birthday?" Aunt Jen asked me. My mom was working late as usual that night, but Charlie was home.

"Good waves!" he interrupted.

I smiled. "Yeah."

"Well, that's the ol' standard," Charlie said.

"*Besides* good waves," Jen said. "There must be something special you want."

I knew right away what I wanted, but I was too shy to say it. I wanted a new swimsuit. One that fit me right—that didn't have a saggy bottom.

"Well, I already have a surfboard, and a wetsuit—thanks to you guys."

"Oh, our pleasure, honey!" said my aunt. "But seriously, anything else you want?"

Uncle Charlie cut in. "Better tell her, or you'll get that typical present you really don't want from your aunt and uncle, but you're like, 'Thanks?'" He acted this out with an expression of bewilderment: eyes wide open, head tilted, shoulders shrugged.

"Well . . ." I began, "I could use a new swimsuit."

Jen took some muffins out of the oven. "Oh yeah," she said, "one that stays on for surfing."

"Yeah," I replied.

"Those are very hard to find," she said. "You certainly don't want those Eeni Meeni ones—those've come off at my first duck-dive!"

"Woo-hoo—I'd like to see that, Jen!" Charlie piped in, raising his eyebrows up and down like Groucho Marx.

Jen ignored him. "Sally and I wear boy's trunks over our suits, rolled up. Sally only wears Offshore. They sponsor her."

"Offshore?"

"Yeah, we can get them at ET," she offered.

"Thanks."

"And we can find something at Beach B's, like the girls' volleyball suits—they're made to stay on while doing sports."

I was delighted at the thought of having a real, grown-up bathing suit, one that fit me snugly and would actually stay on while surfing. Plus it would be from Sally's pro brand, Offshore.

"What color would you like?" Jen asked.

"I don't know." I hadn't thought of that. "Not neon."

"What—you don't want to look like a lifeguard cone?" Charlie joked.

"Oh no, not orange!" Jen said. "We'll find the perfect one."

Jen took me to Beach B's, where I found a light-blue bathing suit that fit me perfectly—no saggy bottom! She also bought me a matching pair of boy's boardshorts at ET Surf to go over the bottoms, just like Sally wore. They stayed on for surfing, even when I ate it. Aunt Jen said the light blue suited me, with my long, dark hair. I never liked to wear my hair tied back in a ponytail while surfing; I let it stay loose. Sometimes it stuck to my face after getting worked and I had to peel it away from my eyes so I could see. When it was crucial to keep paddling to make it out past the impact zone, I would just leave it in my face until I made it outside.

A few days later, I was abruptly awoken by Uncle Charlie knocking on my door. "Wake up, sleepy head!"

I bolted upright. *Oh no, maybe I slept in and the waves are good,* I thought in a panic. But it was pitch-black outside.

I crept into the kitchen, Zuzu at my heels. "What time is it?"

"Time to get on the bus!" he announced cheerfully. "We're goin' south, where that south swell is."

Aunt Jen put a mug of tea and a muffin on the table in front of me. "We're going to camp and stay over too, so bring a change of clothes."

"'Kay." I turned to pack, starting to get excited. But when I remembered it was my birthday the next day, I asked Jen, "Is Mom coming?"

"She can't take off work."

"Hey, but I'm comin'!" Charlie declared.

Aunt Jen glanced at Charlie with a soft smile. "We're lucky Charlie can join us. He's got some days off."

Charlie's blue eyes twinkled at her. He burst into song: "*Ellie Bo-Belly's gonna catch some birthday waves, oh yeah, far out! She's gonna catch some sweet sixteen birthday barrels . . .*" He mimed getting barreled with one arm arched over his head like the lip of a wave, his other arm and head bopping about like he was surfing inside the tube.

Jen and I burst out laughing. "That's the best way to spend a birthday!" she said.

"Can Zuzu come, too?" I asked.

"Of course!" Jen said. "Zuzu loves camping."

We packed up the VW camper van, surfboards on top, and set off into the darkness of the early morning. On the back bench seat, I stretched out my legs next to Zuzu, who was at my feet. The van had lots of space in the back. In front of us there was a little table that could fold up. While driving, Charlie put a cartridge in the eight-track player. I fell asleep to the Beach Boys harmonizing the ballad "Surfer Girl."

I awoke as we arrived at the campground. In the light of early dawn, I could see that we were on high ground above the water. We drove down a winding dirt road and stopped by some rocks. Farther down was the shore, with lots of kelp floating. There were light-blue horizontal lines further out. Following their movement, my heart started beating fast. *Those lines are swell!*

"Corduroy!" I said out loud, the adrenaline kicking in. Zuzu's ears pricked up.

"Yup!" Jen said. "Perfect little peaks."

Uncle Charlie burst out in a jolly tune: "*Zippity-do-da, zippity-day! Ellie's gonna get stoked today—*"

"And so are you," I butted in.

"Ah, nah," he said. "I'm just gonna get some sleep and snuggle up with Zuzu."

I scrunched up my face.

"Just kidding!"

Jen pushed his baseball hat brim down over his eyes. "You're such a ham."

He sat still. "Wait a minute," he said. "I can't see anything!"

Jen pushed her finger up under the front of his cap, lifting it back up.

"Oh wow, thanks." He reached for Jen. "Oh, come here, you. Hey honey, you are cute." He tickled Jen's middle.

She started giggling. "Stop!"

He continued to tickle her. "What? I can't hear you—"

"Ah!" Jen gasped between laughter. "Really, stop!"

Charlie stopped. He popped out of the van and shouted, "Last one in is a rotten egg!" He made a fart sound as he stepped up to take down the boards.

"Was that one real?" I asked him.

He raised his eyebrows and stuck his pointer finger out at me. "Do me a favor and pull my finger."

I pulled it and he blew a succession of raspberries.

"Eww!" I said, cracking up. He had the boards down in a flash, and before I knew it, he'd waxed his board and was ready to go.

The waves were nice and slow to form, with good shape—no walls. My aunt said it was like this because it was a reef break. "That's why we call this spot Old Man's," Uncle Charlie explained. "It's a nice, *slow* reef for us old guys." Charlie meant that he was old, like a parent, and not a kid like me. But he sure made a point of acting like a kid. In some ways it was like he never grew up, kind of like Peter Pan. He was always up for finding fun in the moment. My aunt always said, "Either he's on, or he's asleep." There was no turning his volume down; his intensity was constant, and I never saw him worry. He had a knack for seeing the positive in things. He was the guy who always saw the glass half-full instead of half-empty.

That day, I rode some fun party waves with my aunt and uncle. We all got some really good ones. At one point, Uncle Charlie did a headstand on a set wave all the way to shore. When he came in, he got a request to do it again from some people who'd been watching from their beach chairs. He went back out and did another one, his legs up in the air. Jen teased him, saying, "There he goes, hotdogging," meaning that he was showing off.

That night, Charlie roasted hot dogs on skewers. He offered me one, but I said I'd decided to be a vegetarian like

Jen. We gave mine to Zuzu, which she appreciated. Aunt Jen and I ate cowboy beans—baked beans heated up in a cast-iron pot over the campfire, poured over Jen's homemade corn muffins that had been toasted by the flames. For dessert we made s'mores, my favorite. We roasted marshmallows on sticks, and then melted the Hershey bars and sandwiched them between graham crackers. They were the best.

Later, I learned that the whole back bench of the VW bus moved forward to become a bed, where Jen, Charlie, and Zuzu slept. The top of the van popped up into a little tent-like structure above, where I slept under a canopy of brilliant stars. I felt closer to Dad up there. If he was a star, I thought I'd found the one that was him, bright and beaming its rays of light upon me.

I couldn't believe I was going to be sixteen. "Sweet sixteen," Uncle Charlie had said. I thought of my birthdays in the past. Since it was mid-summertime, we usually were at a cabin we'd rent in the Adirondacks, a few hours north of the city. From there, Dad and I would go on exhilarating hikes that lasted all day. We were in our element—Misiek and Misiu in the wild. Breathing in the refreshing scent of the pine trees, my soul elated and my arms swinging with a bounce in my step, we'd talk about what inspired us, from our research, books we were reading, or anything in the world. We were two philosophers on an adventure; two scientists on an expedition.

Something inside me cracked. It hurt to think about those hikes. Though I tried to hold it back, a fat tear insisted on blurring my vision of the stars. I reached for my Walkman and put on my headphones. My station didn't come in here, so I tuned into 91X with the new song "Every Breath You Take." Dad had loved the Police, but he'd died before this song came out. Tears streamed down my face. It was like Dad was speaking to me through the lyrics, telling me he was watching me from above.

The next morning, I caught twenty-four birthday waves. I counted them. Aunt Jen surprised me with homemade blueberry birthday cake for breakfast—it tasted so good after surfing. Warmed by the sun, the tart blueberries burst in my mouth, a contrast to the sweet cake. I went back out and surfed some more. I wanted to get sixteen times two, like Charlie had said. By sunset, I'd gotten more than my thirty-two and was dog-tired.

When the full moon shone bright and the stars came out, my aunt took me on a stroll to the water's edge. "You know, the stars are all aligned for you on your birthday, so your wishes can come true," she said, her eyes shining.

I breathed in deep, soaking in the midnight-blue sky ablaze with stars. The rhythmic roar of breaking waves resonated through my core: the continual rolling surf, rushing water against the rocky shore, bubbling and popping, harmonized in song. The ocean breeze circled around us, flicking against my skin like feathers.

We sat on a blanket while she ceremonially propped up a white candle in the sand. "I brought this for you, so you could make your wish." Jen tried to light the candle with a lighter, but the breeze didn't let her. We sheltered it from the wind with our bodies, moving in close together. She lit it again, and it glowed. My soul felt like that candle, a little light burning. My heart started beating fast as I made my birthday wish in my head: *I wish to be a good surfer.*

I blew out the candle, and Jen cheered and clapped. The stars twinkled above, tiny windows to heaven. In the rustling wind, I thought I heard Dad whisper, "I love you more than the moon, Misiu."

In August, the summer sun heated up the sand, yards, gardens, and rooftops. Its insistent light streamed in all the windows of the little house. My mom lurked in the shadows. Turning away from the smell of freshly baked goods with a grimace on her face, she'd say, "No thanks, Jen, I'm not hungry." Without her makeup, Mom looked ghostly. Without red lipstick, it seemed her face had no mouth. Her platinum hair blended into her expressionless, pale image. I couldn't see her eyes through those dark sunglasses. It was hard to connect with Mom and have a conversation with her while she wore them, but I didn't ask her to take them off. The sun bothered her and she always had a headache.

"Mom, did I tell you about the dolphins yesterday?"

She pressed her hand into her forehead. "No, but I can't talk about it now."

"Will you please take those stupid glasses off?" Jen shouted from the counter.

"I have a headache," Mom moaned. "My eyes hurt. Do you really have to *bake* in this heat?"

"There's an ocean breeze," Jen said.

"Ugh," Mom grumbled. "Those Santa Anas are killing me!"

She'd usually excuse herself after brewing her coffee each day, taking the mug with her to go smoke a cigarette in the shade of her dark room by the garage. There, she had her stack of art magazines from New York to keep her company. *Bomb* magazine and *Artforum* were her favorites.

Today, she stayed in the kitchen after popping some pills with her coffee. She lit a cigarette and addressed Jen: "So, you're a real Suzy Homemaker now."

Jen looked up from scrubbing a dish in the sink. "Huh?"

"All the baking." Mom spun her finger, coated in glossy

red polish, around to emphasize her words.

Jen smiled. "Yeah, I'm really into baking."

"And you're a gardener now?"

"You already knew that, Julia."

"Well, I just never know what you are. It always seems to change. A waitress, a florist . . . a substitute teacher."

My aunt placed a bowl in the drying rack. "Yeah, I've had a lot of jobs."

"What about your art degree? Are you planning on doing anything with it?"

"I still paint now and then—if that's what you're asking."

"What? Seascapes?" Mom sounded sarcastic.

"Seascapes, landscapes. That's life here, it's what's real. Will you please take those glasses off?"

Mom pushed her sunglasses up on top of her head. "It's not going to get you anywhere, Jen. No one is interested— that's all been done. It's nothing new."

Jen turned to face Mom. "I'm not trying to think up something clever that hasn't been done before—just so I can become famous and sell my so-called art for lots of money. That's not how I approach things."

"Obviously not." My mom pushed her sunglasses back over her eyes. "Too bad, because then I can't help you."

"I'm not asking for your help, am I? Wait, who's helping who here? If you must know, I cleared out my art studio for you, so you could have your own room."

My mom took her glasses off and looked at Jen in total shock. "You didn't have to."

"I know I didn't have to, but I did." Jen plunked a dish onto the counter. "I'm going out for a walk."

She went out the back door, through the garden. I followed after her. She walked briskly down to the Strand by the beach, and I quickened my pace to keep up with her. The cobalt-blue expanse had onshore wind on it, small ultramarine ripples with whitecaps. Jen looked out at it as she wiped tears from her eyes with her forearm. She turned away from me, seeming to not want me to see her cry.

"Are you all right?" I asked.

"I'm fine . . . my big sister can just be a little critical at times." She went on, trying to sound upbeat. "But that's her job, that's the art world—that's what it's all about."

I looked up at her. "I didn't know you were an artist."

"Yeah, I used to paint."

"Are those your paintings in my room?"

"Yup."

"I love them!"

"Thanks."

"Why don't you paint anymore?"

"I will, just taking a break." She looked out at the ocean. "Too bad there's no waves today," she said, changing the subject.

"Yeah, bummer."

"It's like a lake out there," she said with a chuckle. "A windy lake."

"Yeah . . . I think I'll go out anyway and practice paddling."

"You do that." Jen reached her arm around me and gave me a squeeze. I leaned into her. We stayed like that for a few minutes. I let out a big breath. It felt good to be able to offer Jen some of the comfort she always gave me. A twinge of guilt pulled at me; I wasn't doing this with Mom. But we weren't close. Maybe we never had been. Dad and I were. Wind tickled my ear as the ocean's hum beckoned to me.

When Jen turned back towards the house, I followed. I got my wetsuit on, grabbed my board, and paddled out.

I thought Mom had forgotten about my birthday, but she surprised me with a turquoise box wrapped in a white bow. Inside was a silver heart charm necklace with the letter "E" engraved on it, from Tiffany's in New York City. It tugged my heartstrings that she was thinking of me—even though I hardly saw her. I wasn't sure if the "E" was for me or Dad. His name was Emeryk.

I didn't wear the necklace much, because in the water I was sure to lose it. It was bound to get ripped off my neck by the force of the Pacific.

Work kept my mom late more often than before. It wasn't just the gallery openings, but the parties and after-parties she had to go to. I tried to stay up, waiting for her to come home at night. It was hard to do because I was so tired from surfing, from early morning till sundown. Surfing drained me of energy more than anything. Back home, I had played basketball and softball in middle school, but nothing had ever run me so ragged. The Pacific tossed me this way and that, tumbling me into somersaults, scooping me up and spitting me out. But I didn't mind. I liked feeling the force of the ocean. Instinctively, I felt that in order to ride it, I needed to become one with it. Like a rodeo rider has a bond with her horse. When she falls off, she gets back on. The rider is determined to study her horse, to become one mind with the animal—so their movements are in unison. Well, the ocean had the power of a million horses.

I tried explaining this to Mom, but she didn't get it. She couldn't understand why I was obsessed with surfing. I gave up trying to explain it to her. She just didn't get it.

If Dad was still with me, he'd understand. I imagined our conversation:

"*Dad, when I surf I feel connected to the ocean, the strongest force in the world. I feel it pushing me on, through my feet, which sense its changing shape, and up through my center, to my racing heart. I'm flying fast, down a steep liquid ridge, in sync with this big burst of energy. In that moment, I can't help but shout out 'Woo-hoo!'*"

"*Woo-hoo!*" he'd holler back, beaming at me. "*But what about when the waves are huge and scary, mój Misiu?*"

"*I know what it's like to get pummeled by big waves and get held under—when all I want to do is breathe, but I swallow my fear and go for it, because it's worth it—that feeling of freedom. Like when we went on hikes, Dad. I'm connected to nature, to the wild.*"

"*But in this case, it's the ocean,*" he'd say.

"*Yes. The surf. Where the world of the land and the world of the sea meet, I play.*"

"*And you forget yourself,*" he'd say.

"*Yeah. I'm fully in the moment, together, the ocean and me.*"

"*The ocean, she's never the same, always different, each moment, each wave. Like no two snowflakes are exactly alike, no two waves are, either,*" he'd say.

"*Exactly!*"

He always knew what I was thinking.

"*I see you, Ellie. You're one with the waves. They affect you, and they are you.*" He'd flash an understanding smile.

"*Yes! Gliding on the ocean's surface, carving it up, is like dancing. Like when Misiu danced with Misiek; my little feet on top of your big feet, my knees bent with the flow.*"

"*You* are *dancing, mój Misiu!*" he'd agree.

"*Dad, it makes my heart sing. Or jump—like when I go for a really steep drop.*"

He'd let out a Big Bear laugh.

"*But then when I make it, my heart soars. I hold that feeling in my heart throughout the day and say to myself, I'm a surfer.*"

"You are a surfer, and I'm so proud of you." He'd grow serious and continue softly, "And when you're surfing out there, when the colors change from light blues and greens to rich and deep tones, as the sun rises and sets, my star is watching over you—always."

ELEVEN

Surfer Girl Starts Junior Year

I placed my new shorts and t-shirt out on the bench. I'd picked the shorts because they were the color of the ocean in Hawaii from Charlie's surfing magazines. The white t-shirt was given to me by the owner of the local surf shop, Eddie Talbot, who's initials were the "ET" in ET Surf. Aunt Jen and Charlie said to say hello from them, and when I did, Eddie had given me the shirt.

Mom had surprised me by taking me shopping. It was a yearly tradition we'd had, where she'd buy me a new sweater and a couple pairs of pants, mostly because I'd grown out of things. I wasn't sure she was going to do it this year because she was so busy. I couldn't believe I'd be going to high school in shorts. Back in New York, it would start to get cold in September, but here it was warmer than ever. They called this Indian Summer back East, when the heat lingered into the fall—but here it was always like this. My aunt said September was the best month to surf in your swimsuit because both the air and water were warm. It eased my nerves to think about surfing.

While shopping, Mom promised she'd go to the beach with me after school. I was surprised to hear this. She even said that, while I surfed, she'd be thrilled at the prospect of sitting on a beach chair in her big sunhat to relax and read a magazine.

"The sun won't give you headaches?" I asked.

"I think I've adjusted to it now."

I hoped so.

I got in bed and turned the lamp out. Closing my eyes, I saw waves. My aunt said the best way to calm your nerves was to go surf, so we'd gone that afternoon. All that staring out at the horizon had imprinted itself into my mind's eye. I opened my eyes—the room was dark. Out the window, a bright star blazed between the leaves of a tree branch. *Hello, star.* It seemed to say "hello" back as it beamed its light at me, twinkling. *Dad, if you are up there, it's me, Misiu. I'm going to start my junior year of high school tomorrow. Remember when we'd read together in our bear cave, under your desk made of sheets and pillows?* Dad had called it *norka misia*—"bear cave" in Polish. I imagined being little in his arms and falling asleep to his deep, steady voice as he devotedly read to me.

I was up before anyone, even Uncle Charlie. I jerked out of bed and, in the dark, went into the living room, the butterflies a flurry in my stomach. Zuzu didn't stir, but when I opened the cottage door, she looked up. I stepped out, Zuzu at my heels, brushing against my leg.

"Okay Zu," I said. "Let's go." I grabbed her leash and took her for a quick walk down to check the surf. The stars were still shining, but the sky was getting lighter. The ocean called out "good morning" to me with its soothing roar. A gentle breeze brushed against my skin. It was a dark blue-gray, with a little wind on it. Back at the garden, I closed the gate and there was Uncle Charlie waxing his board—a big smile on his face. "Someone's got surf stoke," he said, "that's for sure."

"I couldn't sleep," I mumbled.

"Ah. Well, what're you waitin' for? Let's go!"

My mouth dropped. "But today's the first day of school."

"So? Best to eat cake before dinner!"

"Huh? But I don't know if there's time, I can't be late."

"I've got a watch on," he joked, showing me his bare wrist.

"But Mom won't let me."

"Where's Heels right now?" He tilted his head sideways with his eyes shut to mime sleeping. Opening his eyes wide, he teased, "Hey, wait, who is this person? I gotta convince you to go surf like it's goin' to the dentist?"

"I'll be right out." I rushed into the house to get my new suit on and grab my board. We went down the alley, the sky getting brighter, the waves now visible.

"Small, two-foot fun ones," Charlie said, "and a little sick."

"Huh?"

"Sick—it's got wind on it," he said.

"Oh, yeah." The ocean surface was rippled. Down at the water's edge, tiny peep birds, the sanderlings, nipped at the sand and darted in zigzags. I bent over to put on my leash. Through my legs, looking up at the sky behind us, was the moon, full and bright.

"The moon's still out," I said.

"Surf by the light of the moon!" Charlie called out from the water. "You can do that, ya know . . . surf at night on a full moon."

"Have you?"

"Oh sure —your aunt and I had a blast at the cove one night." He whistled.

"What? You guys are crazy."

"And?" he replied as he began to paddle out.

Walking into the shallows, I marveled at the dawn's light: yellow and pink fading into the silver-blue sky. The waves were breaking in little peaks. A perfect left unrolled and rumbled as it hit the sandbar, echoing in the wind, greeting me.

We caught some fun little ones, as Charlie had predicted. I surfed one all the way to the sand. Then we hurried back up the hill to the house.

Mom was there, all dressed in black and ready—that was a shock. "What are you two doing?" she asked in an agitated tone. "Don't you know what day it is?"

"Huh? It's Saturday, Heels," my uncle teased.

"Ellie—we have to leave in ten minutes!"

"Don't worry, Mom," I called from the outdoor shower. "I'll be right out." I was dressed and ready in five minutes. I grabbed a muffin from Jen, who smiled at me.

Charlie winked at Jen. "Fresh out of the oven—for those fresh out of the ocean!" He grabbed a muffin and twirled her around in a circle, making her giggle.

"Gosh, you guys beat me to it this morning," Jen said, slapping his arm.

"Someone's got surf stoke and was up before me!" He pointed at me.

"How do you feel this morning, Ellie?" Jen inquired, looking straight into my eyes.

"Good," I replied.

"Nervous?"

To my surprise, I realized I didn't feel nervous anymore. "Nope. I'm not."

"That's what surfing does for you," she said, smiling in my mom's direction.

"Ellie, your hair's wet!" Mom scolded.

"It's just water, Julie," my aunt said.

"*Julia!*" Mom corrected her.

"Not like she has to go out with wet hair in the freezing

cold air of New York," continued Jen.

"She looks like a wet muskrat!"

"Whoa, take it easy, Heels!" Charlie said. "This way all the kids'll know Ellie's a surfer, right from the start."

Thank goodness. I didn't want to be the outsider from New York anymore.

"Aren't you going to at least put some makeup on?" Mom urged as we climbed into her car. "A little mascara?"

"It's not pretty when it runs down my face while surfing—I made that mistake *once.*"

"Surfing shouldn't run your life," Mom huffed. "If you let it, it just might ruin it."

On the drive to school, you could cut the tension in the car with a knife. Both of us were fuming. As we walked up to the office, the spike heels of Mom's black suede boots clicked noisily on the pavement. I was conscious of my mom dressed all in black, in contrast to the school's laid-back beach vibe. Everyone was into colors here. Pastels and bright colors were in, not black. Inside the office, we found out which building my junior homeroom was in. It was just around the corner.

"I'll find it," I said.

"Okay," she exhaled in relief. She hugged me too tight. "Have a good day."

"You too, Mom," I said softly, so others walking by couldn't hear. I braced myself for the worst. As I walked around the corner to find classroom number eight, I told myself: *I'm a surfer.*

"Hello," the teacher called to me as I entered the classroom. "Take any seat."

I felt all eyes on me. Glancing at the available seats, I brushed by a few, looking down at the ground. I took an empty seat in the middle, near the back. In a few minutes, the rest of the class filled in and the bell rang. My heart was beating louder than the bell. The teacher stood in front of her desk, leaning back against it. I was surprised at how easygoing she seemed. She wore a yellow blouse and khakis. I still wasn't used to the casual clothes the teachers wore here.

"As I go through roll call and call your name, please correct me if I'm pronouncing it wrong. Then please tell the class something about yourself. Okay, I'll start. I'm Ms. Mathews and I like to run—I'm a runner. Any questions? Raise your hands, please."

One kid near the front raised his hand.

"Yes?" Ms. Mathews said.

"Um, like, have you run a marathon? 'Cause, like, my dad has."

"Yes, I have," she replied.

I knew what I would say when the teacher called my name. That was a relief.

The next boy answered that he liked to "play Pac-Man" before his friend interrupted, "No, Asteroids, dude." Then after a few "play baseball" or "go to the arcade" answers by various boys, and "go shopping" and "go to the mall" repeated by many girls, the teacher called my name. "Ellie Brzozowski," she said, stumbling on my last name. The kids laughed.

"Here," I said, raising my hand.

"Ellie, tell us something about yourself."

"I surf," I said simply, trying to ignore the butterflies in my stomach.

"You what?" she asked. "Can you speak up, dear? I can't hear you."

"I surf, I'm a surfer," I repeated a little louder.

"Oh!" Ms. Mathews said, surprised. "I'm scared of the water myself."

I felt my face get hot, with all eyes on me again. Soon, to my relief, the introductions were over and schedules were passed out. The bell rang and I was sent off to another room for science class.

Later at lunch, Caitlyn came up to me.

"Hey, so you still surf?" she asked.

"Yeah," I replied. She sat down next to me. I was relieved to know someone at school.

"I wasn't sure I'd see you this year. I thought maybe you'd go back home."

"No, still here," I said, picking up my peanut butter and jelly sandwich. "I don't want to go back."

"Really? Why? I'd like to go to New York. All the shows and shopping and stuff. I bet it's fun."

"It's not all that fun when you live there," I explained.

This year, I hoped not too many people knew me as the girl from New York. But I soon found out that they did, which wasn't a good thing. To the locals, being from New York was like being from another planet. My mom sure looked that way to them. Luckily, she fell back on her promise to bring me to school every day. By the week's end, my aunt had taken over for her.

The drive to Mira Costa High School only took about fifteen minutes. I told Jen I could skate to school and back by myself, but she insisted on driving me, saying it was too long a skateboard ride. I told her I preferred to go alone and skate. I was used to it; I had been going to school by myself since since I was eight, in the city, since third grade. But when she mentioned that I'd have to get out of the water a half hour earlier if I wanted to skate, I agreed to let her drive me there and then skate home. I wanted to get as much morning surf in as possible.

Jen said she could get me a bicycle, but I insisted on skateboarding home, even though it was a long and tough skateboard ride with hills. I knew skating would make me a better surfer; I got to work on my balance. The only problem was that my board didn't fit in my locker, and skateboarding wasn't allowed on school grounds. So I had to ditch the board in the bushes surrounding the quad and hope no one would spot it and steal it.

Walking up to the science lab door one day, I overheard one of the popular girls talking loudly to her friends inside. "I mean, like, how can she be a *surfer* when she's from *New York*?" The girl glanced back at me. It was Brooke, one of the girls from my homeroom. Grouped together were all their poofy blonde heads and smiling faces, laughing at me. Bonnie, the leader of their group, responded so everyone could hear: "What a poser!"

A couple of kids snickered at this remark. "Poser!" Brooke spat the word out.

The girls repeated "poser," pretending to cough to cover up what they were saying. April stepped in front of me, blocking the aisle, and said, "You think wearing that shirt makes you a surfer, New York?"

I was so surprised that I froze. As a sick feeling spread through my stomach, I stood still until she moved out of the way. All the girls cackled. As I passed by, another one barked, "Yeah, she probably forgot to dry her hair after the shower *on purpose*, so she could *look* like she surfed!"

"I doubt she even showers," scoffed Bonnie.

"Eww, gross!" Brooke hissed. They jeered, "Eww," and, "Grody."

My heart sank. I was crushed, but I kept it inside all day. I didn't want to give them the satisfaction of knowing that they'd gotten to me. When I got home, I burst into tears in front of my aunt.

"What's the matter?" Jen put her arm around me. It took me a while to respond, I was so choked up.

"They called me a poser."

She frowned. "Huh? I don't get it."

"The girls at school . . . 'cause I'm from New York, they think I'm pretending to be a surfer."

"Oh, *do* they now!" Jen said, getting riled up. "Well, I'll bet *they* can't surf. When they see you out there in the water, you'll show them! Do you know that Sally's friend, Liz Benavidez, just almost won the Op Pro? And two years ago she could've been world champion."

I stopped crying. "Really?"

"Yup, she finished second in the world rankings behind Margo Oberg. She's only a few years older than you. That could be you one day. Those stupid girls don't know anything."

"I just want them to leave me alone!"

"I think," she said gently, "that it doesn't matter what you do—people will always find *something* to pick on someone for. But it doesn't mean you have to take it."

"Huh?" I wasn't expecting that from her. "How do I not take it?"

"Stand up for yourself. Tell 'em, 'Buzz off, kook!'"

"Kook?" I looked up at her quizzically. "Like what that old man yelled at me in the water?"

"Yeah, but *these* girls deserve it! Give it back to them." She swung her fist in the air to emphasize her point.

"I can't," I agonized, collapsing onto the sofa.

My aunt sat down next to me. She must've known I was too shy to fight back, but still she pressed on. "If you think you can't surf that big set wave coming at you, and you don't even try and paddle for it . . . well, then you *can't* surf it, can you?"

My brow furrowed as I thought about that. I would never *not* paddle for it, but it wasn't fair to bring surfing into this.

"Well," she continued, "you and I know the truth of who you are, surfer girl. And one day they'll know it, too, and feel ashamed for being mean, rotten teenage girls."

I doubted they'd ever be sorry for how they acted. A few minutes later, I made a solemn pact with myself while sipping tea with Jen: *I'll become a good surfer one day and prove them all wrong.*

When my mom heard about what happened at school, she reacted in a way I didn't expect. She went on a rant. "Obviously these teenagers have no awareness of culture, since there is none here. Of course they don't understand anyone different from them. I mean, you're sophisticated, you're from the big city! Ugh." She held her hand up to her forehead dramatically. "Maybe we should seriously consider going back to New York."

"Mom, I'm not different," I maintained.

"Yes, you are. You should be proud of that—you're not white Wonder Bread from some hick beach town!" She slapped her hand down onto the table. "I mean, have they ever even seen a black person?"

"There's black kids at my school," I answered. I didn't want to admit it to her, but there was only one African American girl in my homeroom, Aisha—the rest of the girls were white, and mostly blonde. There were two African American boys who were brothers, and a few handfuls of others. But the entire high school was predominantly white.

"I don't want to go back to New York!" I spoke from my

heart. "I like it here. I like surfing."

"Well, we'll see . . ." She studied her red fingernails. "You may get bored of surfing soon."

I protested, "No, never!"

Mom spouted on about how small the art scene was in L.A., how she'd tried to no avail to bring all her artists from New York to the gallery's roster. "There's no Julian Schnabel here, or Mark Tansey," she whined, going on about how Andy Warhol's Factory and her gallery in SoHo were visited by all the current who's who. She continued speaking, though no one wanted to hear her. "I mean, Keith Haring and Jean-Michel are making art in the streets of the city—but who's doing that here? There isn't even a subway! If I tried taking public transportation, it would take me three hours to get to the gallery, and I hate driving."

I stood stiffly in the middle of the living room and let her talk without interruption. Aunt Jen had gone out back with a pile of laundry. Later, in my room, I made another pact with myself—that I would never mention any bad stuff about school again. If Mom heard, she might threaten to move us back to New York again. I didn't want to go back, not now or ever. My heart was set on surfing.

That Monday, Mom had the day off from the gallery. She had the idea to humor me by joining me at the beach after school. The plan was that I would surf, and she would flip through that thick, smelly magazine of hers.

"It's too hot," she scowled, peering out from under her black wide-brimmed hat. She was wearing all black. The gloss of the magazine page reflected the sun and blinded me with its glare for a minute. Wet and trying to catch my breath, I gripped the heavy Banana surfboard under my arm. I couldn't think of how to respond.

"The water's nice," I said finally.

Mom huffed. She shifted uncomfortably on her towel. We both knew she wouldn't go in the water. She never did; she didn't enjoy partaking in anything outdoors. New York City was her ideal, with all its culture and the arts—something she was beginning to believe this beach town had none of. Los Angeles was substantial, and I thought she would find all of that here. But she said the art scene here was so small, it was a joke. And it was too hot.

"No really, the water's pretty warm," I continued, feeling like I was talking to myself.

"Oh, I'm sure it's too cold for me." Mom turned a magazine page and a waft of perfume invaded my nose. I was going to ask if she saw me on my last set wave, but I didn't, because I'd looked to see if she was watching after each wave, and she hadn't even looked up once.

TWELVE

What Happened in Venice

I was determined to be a good surfer. I had made a pact with myself, a solemn promise. But there was more to it, too. I needed it—I was addicted to it. At dawn and dusk, I filled up that empty space in me with ocean. I went surfing every morning before school, and every afternoon after school. Wilkies had said to me, "You only get good if you surf every day—and then it takes four years of that, surfing every day, to get good."

I was doing just that. It was all-consuming, all I thought about. I wanted to prove to myself that I could be good, and to prove the kids at school wrong. There was something else, but I wasn't fully conscious of it yet. I needed to surf like I needed to talk to my dad each day, but couldn't. I was heartsick, but I couldn't talk about it. What I did instead was get up each morning in the dark before the sun rose so I could get in as much surfing practice as possible. I only had about two hours to surf in the morning before I had to go to high school.

By the time my toes hit the cold water, the dawn's light illuminated the ocean before me, creating a milky blue haze. I felt like I was looking over the edge of a cliff, into infinity. The continuous "shh" sounds of the ocean were soothing. Its tinny hum drew me in, and when the crashing surf pounded the sand, its thunder bursts caught my attention. Jumping in,

I submerged my body, washing away sleep. Coming up to the surface, I awoke, water flowing through my hair, my eyes open. Arms flailing in the cold foam, I paddled hard, telling myself that I had to make it out as quickly as possible before the sets came. My arms ached, but still I made myself paddle, my neck straining, my jaw clenched at the menacing thought of giant overhead sets breaking on me. This pushed me to dig my arms deep, to keep focus, to keep going.

When I finally made it out, I allowed myself to rest and catch my breath. My heart pumping, the adrenaline rush merged with the pride that I'd made it out. I soaked in the beauty around me. Infinite, shimmering, silvery-blue ocean, reflecting the endless sky. To my left, the black silhouette of the pier stood out against the mauve peninsula of Palos Verdes, and beyond that, the lavender outline of Catalina Island. An oil tanker sat permanently out at sea. Behind it, the purple Santa Monica Mountains stretched to the candy-cane red-and-white-striped smokestacks of the steam-generating plant to my right. The sun, rising gradually behind me, lit up the face of the waves like green glass. When rainbows appeared in the back spray of breaking waves, my eyes welled up with tears. *It's so beautiful!*

Because it was so early, sometimes I spotted a squid boat, lighting up the water below it in shafts, beaming headlights up top. On occasion, a bird came by. The small grebes looked like black baby ducks floating on the water's surface. As I paddled past one, I noticed that its eyes were red. I once mistook a similar bird for a snake, because it had a long black neck that stuck out of the water. It plunged its beak under, foraging for fish—and then I saw that it was a cormorant, sitting with its bottom submerged in the water like a surfer on a shortboard.

When a group of pelicans appeared in a "V" formation,

swooping and gliding just above the breaking surf, down the line and the length of the beach, they took my breath away. It looked like they were surfing the wind. And every time I spotted dolphin fins on the horizon, my heart skipped a beat.

It was always hard to get out of the water to go to school.

One day, after getting worked a lot during my morning surf session, I bent down to pick up my books and water dripped out of my nose. Again. It continued to drip when I stood up.

Sheila, a blonde who sat in my row, saw my nose dripping. She exclaimed in disgust, "Eww, what was that?" I quickly covered my nose with my hand in embarrassment.

"My nose drained," I said, "from surfing."

"Oh," she said with a grimace, but I could tell she didn't believe me. I hoped she didn't tell anyone about it like April had last spring, but somehow, the mean girls found out and constantly teased me about it again. I tried to ignore them.

Each morning, I arose in the dark to surf. At the water's edge, I stopped and bent down to tug up the legs of my wetsuit, still damp from the day before. My nose always drained water from the last night's session. Sunlight filtered through cracks in the clouds in patches, streaming down its golden rays. Immersed in water, I felt protected by my wetsuit, like it was a seal's skin.

I paddled out through the impact zone. Out there, I called to the dolphins, rubbing the rail of my board. I imagined that their senses were so fine-tuned, they knew the unique sound of my board with its fin trailing through the surf, and knew it was me. When they came to say hello, I felt something like electricity throughout my body. There were always three or four of them together, side by side, diving and springing up in unison. As they passed, I scanned the patterns of marks and nicks on their bodies, searching for the dolphin with the crescent moon scar. I would try to communicate with them telepathically. In my mind, I'd say hello and thank them for coming.

One morning, I got a black eye from my surfboard. I surfed to shore, jumped off, and just when I turned around to pick up my board, another batch of whitewater shot the board out at me. It hit me hard on my forehead above my right eye. The bruise formed all around my eye, black and blue that faded into purples. *Great, Calamity Jane*, I thought. I put my mom's cover-up makeup over it, but it still showed.

Of course, the kids at school teased me. "Huh! Somebody told you!" a boy commented as we passed in the outdoor hallway. Another boy taunted, "Ha! Who punched you?" Not waiting for the answer, he said to the other boy, "Bet it was her dad." They both laughed.

My jaw clenched. I wanted to yell back at him that it wasn't my dad, that he'd never lay a hand on me. *How dare he say that! My dad's dead! It was a surfboard, kook!* But I didn't. I couldn't. My mouth went dry. I just walked by, ignoring them.

Girls with big, blow-dried hair and collared shirts with little green alligators on them whispered among themselves as I passed them. My face grew hot. When I entered the classroom, I was afraid I'd blushed the color of Bonnie's hot-pink shirt. She scowled at me, shaking her head as she hissed, "Beach trash."

April blocked the aisle to my seat and, with a smug look, sneered, "Like, where do you get your clothes?"

"At the Salvation Army, can't you tell?" Brooke scoffed. They all laughed. I kept walking past them, wishing that school was over so I could be out in the water. But it was only just before lunch.

Later, I scanned the cafeteria, looking for a place to sit. I saw my one friend, Caitlyn, sitting next to Sheila at an indoor table by the open doors. I sat down opposite her, next to Aisha.

"Hi," I said to Caitlyn, but she didn't respond. I figured she was in the middle of chewing or talking with Sheila.

"Hi," Aisha said.

"Hi," I said back to her, grateful that she responded.

Aisha's astute eyes lit up when she smiled. Her copper hair was in a half-up style: curly bangs in front, with the rest pulled back and curls tumbling down to her shoulders. Her brown skin had a golden tone in the sunlight. She was really pretty.

Caitlyn looked up at me. "Hi," she said unenthusiastically. Sheila didn't say anything.

We ate our lunch quietly. It was a little awkward, until Aisha broke the silence.

"You know, *why* the boys still think blowing milk bubbles is entertaining is *beyond* me," she said.

That made me crack up. "Do they do that?"

"Yeah, look. Over there, Danny, Liam, and them," she replied.

"Bogus . . . they act like they're in kindergarten, not high school," Sheila remarked.

"Eww, did you see that?" Aisha said, her hand covering her nose. "Dave just blew bubbles out his nose."

Sheila stopped chewing and gave them a dirty look. "Grody!"

I thought it was kind of funny. I giggled. Caitlyn glared at me, red-faced.

"You're just as bad as them, Ellie," Sheila snapped. "I saw stuff pour out of your nose the other day."

"What?" I said, caught off-guard. "Oh, that was ocean water, from getting held under on a big wave."

"Eww, gross!" whined Sheila. "You mean it stayed up your nose for hours, then came out?"

"I guess so."

Caitlyn frowned at me. They both did. "What happened to your eye?" questioned Caitlyn.

"I told you, I got hit right here on my forehead by my surfboard—it's a longboard."

Caitlyn pushed her chair back, making a loud sound as it scraped against the floor. "Like, gross me out the door . . . I'm leaving," she announced.

"Me too," said Sheila. "Grody to the max." They got up, took their trays to Bonnie's table across the room, and sat down. Bonnie and her friends pointed at me and laughed derisively.

"What's their problem?" said Aisha.

"Me," I said with a sigh.

"No, they're stuck up. I know it when I see it. They think they're better than everyone else because they have money to buy designer clothes. Stuff like that . . . now they got to go and join the worst of them."

I wasn't hungry anymore. My stomach had tightened into a knot. *Is it my black eye? Or that my nose drained?*

Then I had a bigger shock. I spotted Mom walking around the outdoor cafeteria. She appeared to be looking for me. She was wearing big sunglasses and a black leather mini-skirt suit with bright-red stockings and high heels to match her lipstick.

She spotted me and started walking towards me. "Ellie," she shouted out. My hands were sweating. *Oh no, please don't cause attention!* I stiffened. Bonnie and her friends were pointing at Mom and snickering. Caitlyn looked shocked.

I leapt up and ran past my mom towards the office building, my heart racing.

"Ellie!" Mom called out. "We have to go, you have a doctor's appointment."

I could hear Caitlyn say to Sheila, "That's her mom?"

Sheila put her hand over her mouth.

When Mom caught up to me, I quickly told her that I'd meet her in the parking lot. My face was burning; I couldn't look at anyone as I escaped to the lockers to get my bag.

As I grabbed my skateboard hidden in the bushes, I spotted the bright-red Porsche 944 with Mom standing next to it, smoking. Didn't she know smoking was against school rules?

When I got to the car and we climbed in, Mom turned to me and smirked. She put her finger over her mouth. "Shh— you don't have a doctor appointment."

"What? You lied?"

"Is that a crime?" She started driving. "I just want some special time with my daughter. I never get to see you, and I have the day off. There's this chic café in Venice I want to take you to."

"But why didn't you tell me? I wouldn't have come to school today." I was regretting that I'd had to leave such good waves that morning—but didn't dare mention it.

She cursed. "I thought you'd be happy to play hooky from school!"

"I am." I let it go that she'd just completely embarrassed me, because I had longed to spend time with her.

Soon we were speeding north on Vista Del Mar, with the beach to our left. Mom turned on the radio, but "Total Eclipse of the Heart" was playing so she switched to another station. "Flashdance . . . What a Feeling" blared out, so she turned the dial again, landing on David Bowie's "Let's Dance." *Mom does have her red shoes on*, I thought. The memory flashed in my mind of Mom and Dad slow dancing together in the loft. Mom had been wearing red shoes. That night, they clung desperately to each other. *Is Mom remembering the same thing?* It was a rude awakening when the song "Maniac" came on, so I switched the dial to 106.7, even though it was too early for Rodney on the ROQ. The mesmerizing synthesizer and harmony of the new hit "Sweet Dreams (Are Made of This)" by the Eurythmics blasted out as we passed the marina and then made our way up Pacific Avenue to Venice.

She turned left on North Venice Avenue and parked. We walked across the street to the West Beach Café. Inside, everything was white except for well-lit art on the white walls, like a gallery. Each table had a white vase containing a single white flower on top of a white tablecloth. We sat at a table in the corner.

"This place looks expensive," I said, slouching in my chair.

"It is," smirked Mom. "Basquiat's silkscreens were showing when I first came here with the gallery owner."

"I thought we needed to save money."

"I wanted to take you someplace special, darling. I've been so busy with work, I know I've let you down. I want to celebrate you. My girl. Your dad always did." She reached for my hand and squeezed it. Hers was shaking. Her eyes welled up with tears, pink at the edges. My heart was beginning to unravel.

A man who'd been sitting at the bar walked up to us, carrying two full champagne glasses. "Julia," he exclaimed, his arms opening wide to embrace her. He was wearing a white suit jacket with a black t-shirt and jeans. He gave her one of the glasses. "Fancy meeting you here." The way he said it, I could tell it wasn't a coincidence that they were here at the same time.

She stood up and air-kissed his cheek while he embraced her. "Mark, so great to see you!"

"And who might you be?" he asked me, tilting his head and squinting. "Is this your sister you've been hiding?"

"No, this is my daughter."

"You have a grown daughter? How's that possible? You're

no older than what, twenty-three?" His exuberant eyes devoured my mother.

"Uh-huh," Mom said, smiling, her shiny red lips wide open. *Oh God, they're flirting.*

"You are a beauty, just like your mother. Some shiner you've got there—I'd love to paint you." He raised an eyebrow, staring at my black eye. "I know this one can crack the whip, but I didn't think she'd turn it on her own flesh and blood." He was so amused with himself that he cackled with laughter. He was odd. He had a pasty-white complexion, though he was handsome in a boyish rocker way with his shaggy hair. He had a magnetism about him. Mom obviously liked him, but I wasn't sure about him.

"Mark's an artist at the gallery, a rising art star in L.A.," she explained.

"Thanks to this force of nature." Mark raised his champagne glass to Mom. "She's like that tornado that swept through downtown L.A. this March. Do you know what she's accomplished? Quite an impossible feat in, what, five months? She's got the entire L.A. art scene wrapped around her pretty little finger."

Mom waved him off with a hand gesture, but I could tell from her satisfied expression that her ego was eating up all the praise. She chimed in, "Listen, you deserved to be *LA Weekly*'s 'pick of the week.' Next is an interview with *Artforum*."

Mark raised his glass again. "Cheers to your MOCA committee invite!" He smiled devilishly. "And . . . maybe a future board member?"

"Maybe." Mom looked smug as they clinked glasses. "Thank you," she said flirtatiously before taking a sip.

"Wow, really, Mom?"

"Oh yes, everyone wants Julia, she's simply irresistible,"

Mark gushed, eating her up with his gaze.

Mom suddenly bolted up. "Mark, we need to talk about the LACE show." She turned to me. "Darling, I'll be right back." Then she scooted off with Mark to talk alone at the bar.

I waited. Finally, Mark left the café and she came tottering back in her heels and sat down. "Want an egg cream?"

Her words tugged at my heart. We used to go out for egg creams with Dad at the Ukrainian deli in the East Village.

"Sure," I said. "They have that here?"

"Probably not. You hungry? They don't have pierogis here, but they do have a *divine* pesto caprese salad."

I missed pierogis. Dad's potato pierogis were the best, his mom's recipe from Poland. He'd make them on holidays.

The waiter was already standing at attention at our table, a crisp white apron around his waist. Mom looked up at him. "We'll have two egg creams."

The waiter, who looked like a member of the Stray Cats with his rockabilly hairstyle, cleared his throat. "Excuse me?"

"Oh no." She waved her hand furiously in front of her face. "I mean, we'll have two . . . Screaming Orgasms."

The waiter glanced at me, blinking, his lip curling up into a side smile. I flushed hot with embarrassment.

"Water's fine," I said, looking down at the tablecloth. *I'm too young to drink legally, Mom.*

"Oh, let's celebrate a little," she whined, pouting. "It's like an egg cream, you'll like it."

I glared at her.

She peeled off her leather jacket and sat up straight, partially revealing her boobs pushed up by her bustier. "We'll have two Screaming Orgasms," she announced again. The waiter looked hesitant. "Okay, fine, one virgin," she added.

"That's basically milk," he quipped back.

"Do you have seltzer?"

"What's seltzer?" he asked, shifting to another hip.

"Soda water."

"We have that."

"You take milk, add chocolate syrup and soda water, and you've got an egg cream."

"What's that?"

"A New York drink."

"We don't have chocolate syrup, but I'll see what the bar can do."

"Thank you," Mom said with a huff, straightening the oversized brass art piece she called a necklace. She excused herself to go to the restroom.

The waiter carefully placed our tall white drinks onto the white tablecloth. "Let me know what you think," he said.

I took a sip. It didn't taste right—it was kind of bland— but when the waiter came back to ask how it was, I said it was good and smiled. I drank some more. I waited a long time.

The waiter came to ask if I wanted anything from the menu. Everything was expensive. I said I'd wait.

When Mom finally came back, she sat down and picked up her drink to sip from the straw. Her designer purse slipped off her shoulder onto the floor and one of her red heels slipped off her foot. She didn't notice.

"This is nice," she sighed, focused entirely on sipping.

"Some girls at school ignored me today," I told her.

"Umm . . . that's nice," Mom said between sips, slurring her words.

"They thought I was gross because water came out my nose." Waiting for a response, I realized Mom had fallen asleep while sipping her Screaming Orgasm.

"Mom? Mom!" I shook her shoulder. "Mom!"

She jerked her head up. "Ah-ha . . . nice," she drawled.

I stood up. A chill ran down my spine as I watched Mom nodding off in her drink again. *What is wrong with her?* I knew she was working a lot, but was she really that tired?

"Mom, you can't sleep here," I protested.

She didn't stir. My heart sank. I picked her head up, heavy in my hands, and pushed it back as I moved the drink out of the way. "Mom, get up."

Abruptly, she jerked up again and sighed. "Okay."

I stiffened against the lightning bolts of shock, worry, and frustration as they each struck my core. Her gradual movements were puzzling. She sank languidly towards the table, very slowly—the weight of gravity pushing her down. She was moving so slow it looked comical, like it was a joke she was playing on me. But she wasn't joking. I had never seen her like this. I had never seen anyone like this.

"What's wrong with you?" I pleaded. She continued her steady, slow slump. *What should I do?* My heart started to race. I glanced around the near-empty café. *Does anyone notice?* A wave of embarrassment swept over me. Then I grew bitter, and something inside me snapped.

"Okay, sleep at the table for all I care!" I whipped around and left the café. I walked down the block, fighting back tears, though my face was wet with them. I saw a pay phone and called Aunt Jen. No one was home. Then I remembered she was installing a garden today. No one would expect me home until after school, and it was the middle of the day. I tried calling Charlie at the fire station, but they said he was out on a call. *What should I do?* I wished I knew how to drive so I could take Mom home.

I decided I had to go home and get help. I went back to the café and got Mom's car keys out of her purse. Then I went to the car and grabbed my skateboard. When I went back to return her keys, she was awake again, sipping on her drink as if nothing had happened.

"Mom, you fell asleep a minute ago. Are you okay?"

"I-I'm fine," she slurred.

"You're not fine, Mom. I'm going to go get Jen or Charlie to drive you home, okay?"

"Just so tired," she mumbled. Gradually, painfully, she slid forward bit by bit, as if in slow motion. Her head finally landed on her bent arm, resting on the tabletop.

I skated down the block to the boardwalk by the ocean. It was crowded with all kinds of people dressed in all different ways; a guy with an Afro and headphones on roller skates, a punk with a green mohawk, a very tan, blond woman with a terry cloth headband jogging in a pink leotard, and a guy with cornrow braids carrying a big boom box, blasting the hip-hop song "The Message." It reminded me of Eighth Street or St. Mark's Place in the Village in New York City.

I skated south. It was a long way home, but I would get there eventually and get help. To my right, the afternoon seas were sick, rippled by the wind. My left leg grew tired of pushing. I had gone about two and a half miles, and still had seven miles to go.

I followed the way we'd driven up, going inland and curving around the marina. I skated on the street because the sidewalks were too bumpy. My feet hurt, and my legs burned. I knew the path would lead back to the beach after the marina. Charlie and Jen had told me about it. Sure enough, after crossing Ballona Creek, I was back on the Strand, though I was two towns north. I skated faster now, my chest tightening against the wind. It was deserted in El Segundo. *Why did I leave? What was I thinking? I should've stayed with her!*

Tears were really flowing now. I tried to concentrate on skating, but I was so upset and exhausted that I kept falling. After tripping and falling the fourth time, I collapsed and cried. I cried so hard I thought I would puke. I bent over and started gagging and coughing. Out on the ocean, the choppy blue-green peaks were now a dark gray-blue. The sun was beginning to set. Streaks of peach stretched across the pale sky. *What time is it?* I wondered. *What am I doing? This is crazy.* I wasn't sure I could go on. My legs were worn out.

The black silhouette of a dolphin fin appeared on the horizon. As the dolphin leaped through the air, my spirits lifted. *Is that you, Crescent Scar?* Many more fins appeared. It was a big pod of dolphins. They continued to leap. They were traveling south. I hadn't seen so many of them before. I felt like they were cheering me on. "Keep going!" they seemed to say.

I got back on my board and skated, following the dolphins. It felt like the wind was behind me, pushing me, making it easier. It took less effort to skate. Gliding south, I breathed in the fresh sea air. Soon I was past the steam power plant at El Porto, back at last. The outlines of dolphin fins faded as they traveled further south and out of sight. I hoped Mom was okay. I was really mad at myself for leaving her now.

I struggled up the hill to the house, my legs heavy. My calves had begun to cramp. Zuzu greeted me at the gate, licking my legs as if to heal them as I trudged on. "Thanks, Zuzu," I said. The light was on in the cottage. *Thank God, Aunt Jen's home!*

I burst in the back door. "Jen, Mom fell asleep in the restaurant. It was weird. She needs a ride home."

"What?"

"In Venice. We have to go get her."

"She's here. In her bedroom." I stared at her in disbelief.

"She got back about an hour ago."

I rushed back through the garden to the door to her room. Out of breath, I opened the door a crack and looked in. She was sleeping. I slammed the door and turned around, heading for my room. Jen had followed me into the garden.

"What happened? Did you skate home?"

"Yes, from Venice Beach."

Her jaw dropped. "What? That must've taken you hours!"

"I tried calling—you weren't home and Charlie wasn't at the station."

"He wasn't?"

"No, he was out on a call. I'm never going anywhere with Mom again."

"You just left her and skated home?" Jen's face crumpled into a frown.

"What was I supposed to do? She couldn't possibly drive home. She wouldn't snap out of it." I started limping towards my room.

"But why didn't she tell me you were with her when she got home? How could she have just driven home—without you?"

"I told her I was going home to get you or Charlie to drive her."

Ignoring Jen's wide-eyed, insistent stare, I hobbled to my bedroom, slamming the door shut. I got my wetsuit on, grabbed my board, and stumbled down to the beach, though it hurt to walk and it would be dark soon. I needed some waves to calm down. Outside, I sat on my board, rocking, drifting, a floating black dot to someone looking back from the Strand like I once had. I used to look out and long to surf; now I was out here.

I let out a big breath. The darkening ocean before me had

no limit. At the horizon line, the orange skies faded to gray above. Streaks of electric-pink clouds stretched without end. Behind them, the setting sun peeked out at me and glared into my eyes so I couldn't see the influx. It swept me with it and broke all over me, gushing, flooding around me. I rode the sea foam in.

Undoing the gate latch, my pruned and numb fingers fumbled, my legs wobbling. Later, resting against Zuzu by the fire's warmth as I drifted off to sleep, I thought about that one set wave I'd made. I sighed in relief; tomorrow was Saturday, I didn't have school. My aunt gently let me know that I'd fallen asleep and asked me to brush my teeth and climb into bed, which I did. Sinking into the softness, I felt the weight of being bone-tired and, at the same time, of my cells growing and expanding. Sore, aching muscles were a distraction from thinking about what'd happened with Mom earlier. They brought on a good, deep sleep.

THIRTEEN

The Green Room

The next morning as I was about to enter the kitchen from the hallway, I overheard my aunt arguing with Mom. *I must've slept late if Mom is already up.*

"What were you thinking? Can you please tell me why you'd leave Ellie alone in Venice? That is not a good area to leave anyone in."

"She's the one who left *me*."

"Did you even look for her?"

"She told me she was skating home."

"Do you know how far that is? How long it took her?"

Mom huffed. "Listen I don't need to listen to this—she was very independent in the city. I'm going back to bed, it's too early to go in to work." It sounded like she pushed her chair out, so I flattened against the wall.

"What exactly happened?" Jen demanded. "Ellie said you fell asleep, and she couldn't wake you up. How could you even fall asleep? Did you take sleeping pills?" A sinking uneasiness crept in my stomach.

"No . . . you know, I guess I was up too late the night before—there was a gallery party, and an after party, remember?"

"But how long did you sleep? Julia! Don't just walk away, this is serious."

"Oh please, you're making a mountain out of a molehill. I was just so tired—maybe a little hungover. I even visited some artist studios on Main Street after."

"Really?"

"Yes."

"Whose?"

"Oh, James Turrell, Sam Francis, Diebenkorn, and Garabedian's."

"Wow," said Jen.

"We went to the Circle Bar after."

I slid back into my room before Mom could see me, listening as she stomped by and slammed the door shut behind her.

My legs were so sore that day, I could hardly stand up on my surfboard. I paddled around for a while, then went home and pored over the piles of surfing magazines that my aunt and uncle had collected. I had my nose in one when Charlie walked by. "That's Benny," he said. "Mike Benavidez. Right here at Hermosa Pier—he's pro, on the Kanoa team, and before that, was the number one amateur in California. Really nice guy. His sister's pro, too. We call her 'Brutal Videz.'"

My mouth opened in awe. "That's a cool nickname. She's Sally's friend who almost became world champion, right?"

"Yup. She's got more balls than most guys—fearless. An amazing surfer." The magazine's *Surfing* title was in gold type, with a grid of nine photos and a caption underneath: "To Experience Surfing."

"That's Benny." Charlie pointed to the middle-left photo. "In the barrel." There he was, in a tunnel of water, majestic. It was the August/September 1979 issue.

"Barrel?" I asked.

"Yeah, look, he's getting tubed," Charlie said. "And that's Michael Ho and Reno Abellira. There's an even better shot of him on the cover of *South Bay Surfer*." He rummaged through his magazines to find it. "Here." He handed me the December 1982 issue. The cover photo was Benny inside a barrel with a pink banner across it that read, "Danger and Excitement with Benavidez."

"Wow . . . and he lives here in Manhattan Beach?" I asked.

Charlie was looking through the pile of magazines as he replied, "In Hermosa, at Doc's house. All the pros stay at Doc's when they're in town. His buddy, Chris Barela, lived there, too. Their surf shop, Fireline, is here in Manhattan Beach."

I was just about to say that I wanted to go there when Charlie handed me the January 1983 issue of *Surfing*. "Here, Barela is on the cover this year." He was mid-cutback, and the type matched his yellow-and-turquoise boardshorts. Charlie handed me the more recent May issue, turning to an article inside titled, "Conversations, Chris Barela."

"He talks about how all the goofy-footers dominate California surfing—like you, Ellie." Wrinkles formed at the corners of his eyes as he grinned.

After reading the article, I flipped through many of the magazines, finding Benny on the cover, or his name on the cover, or photos of him featured. There were so many. He was on the cover of this year's May issue of *Pacific Surf*. The June 1980 *Surfing* issue's headline read: "Profile: California's Joey Buran and Mike Benavidez." Inside was an eight-page spread titled "California's Golden Boys Battle for Fame and Fortune on the IPS World Circuit." The caption under his photo read, "Benavidez cuts his teeth in Hermosa juice . . ."

He was also featured in the February 1980 issue of *Surfing* and the May 1980 issue of *Surfer*. In the January 1981 *Surfing* issue, which covered the Stubbie's contest, Benny was pictured on the podium placing second. The December 1977 issue feature, "California Surfing," contained an awesome full-page photo of Benny in the barrel. The caption read: "Mike Benavidez surfing a Southern California beach break." *Could it be right here out front?*

I picked up *South Bay Surfer*, turning to the Benny feature. It said he was number twenty-three in the world. A quote from him in big type read: "The main thing is that I never give up." I agreed; I wasn't about to, either. The April 1977 issue of *Surfing* had a double-page-spread of Benny getting tubed. It said he was sixteen at the time. *He was my age! What's it like to surf through a tunnel of water?*

I didn't have to wonder about it for long. The next morning, I found out when Uncle Charlie took me to the Hermosa Pier.

"Are you up for it?" he asked as we surveyed the seascape before us. It was big. There were overhead sets. My heart started racing.

"Yeah!" I answered, though I had butterflies fluttering around in my stomach.

Charlie had me wait until between sets to paddle out. I made it out by paddling as fast as I could in the current next to the pier. My board was nine feet long, so it paddled fast. Once I got outside, I could relax for a minute. But my heart began to pound when I noticed that the boy with the checkered board was also sitting in the lineup.

Uncle Charlie took off on a left. And then I saw it—a massive wedge of ocean heading my way, a giant set left. I positioned myself on my board and paddled, angling left. I felt the force of it move me. I popped up and then, all of a sudden, there was a huge wall of ocean next to me. It formed an arch over me as I soared faster. I could see Uncle Charlie framed by it, on the other side of the tunnel of water. He was looking straight at me, his mouth wide open.

"Woo-hoo!" I screamed. The board blew out from under me. Plunging into the cold water, I remembered to relax. Surfacing, I tugged my leash, pulling my board to me, so I could grab it. Paddling back out as fast as I could, I didn't even feel my arms thanks to the adrenaline rush. My heart pounded, bursting and energized from that wave.

Charlie was hooting and hollering and grinning broadly, his hands up in the air. "Wow, Ellie, you were in the green room! You got barreled!"

I was beaming. As I paddled toward the boy with the checkered board, he shouted out, "That was rad!"

"Thanks!" I was grinning from ear to ear, exuding joy and satisfaction for getting barreled for the first time. When I passed by the boy, I locked eyes with his and got lost in their beautiful sea-glass green.

"Nice one!" he added. An impish glint shone in his lovely eyes that made my body feel like it was on fire.

"Tah-wee!" Charlie cheered. "Ellie Bo-Belly got tubed!"

Another boy on a green shortboard shouted out, "Nice wave, dude!" amongst Uncle Charlie's hooting and hollering.

"Thanks," I responded, smiling in his direction.

"Wait till Jen hears about this!" Charlie exclaimed.

Later, back at the house, he told the story to Jen. I was all smiles, relishing each word of praise.

"You were looking at Mike Benavidez on the cover of surfing mags, and then the next day—boom! A big barrel! I couldn't believe it, Jen. I look and there she is, smack-dab in the middle of a big outside set tube. She's a charger—just like Benny."

"This is a cause for celebration!" Jen announced. Charlie took her in his arms, and they started dancing. He kicked his legs in all directions, looking like a rubber band. He spun her around. Jen laughed, and so did I. The way he danced reminded me of the scarecrow in the *Wizard of Oz* movie.

"El Terasco's all around!" he exclaimed. "Who wants a bean and cheese burrito?"

"Me!" I said.

"Me too," said Jen.

"I'm going to walk Zuzu to pick it up. Wanna come with me to get it?" Not waiting for my response, my uncle grabbed Zuzu's leash, leaned in to kiss Jen, and said to her, "She needs a shorter board."

"Okay, she can try one of mine." Jen's eyes met mine, shining bright as she showered me with a radiant smile. I beamed back at her.

"Oh yeah, woo-hoo, Benny—watch out!" Charlie sang out, then turned around by the front door and directed his question at me: "Coming, Charger?"

"Sure." *Now I'm Charger!* I was relieved to have a new nickname. I hoped it would stick.

As Zuzu, Charlie, and I walked to the restaurant, Charlie crowed, "Woo-hoo, grimmie in the green!"

"Grimmie? What's that?"

"An older word for grom," he explained. Then he made up a song, singing exuberantly. "Grom in green, woo-hoo! Ellie Bo-Belly's gettin' barreled, oh yeah. Gettin' tubed, grimmie in the green, yeah, that's my Ellie in the green room."

I wished my mom were around so I could tell her about my barrel. But she was at work. I thought I'd burst, having to wait until I saw her the next day. When I told her, she replied, "Ellie, that sounds dangerous, like it was a giant wave."

"Yeah, but I can handle it."

"But maybe you can't one day, and then . . ." She turned away from me.

"Then what?"

"I can't lose you," she whimpered. "Not you *too*." Tears streamed down her face. I put my arms around her, and we stood there awkwardly. Mom wasn't comfortable being emotional.

I tried to explain. "I know you don't understand, but I have to surf."

"Nothing's worth risking your life. If my sister wants to, that's her choice." Mom wiped her eyes and stood up. She took a cigarette from her pack, lit it, and started smoking, standing just outside the door to the garden.

My insides twisted up. It bothered me that she smoked. She looked weak without her heels on, barefoot. She took a long drag from the cigarette. I noticed that her hand was shaking. I thought about how she'd ignored the incident in Venice, like nothing had happened.

"Is Peter okay?" I asked.

"He's home from the hospital."

"Good."

"It's not good, he's not good, they can't help him." Mom's words about Peter cut into me like a knife to the gut. But before I could express my worry, she took another drag, then continued: "Why my sister would want to waste her time in such cold, dangerous water is beyond me."

It felt as if she was talking about me—like she didn't

understand me. She went on with more agitation in her voice. "I swear, this house is going to fall down, come the next storm . . . forget it if there's an earthquake!"

I stood up. I couldn't bear to listen to her. "I'm going to walk Zuzu."

Mom went to the kitchen and took out a bottle of vodka from the freezer. She poured some in a glass, then took a few pills out of her pocket and swallowed them, still holding her cigarette in her shaking hand.

"Do you even have a headache?" I asked her. Her mascara had run down her cheek.

"Huh?"

"The pills."

"Oh . . . yes, it's been bothering me." She held her hand up to her brow, took another gulp and continued on a rant. "Jen asks why I don't have dinner here. Well, *hello*, would I be able to bring a client *here*, to this run-down beach shack? I don't think so! Why anyone who's anyone would want to come to this sand pit—"

"Mom, stop!"

"What? If Jen doesn't care to go to the salon and would rather leave her hair a mess, looking like a bum—I guess that's her prerogative."

"Mom!" I shouted, my fists clenched.

"I'm *making* something of myself," she snapped. "Making money for your future and education so you can go to college."

I stormed into my room. *Why does she always have to criticize Jen? And for the dumbest things. Why does it matter how her hair looks?* I punched the bed. I needed to surf more than I needed to walk Zuzu. I got into my wetsuit, grabbed my board, and headed out the door.

Floating in the midst of the blue-gray glass, I was able to

let go and breathe. I thought about how Dad used to cook and do things for Mom, like have her coffee ready when she stumbled into the kitchen in the mornings. *Dad really loved her. He did things to please her all the time.*

Suddenly, a spurt of water blew up from the ocean's surface, fifteen feet high into the air. I gasped, shaking.

A guy near me shouted, "Whale!"

It's him! The boy with the checkered board!

"A whale!" I repeated out loud. I couldn't believe it. Just then, there were two more spouts.

"A baby!" he exclaimed. "Sweet!"

"Cool!" I shouted out, my heart beating fast. Normally I would've been too shy to talk in the lineup, but the whales were mind-blowing and they were so close to us. We watched them, gigantic, beautiful beasts floating near the surface together. The baby breached about twenty feet from us, jumping up into the air, and then it went back under. I screamed, and the boy shouted, "Whoa, far out! Totally awesome!"

He continued to talk the whole time we were surfing. To the seagulls flying above, he called out, "Stellar." To the waves as they formed and loomed closer, he said things like "Totally," "Mega," and "Most triumphant." He waved his arms up and cried out "Radical!" as a pelican soared overhead, so close it almost touched his fingertips.

I was trying to figure him out. He seemed to catch any wave that came by on his checkered shortboard, which I noticed had a colorful hand-painted addition to it. He was so fast, carving up the face of each wave and flying down the line. He'd go off the lip, back up to the lip vertically, then turn back down at the steepest part. Then he'd snap back, re-entering the force of the wave again and again, ripping the wave up. He beamed at me after a particularly good one. I couldn't help but get caught up by his energy and smile back at him. He had a high-spirited yet easygoing way about him.

"Hey," he said to me, "here's one for you. Righteous!" I turned around to see a big mound. I flung my arms, shoveling the water behind me. When I felt its full force under me, I popped up and was riding it, the fastest I'd ever gone. "Woo-hoo!" I hollered as I jumped off.

I learned the boy's name, Nick, after he asked me mine. Then I asked him if he had painted his board himself, and he said he had.

"You like it?" He jumped off and held it up out of the water. Close-up, I could tell that the black-and-white checks on it were drawn in black marker. There were graffiti letters spray-painted in pink and turquoise, though I couldn't make out what they said.

"Yeah," I said with a smile. "What does it say?"

"It says gnarr, short for gnarly." He got back on his board, turned, and paddled into a right, attacking the wave all the way to the lifeguard tower, where he ended it in a floater. I knew "gnarly waves" meant they were heavy or difficult. I guessed he had no problem surfing them. We surfed together for about an hour. He went in, but I stayed out another half hour. I hoped to see him in the water again. I wanted to try a smaller board like his.

The next day, my wish was granted. Well, one of them, anyway.

First thing in the morning, I overheard Jen and Charlie talking in the garden. My bedroom window was open.

"Do you think my sister's okay?"

"It doesn't make sense," said Charlie. "You don't just fall asleep randomly . . . unless you have narcolepsy or something."

"I know. I'm really worried about her."

"I don't know, your sister . . . ha! She's certainly unique, let's just say."

"Yeah, there's no one like her, that's for sure."

Unease crept down my spine and settled heavy in my stomach. Jen was worried. Mom didn't seem *too* sad, like when she had been in New York. I didn't want her to have to go back to the hospital or anything. But something wasn't right with her when she fell asleep at the café.

Pushing my thoughts aside, I went to the kitchen to make tea, in anticipation of going surfing.

Jen burst into the kitchen. "Want to try this one today?" She held up a multi-colored shortboard. It had two fins at the tail, one near each rail.

My heart leapt. "Sure! Oh my God, thank you!"

"It's one of Don's custom boards. Charlie calls it the Easter Egg."

"I love it. Wow, Don made it?"

"Uh-huh."

Don Kadowaki, who shaped for pro surfers like Sally, made this board—and I'd get to ride it. The wild brushstrokes all over it, in ultramarine-blue and hot-pink, did look like a hand-dyed Easter egg, or an abstract painting.

"It's got two fins," I remarked.

"Yeah, it's a twin fin, and it's got channels to give you speed and a winged swallow tail to help grip when you turn." Jen put it in my arms. "Here."

"It's so light!"

"Yeah, it's only six feet. I think you're ready for it, after hearing about that barrel." She was glowing. *She's proud of me,* I realized. Her voice grew bubbly. "And you can duck-dive it. It'll be easier to make it out when there are bigger waves."

I breathed in deep, taking in her shining gaze. "I'd like to learn that . . . can you teach me?"

"Sure." She chuckled. "I'll strap a new leash around it for you, too."

I only knew how to turtle my board. Duck-diving was diving under the wave, like a dolphin did.

My aunt gave me a duck-dive lesson between the white-wash and the lineup, in the impact zone. This wasn't a place you'd normally like to hang out in. But that day it wasn't critical; it was small. It was hard to push the nose down underwater. I tried again and again, but the force of the wave coming at me was too strong. I got frustrated. I kept getting pushed back. Jen showed me how to keep my arms straight from a push-up position, to add body weight when I pushed down. Still, I couldn't get the nose far enough under the water, with the topsy-turvy foam fighting me.

Finally, I was able to get the nose to dive under, but I didn't know when to come up. Jen suggested keeping my eyes open underwater so I could see when I was clear of the wave. I was surprised the water didn't sting my eyes. I could see whirling white above me and kept moving forward, hugging my board till I was in clear water. I pointed the nose straight up, and it worked.

I practiced over and over that day, the next, and the next, and for weeks afterward until I'd gotten the hang of it. The shortboard was harder to paddle out. It took more arm strength, so it took more time for me to make it out. The longer it took to make it outside, the more waves I would need to duck-dive, so I got lots of practice in. Then, once I made it out, it was harder to paddle into waves, but the force of the wave from just inside the peak was enough to push me down the line.

It was so much easier to turn a shorter board. In fact, I

turned too much a few times, and threw myself out the back of the wave. Soon I got the hang of it, though, and was carving down the line in curves.

I kept hoping to see Nick again. One Saturday, a few weeks after we'd officially met—when we'd seen the whales—I paddled out, and there he was. It hit me to the core how majorly attractive he was. The two of us were alone at the peak.

"Hi," he said as he paddled in past me, chasing a wave. His dark brown hair looked scruffy, not yet matted down from the water.

"Hi," I muttered, helpless to my quickening heartbeat and the warmth shooting through me.

"There are some fun ones today, for sure," he said after he'd caught and ridden one nimbly. My heart fluttered at the sight of him flying down the line—he was so in tune with the shape of the wave.

"For sure," I agreed.

"Hey, nice board!"

"Thanks—it's my aunt's." I gazed down at it, pleased.

"Did you paint it?"

"No, my aunt did."

When I met his bright-green eyes, he smiled warmly. "Radical! Bet you're stoked to ride it."

"Yeah," I said, beaming back at him. I *was* stoked to ride it now that I was getting better at my duck-dives. I made it out quicker, and it was nice having less board to deal with. It felt so light, it reminded me of riding a skateboard.

The south wind picked up, spurting dents all along the once-glassy surface. The cool breeze kissed my face. Behind surges of water in the distance, a dark-gray fin appeared.

Ripples of excitement surged through me. I rubbed the rail of the Easter Egg, and within a few minutes, there were six dolphins circling. I drifted toward them in the rip current. A baby floated with its head out of the water and its mouth open, the mother right by its side. Seagulls flew about in a frenzy. *The dolphins must be feeding,* I surmised.

A set was coming in, and a dolphin way out was moving to meet it. I turned around and started to paddle to try and catch the wave. I couldn't make it; I had drifted too far out with the dolphins. I watched the wave go all the way south of the tower, almost to shore, and then a dolphin leapt out from the shallows. *It rode that big set all the way to shore!*

"Oh my God, did you see that?" Nick shouted as I paddled in towards the lineup. "That dolphin surfed the wave! He got tubed! Bitchin'!"

"Wow," I cried out. "Amazing!"

Nick turned to me, his mouth open in awe, and raised an eyebrow. "That was a righteous wave."

"I can't believe that dolphin got barreled." I met his friendly gaze and giggled. He threw his head back with a hearty laugh.

That session, we took turns, each of us getting one of the sets. Nick was really good. I wanted to learn how to hit the lip like he did. I tried, but I couldn't turn my board with enough speed and ended up falling off. I came up laughing at my mistake. From the inside, I watched Nick catch a big one and go speeding down the line, cut back up to the top, and rip the face, shredding it. Then he rotated all the way around—three hundred and sixty degrees—before continuing on the wave like it was nothing to do the most awe-inspiring spin ever.

"Woo-hoo!" I shouted out. I wanted to learn how to do that, too.

We stayed out for hours. We split the peak a few times.

He went right, I went left. When my arms had turned to noodles—what Charlie called arms that were exhausted from paddling—I caught one in and waved good-bye. He waved back. My heart raced.

Heading home, I struggled against my useless arms to not drop my board. *He's so confident*, I mused. *But not cocky at all.* Like how just being in the water makes you happy . . . that was him, pure cheerfulness. I wondered where he went to school. He looked like he could be in college. I decided I would ask him next time I saw him in the water. I hoped that would be soon.

FOURTEEN

The No Beach Trash Club

At the beginning of November, a heat wave hit. During the day, it was too hot to walk Zuzu. She lay inside panting, looking like she was suffering under her heavy coat.

Nightfall brought some relief from the constant, intense heat. I got Zuzu's leash and took her out. In the back alley, above the treetops, dark clouds hung suspended, the moon hidden behind them. Everything else was black. As we walked, I thought about having to go to school the next day. I clenched Zuzu's leash, my hands sweating. I didn't know what the girls in my homeroom talked about during lunch break in the quad. Caitlyn was hanging out with them now, and so was Sheila. My shoulders hunched.

A cat sat motionless under a street lamp, watching Zuzu and I pass by. A gentle breeze blew the hairs on my arms. I thought about Aisha. She seemed nice. She usually sat and read a book during lunch. I thought I'd do the same, so my table wouldn't seem so empty. My stomach clenched. I dreaded going to school in the morning.

The next day during lunch, I sat alone at a table outside in the quad, reading. Someone tapped my shoulder, hard. I glanced behind me and was surprised to see Bonnie, followed by a pack of ten girls from my homeroom.

"We, like, need to talk to you," Bonnie informed me.

"Now? I'm in the middle of a book." But they lingered there, behind me, in a clump.

"In the middle of a book," April mimicked me. "What a nerd."

"Duh, like, now!" Bonnie insisted.

Thinking it was an emergency, I put my book down, stood up, and turned around. "What's wrong?" I asked.

Bonnie shoved Caitlyn forward, "Say it, Caitlyn." Caitlyn looked down at the ground. "Say it," Bonnie repeated. Caitlyn muttered something.

"What? We can't hear you!" Sheila prodded. All eyes were on Caitlyn. She froze, looking down at the table.

Bonnie huffed, pushing in front of Caitlyn. "We don't like you, beach trash. We don't like posers from New York with black eyes and bruises coming here, spreading your grody hobo germs out of your nose."

"None of us like you," Brooke taunted.

Reeling, I felt like I'd been punched in the stomach. But I said, "That's not true. Caitlyn's my friend."

"No, she's not. Caitlyn, say it!" Bonnie demanded.

A prickly chill went down my spine as I tried to make eye contact with Caitlyn, but her gaze remained fixed on the ground.

"Are you friends with this trash?" Bonnie pressed.

And then I heard her say it, a mumbled "no." I stared at Caitlyn in stunned disbelief. She had betrayed me.

"See!" Brooke scoffed. "Like, no one likes you."

My stomach clenched into a tight pit. I glanced around the empty quad, hoping to see someone, anyone, who wasn't a part of this.

April stepped in closer and spat out, "Who are you looking for? You don't have any friends."

Bonnie crossed her arms and asserted in a matter-of-fact tone, "This is *our* school. You don't belong here, trash. None of us will tolerate you from now on. We've formed a club."

"Yeah, the No Beach Trash Club," Brooke said, making sure to pronounce each word clearly, like she was talking to an idiot.

"Yeah, like, go back home, New York!" April said with contempt. The other girls laughed at me.

Sheila joined in. "Like, totally gross!"

"Poser!" Brooke jeered, as the others snickered.

"I'm not a poser," I replied. "I surf."

"You're nothing but grody beach trash," Bonnie hissed, turning her back to me. They all laughed loudly at that as they took off in a clump toward the classrooms.

Suddenly lightheaded, I turned around and reached for the table to brace myself. Weak-kneed, I slumped onto the bench. I opened my book, but my eyes couldn't focus on the type. My head was in a whirlpool of confusion, my thoughts all jumbled up, shadowed by a sense of doom. I had a horrible feeling in my stomach that I'd done something wrong. I didn't cry, not wanting to give them the satisfaction. I just pretended like what they said didn't matter to me. I held it in all day, but when I finally arrived home, I burst into tears in the living room. Aunt Jen put her arms around me. I couldn't stop crying.

"It's okay, sweetie," she said. "Did something happen at school?"

I wanted to tell Jen what had happened, but I was scared that if Mom found out, she'd want to move us back to New York. I needed everything to be fine at school, so I could stay here and surf.

"Is it those spoiled brats at school?" she asked.

I shook my head, knowing it was a lie. *They all hate me.*

"Is it your dad? Do you miss him?"

I nodded. I did miss him. *I miss you so much, Dad! Can you stop this from hurting so much? Why do they hate me?*

"Oh Ellie, it's okay, let it out. It's okay to cry." Jen hugged me gently.

The only friend I had in high school had betrayed me. I had no friends, it was true. And Dad was gone, so I could never talk to him about this or anything again.

As I wailed, Aunt Jen stayed with me. Zuzu rubbed up against my back, pushing her wet nose into my elbow. She nudged me so hard I lost my balance, and Jen and I both fell over on our backs. Startled, I started to laugh. Jen laughed with me.

"I know what you need," she said. "Some good waves."

I turned to face her and nodded, tears streaming down my cheeks.

"Right!" she exclaimed as she shot up and reached out her hand to me. "Let's go!"

I took her hand, leapt up, and was in my wetsuit in no time. Jen was already in the garden, waxing her board.

I was able to forget the events of the day a little, because I had to concentrate in order to surf. My whole being relaxed in the soaring speed and power of the waves. All my senses were activated, from the bottoms of my feet up to my head, in tune with the unpredictable movement. I stayed out until the sun was setting and there was only the occasional set wave due to the rising tide. When I could no longer feel my fingers and toes, I caught my last wave in and joined Jen, who was waiting on the beach. The sunset was the kind I'd seen in books at the library in New York: bright pink, yellow, and orange, with purple streaks over the ocean.

That night Mom didn't come home. I stayed up looking at the stars twinkling between the tree branches, trying to talk to Dad. My head spun and the empty space inside me ached. Dad seemed so very far away. *What should I do? I don't want to go back to school.* I tried to sleep, but kept waking up to Bonnie's bratty voice repeating, "We don't like you."

I was strangely numb from not sleeping much in the morning. The wind was already strong, but I paddled out anyway. I sat out there in the blue-gray chop, bobbing on the water like a buoy. As I searched for waves on the horizon in the cold mist, I longed to stay out and skip school, but I knew I'd have to go back and pretend everything was okay. If Mom found out about the No Beach Trash Club, I was sure she'd move us back East. That had become my worst fear, and I was determined to not let that happen. I needed to stay in California. I couldn't stop surfing, not now, not ever.

After Jen dropped me off, I was careful to keep my head down as I approached school, focusing on the ground to avoid eye contact with anyone. I was early today—that was a first. I sat on a lone bench at the edges of the quad.

Aisha Davis approached me. She sat down next to me. "I'm not with those girls," she said, breaking the silence.

I looked into Aisha's beautiful amber eyes—they were sincere. "I'm not a part of their stupid club," she said.

My eyes welled up with tears. Her words cut through the fog of doom and confusion overwhelming me. I didn't know what to say, but I managed, "Thanks."

The bell rang and as we got up, I thanked her again, looking into her eyes this time.

"No need to thank me," she said with a warm smile.

We turned to walk into school together. It was a big relief to not have to walk in alone.

That day, the girls did their best to try to get at me, but I didn't let them know they did. While walking from the science lab back to homeroom through the hallway of lockers, the heavy hall door suddenly swung out at me. A boy named Liam bolted forward and blocked it just in time, before it hit me in the nose. Bonnie was on the other side of the door with Brooke and April, laughing. They had deliberately tried to hit me in the face with the door.

I gave Liam a thankful glance for saving me. He was tall and lanky, with long blonde hair. I ignored the onslaught of jeering girls as we passed by. I ignored the remarks of "Go home, New York," "Loser!," "Poser!," and "Eww, gross!" In the weeks and months that followed, they said those things to me every chance they got—out of earshot of teachers, of course.

All of the girls in my homeroom class were part of the "No Beach Trash Club," except for Aisha, apparently. I was wounded by Caitlyn's betrayal, but I didn't let her know it. Nor did I let any of the girls know that what they said or how they acted hurt my feelings. I wouldn't give them the satisfaction. They gave me mean stink-eye looks from across the cafeteria and quad, snickering among themselves during lunch. Bonnie, Brooke, April, Sheila, and now Caitlyn, along with the other girls from homeroom.

I sat at an empty table. Aisha sat down next to me and blew her breath out in a huff.

"I think Bonnie must've farted, 'cause that table stinks,"

she said.

I smiled at that. "Really?"

Aisha waved the air away from her nose. "Uh-huh, totally. I smelled it as I passed by. Bogus." She shook her head and pinched her nose.

"Eww! I'm glad we're over here."

"Yeah." She drew in a breath. "Big time."

We opened our lunch bags. Hardly anyone got lunch from the cafeteria; it looked like slop. A girl from freshman year came up and stared me in the face. "Why are you homeless?" she asked me with a grimace.

"I'm not."

"What's your problem?" Aisha said to the girl.

"It's just, those girls said she was," she said, pointing to Bonnie's table. They were laughing, jeering, and gesturing.

Aisha squinted at the girl, giving her a cold look. "Get bent! Go on, kick rocks!"

The girl skipped away with a smirk on her face, her blonde hair flopping behind her.

"What jerks, they're so lame," Aisha said in disgust.

I stared at my peanut butter and jelly sandwich. I wasn't hungry anymore.

When the bell finally rang at the end of the day, on my way out I turned the corner and, to my surprise, there was Uncle Charlie. He was standing just outside the office in his fireman uniform, a navy-blue jumpsuit. He had a serious expression on his face, but when he saw me, he grinned and waved at me. I was relieved to see him. I wouldn't have to run into those girls alone.

"Hi," I said. "What are you doing here?"

"I was just goin' to ask you the same question, Ellie Bo-Belly."

I tilted my head sideways, trying to figure out if he was joking or not.

"Okay, I admit it," he announced. "I've come to take you to try the best root beer float you've ever had."

"Like an egg cream?"

"Now that sounds terrible—must be some New York drink with eggs in it. This is way better, 'cause it's got ice cream."

Inside the yellow VW bus, Charlie blasted a cassette in the eight-track player. "Misirlou" was a riveting song of guitar frenzy. I had never heard anything like it before.

"What is this?" I asked.

"Dick Dale and His Del-Tones," Charlie said, a look of disbelief on his face that I didn't know it. "Dick Dale, the legend—it's *surfer* music! Can't you see yourself surfing?" He shook his head from side to side to the beat, drumming his fingers on the steering wheel. He mimed being covered by a wave in the barrel by lifting his arm over his head. That started to crack me up. We pulled into a spot on the street in front of the diner on the corner. Charlie opened the door for me, and I jumped out. We went inside and sat in a booth. He ordered two root beer floats.

"Anything else?" the waiter asked.

Charlie looked at me and asked, "You hungry?"

"No thanks. I want to be able to surf."

"That never stopped me from eating," he said with a chuckle, and then turned to the waiter. "I think we're good, man. Thanks."

When the waiter left, he asked me, "Everything okay, Ellie Bo-Belly?"

I paused. I stared at his name tag, which read "MacGreg-gor," and then down at the wooden table top. "Not really," I answered.

"What's wrong? Did some old fart snake you this morning? I'll have to have a word or two with 'em. Calling my niece names—you're the kook, kook!"

Normally I would chuckle at that, but I was serious now. "Do you promise not to tell my mom?"

"Definitely."

"Pinky promise?" I asked, holding out my pinky finger.

"Pinky promise." We shook on it.

"Okay, well . . . all the girls at school hate me."

"Hate you? That's impossible."

"They do. They formed a club against me."

He shook his head. "Girls can be so mean . . . at least guys'll punch it out with each other, and after that, sometimes things are okay. Maybe you should take a swing at 'em?"

I slumped in my seat and sighed. "That won't help."

"It might make you feel better. How's your right jab? Your left hook?"

I looked down at my lap.

"Surely not every girl is in cahoots with this," he said. "There must be a leader, a big bully."

"Yes, they all are. Well, all except Aisha."

"You see," he said. "That's all you need—one friend. And you have many more friends. Me, your aunt, and the all the local surfers, lifeguards, and firemen in this town. That adds up to about . . . five hundred people. And don't forget Zuzu, your faithful canine companion."

But I couldn't smile.

He leaned in towards me and whispered, "Ellie Bo-Belly . . . you're a wonderful girl. And you're a surfer girl. That's like the coolest. Don't listen to those stupid girls—don't let them hurt you. If they get at you, they've won their catty game. That's what they want. Don't let 'em."

"I know," I said, "but I'm afraid if Mom finds out, she'll use it as an excuse to move us back to New York."

"Don't worry, I won't spill the beans, pinky promise," he said holding up his pinky finger. His bright-blue eyes brimmed with empathy, then crinkled at the edges into a warm smile.

Encouraged, I confided in him, "I don't want to ever move back there. I just want to surf. I want to get really good."

My uncle put both hands down on the table in front of him and looked me square in the face. "You know who the best surfer is?"

"Who?"

"The one having the most fun," he said with a wink. "Geez, I can still picture you smack-dab in the middle of that barrel—gremmie in the green!"

I smiled, remembering it. "That wave made me happy for a whole month."

He ducked his head, grinning from ear to ear. "I understand completely." Then, in a serious tone, he said gently, "You know, your Aunt Jen and I want you to stay with us forever."

I couldn't believe it. In that moment I realized not only how much I wanted to stay in California, but how much I wanted to stay with them. My eyes welled up with tears, soaking up the sincerity in his gaze. "Really?"

"Uh-huh. My lips are sealed, cross my heart, pinky promise, I won't mention a thing to Heels—gosh, how does she walk in those things? They just sink into the sand."

I couldn't help but crack a smile at that. It was funny how her "Heels" nickname had stuck.

The root beer floats arrived. I sipped mine with my straw—it was creamy and delicious, better than an egg cream.

"Like it?" Charlie inquired.

I had already sipped half of it down. I nodded and drank

the rest down quick, eager to surf.

Driving back to the house in the van, Charlie played the Beach Boys' "Surfin' U.S.A." in the eight-track player. Listening to the lyrics, I realized that all the surf spots they were singing about were right here.

When we hit the afternoon waves there was some bump on it, but I didn't care. I dove deep into the chilly ocean, cleansing myself in the saltwater, washing off all the stuff from school. Forced to focus on each maneuver while surfing, I forgot about it all for a few minutes, especially when riding a wave. In those few seconds of elation, I was akin to the gulls soaring overhead, suspended in flight. One with the water's movement, I succumbed to its force, which was much more powerful than me, and let go. I let go of everything—all my worries and fears and sadness—for a moment.

I rubbed the rail of the Easter Egg and waited. I gazed out at the azure horizon, my back to the town, the school, the land and everything on it. I sat at the edge of the earth, facing the vast blue. The wind tickled my ear as the roar of the erupting surf warmed my heart. The resonance of the gushing, rolling, bursting whitewash cleared my head. Each wave release was the ocean sighing, bringing its message from across the sea.

Suddenly, a momma dolphin appeared with her baby and another older one, maybe the aunt. The baby was curious and swam close to me. My heart pounded in my chest. I dove down and swam with my leash strapped to my ankle. In the cloudy brine, I couldn't see anything but shadows and patches of light, but I could hear them. They were talking in their own language. A high-pitched tune echoed in the water, then another, and then clicking sounds.

I blew bubbles in reply. *Thank you for saying hello to me. Want to play?* I imagined that the baby said, *Yes, I do!*

I came up for air and slid onto my board. A wave was coming. As I turned and paddled, the baby dolphin popped up a few feet from me, deep in the wave. I turned to angle the other way. I felt the momentum and stood up, knees bent, my hand skimming the water wall's surface as I flew by.

Back in the lineup, I shouted to Charlie, "Did you see that?"

"You split the peak with the dolphin!" Uncle Charlie howled. "Tah-wee! Woo-hoo!"

"Woo-hoo!" I called back. Just then I noticed that there was a girl in the lineup. She wore a bright-yellow swimsuit and had long, white-blonde hair. She had seen it, too.

"That was totally awesome!" she shouted over to me.

"Yeah, the dolphins are so amazing!"

"Hey, what's your name?" the girl asked.

"Ellie . . . what's yours?"

"Chris."

I was beyond happy to see another girl in the water. A set came, and Chris took it with such force. After a strong bottom turn, she ripped the wave to shreds, carving bottom to top and off the lip, again and again with snappy cutbacks.

"Wow, you're so good!" I shouted when she paddled back out.

"Thanks," she said, smiling. "Will you be here tomorrow?"

"Yeah."

"Me too. I hope there's good waves."

"Yeah," I agreed, smiling back. When I finally got out of the water, though I was bone-tired, I was excited to have met another girl who surfed. I wasn't sure how much of a girl she was; she looked like a woman. She had curves in all the right places. I didn't know how she wore just a swimsuit in that freezing cold water.

As we walked back up the hill to the cottage, Charlie said in an upbeat tone, "Hey, that girl rips. Maybe she'll be here tomorrow."

"You think so? She said she would be."

He brushed the top of my head with his hand, messing up my hair. "I bet. I think Ellie Bo-Belly just made a new friend. And a surfer girl, too—Ripper."

Sure enough, Chris was there the next day. Charlie's nickname for her stuck—Ripper. She did really rip. I learned later that she biked the whole Strand, seven miles from Torrance Beach to here in Manhattan Beach, every day after school, holding her ET thruster under one arm. She could've surfed closer to where she lived, at Rat Beach or the Avenues. But when she met me, she decided she'd surf here. We were the only teen girls we knew that surfed.

Chris was a year and a half older than me. She'd been surfing for a few years, and was starting to compete in contests. Her tanned brown skin was partly due to her Latin heritage, her mom being from Mexico, but mostly from surfing without a wetsuit all year round. I didn't know how she did it, but she never seemed to get cold. She'd inherited her long blonde hair from her dad, and it was bleached white from the sun.

With our shared surfing obsession, we became fast friends. Between Aisha at school and Chris at the beach, I was able to deal with Bonnie's stupid group. Uncle Charlie kept his promise, and never told Heels about my problems with the girls at school. Things were looking up.

During lunch at school one day, Aisha and I were sitting at our own table as usual when Liam came over with some canned sodas in his hands. "Anyone want a Like cola? An extra one came out of the machine."

"Sure," Aisha said. "When did they get *that?*"

"I think just today," Liam answered as he gave her one. "It says it's ninety-nine percent caffeine-free."

"Like, totally," she said, opening the soda can. "Like, I can't believe there's a soda named Like." We all cracked up.

"Like, yeah," he said. He stood there with a sheepish grin.

"We can share it, Ellie," Aisha said before she took a sip.

"Sure," I said, then turned to Liam and said, "Thanks."

As he turned to go, he whipped his head around and his chin-length blonde hair sprayed in the air.

Aisha whispered in my ear, "Can you believe him? He thinks he's in a shampoo commercial."

"I mean, like—thanks for stopping the door the other day," I blurted out.

Liam turned back to face us. "Oh, no worries," he said. "Actually, I believe one should hold the door for a lady, that's the proper way." He bowed and smiled.

"Uh-huh," Aisha said in agreement, giving him an approving smile back.

"Hey, have I seen you in the water?" I asked him.

"Yeah," he said. "I saw you get a barrel one day at the pier."

"Oh yeah," I remembered. "You've got a green board . . ."

"Uh-huh, Lucky Charms," he said.

I must have flushed pink. I hadn't recognized him out of the water. *People look so different in normal clothes with their hair dry.*

Aisha raised her eyebrows. "What is it with you surfers? Giving your boards names like pets."

"Yeah, um, or like, your favorite cereal," he said, his smile turning a little goofy. "Do you surf too?" he asked Aisha, leaning in towards her.

"No way. I don't like the cold water, nuh-uh."

"Are you sure? I could teach you sometime," I offered.

"No way am I going out in that freezing water!" she said.

"Yeah," said Liam, "I like summertime when you don't have to wear a wetsuit."

"I like the cold," I said.

"You're crazy," Aisha remarked.

"I like to wear a wetsuit, it's like a second skin," I explained. "I feel protected, like I'm a seal."

"I like skateboarding," said Aisha.

"Really?" I said. "Me too! My aunt's friend Sally gave me a skateboard this summer."

"My older brother taught me to ride," she said. "He graduated last year. Now he's at El Camino College. He skates pools and stuff."

"Swimming pools?" Liam asked.

Aisha nodded. "Him and his friends are kind of gnarly. They find abandoned houses, drain the pools, and skate them."

"Rad!" said Liam. "I skate, too—"

Just then, something wet and slimy landed on my head. As I touched it, it stuck to my hand. "Ugh!" I gasped. I turned around and saw some of the mean girls scurrying away in a clump and snickering.

"What is this?" I said, stunned, looking at the clear bright green stuff stuck to my hand.

"Looks like Jell-O," said Aisha. "Those jerks. That's so immature." She got up to wipe it off my hair with a napkin.

"Jell-O? Who'd do that?" said Liam, taken aback.

I summoned all my effort not to cry. "Bonnie and her group."

"The preppy girls?" he said. "They think they're better than everyone else. They're so lame."

"Yeah," said Aisha. "They're so fake and plastic, like Barbie dolls. Wait, not Barbie—Barfie dolls!"

"Ha! Barfie dolls . . ." chuckled Liam "That's good. You know, they're all big-time partiers. They used to be cheerleaders, but now they spend all of daddy's money on coke."

"I doubt they have spare brain cells to burn." Aisha brushed the napkin into my hair harder. "They're a bunch of imbeciles. They really piss me off."

"They call me—" I started and then stopped, my voice wavering. "They call me beach trash." I was beginning to feel like trash with garbage in my hair, like I was no good and didn't amount to anything. Maybe they were right. I was displaced, far from my life in New York City. Maybe I'd never fit in here.

"Well then, I'm beach trash, too, and proud of it," stated Liam.

Aisha smiled at him, taking a break from getting the Jell-O out of my hair. "Really?"

"I kid you not, the beach is where it's at!" Liam said. "Since I was a mini-grom, before I could walk, even. I mean, like, what place is more beautiful than the beach?"

Aisha's amber eyes lit up as she leaned in towards Liam and said softly, "You're kind of brill, dude." The corners of her mouth raised into a genuine smile and Liam, grinning, blushed pink. Aisha turned back to my hair and sighed, gesturing with the napkin in the air. "I can't get it all out. I'm sorry, Ellie."

I felt my hair. It was still sticky. "It's okay," I said.

"I'd like to punch those stuck-up airheads," she said as she plopped back down in her seat.

"I would if they weren't chicks," said Liam.

Aisha's eyes met Liam's, still blushing. He quickly looked

down at the ground, his long hair falling into his face. He whipped it back.

Aisha gave me a look, as if to say, "He's done it again—the hair thing."

"I'm going to go wash this stuff out," I said, getting up.

"I'll help you," Aisha said.

I didn't really care about the Jell-O in my hair. I knew it would wash away in the surf later.

They can't make me cry. They can't take surfing away from me.

From then on, during lunch breaks, I joined Aisha on the stairs to the parking lot at the edge of school, away from the quad. It was under a big oak tree, and we read and talked there while we ate our lunch. I started skateboarding home with her, too, since her house was halfway home on the way to mine. And in the mornings, Jen dropped me by her house so we could skateboard to school together.

Liam began visiting us during lunch every day. He liked to act the part of heroic protector towards me and Aisha, joking about blocking flying Jell-O. I started to think he had a crush on Aisha because of how he looked at her. I thought they would make a cute couple, but wasn't sure if Aisha liked Liam that way. But he lightened things up considerably at lunchtime.

The No Beach Trash Club started calling me "Lezzie" for being the only girl from our high school who surfed. I found that odd, because I'd just found out that Chris was a lesbian. She'd confided in me that she had a girlfriend during our last surf session. They'd met in high school in Torrance. Now they were both seniors. But if I was a lesbian, too, did it matter? I didn't like being called names. And being gay wasn't anything to be shamed for or ashamed about.

Bonnie's group was so backwards. Growing up in New York City, our family dinner table was permanently occupied by my parents' artist and writer friends every Saturday night, many of whom were gay. I'd grown up with them. Peter was like my uncle, just as much as Uncle Charlie was. It hurt to think about him being sick and that the hospital couldn't help him. I pushed it out of my mind.

In middle school, I'd kissed a boy I liked, Josh. We would go up on his roof to kiss during one month in eighth grade. I'm not sure he liked it that much, because he came out as gay two years later. We were friends my sophomore year, before I left. Thinking back, I was so overloaded with homework and Dad being sick that I didn't have much time to hang out with friends outside of school. I'd only begun to make new friends in high school when I had to leave.

I thought of Nick, and my heart began to quicken at the thought of us kissing. *Would he like it?* Just imagining kissing him was too much for me to handle. I quickly erased it from my mind.

FIFTEEN

Lowers and Lucy

No one was more thankful than me when Thanksgiving week arrived. I really needed a break from the constant mean things Bonnie's group said and did to me at school. Besides calling me "Lezzie" for being a girl who surfed—which didn't make sense, because they simultaneously called me "Poser" because they didn't believe I was really a surfer—their latest thing was attacking my mom. They called her trashy. I had to admit that she did dress slutty; it was embarrassing.

April and Brooke seemed to be in a contest over who could do the best stink eye at me from across the desks during homeroom. Caitlyn bragged loudly to Sheila about going to parties on the weekends with Bonnie and April and their group. I was never invited to a party. I told myself I wouldn't want to stay up late at parties anyway, because I'd be too tired to wake up early for dawn patrol.

Early one morning, my aunt and Charlie took me and Chris to surf a new spot down in San Onofre called Trestles. Charlie said this spot was north of Old Man's, where we'd surfed on my birthday. In particular, we were going to check out Lowers, a really good reef-break that was considered by many to be the best surf spot in California. I was stoked. Charlie said it was known for its "long, steep right." I was the only one in the group who was goofy-foot. That meant I'd be backside, not facing the wave, which was considered more difficult. But I looked forward to working on my backside, and maybe even getting a backside barrel.

Charlie dropped us girls close to the beach, at the short path, and Jen called him "a gentleman" and gave him a kiss. Charlie whistled at us, blasting Jan and Dean's "Surf City" as he drove off to park far away across the highway.

When we got down to the beach, Jen said it was "epic" and that the right was on fire.

The guys out in the lineup tried to ignore us, but Jen's smile was contagious. We girls waited in the wings of the peak. Two guys had just caught waves, and a rogue outside set had washed everyone in but us. I had concentrated hard on duck-diving it and was surprised how easy it was to pierce through the back of the wave. The next one was building into another set wave. Jen paddled out toward the peak and caught it; she was in the spot. After a perfect take-off, she sped down the line, trimming it expertly in front of all the guys who were trying to get back on their boards in the whirling wash, making it almost all the way to shore.

Chris took the next one. It was a bit smaller and peaked further in, so she didn't have to paddle out to it. She did a big bottom turn and stalled a little. Then I couldn't see her—she was covered in water. When the top of her white-blonde head shot out, I quickly turned back to face the horizon, knowing not to keep my back to the ocean. Waves could sneak up on you.

When Jen made her way back out, I felt relieved to not be alone. The old guy next to me cleared his throat and shouted, "Nice wave!"

"Thanks," she said with a smile, and continued paddling over to me.

"Did you see Ripper?" she asked. "She got barreled and came out the other end."

"Really? Wow!"

"Your turn," Jen said with a grin. I had butterflies in my stomach. This was a new place, a reef, and there were powerful overhead sets. "Next one," Jen said.

I braced myself for it, scanning my peripheral field. Dark lines were out there, a giant sweep moving towards me. Ignoring my butterflies, I paddled north towards the peak. Jen could've gone, but she was telling me to go, so I turned and paddled with the incoming mass. I couldn't help glancing over my shoulder. It looked really big, and it was growing. A pang of fear shot through me as my heart pounded, but I knew timing was crucial. If I hesitated and dropped in late, I could get worked. Though my muscles were trembling, I kept paddling as I angled my board to my right.

Jen shouted, "Go, Ellie!"

I felt the force of the wave under me and ploughed through with two more strokes to be sure to make it. Keeping up with its speed, quick as I could, I got to my feet as a wall of water formed to my right. The instant the thrill of the drop overcame me, something let go in me. I soared as the wall rose and formed a lip over me. Speeding through, I squatted low, my left hand holding onto the rail as my right reached out to touch the water wall. I marveled at the ocean tunnel. Amazingly, it held its canopy. Though it was only a second or two, it felt longer, like time had stopped. And it was quiet here, the roar of the surf hushed.

Before I knew what had happened, I was falling. I hit the water's surface and plummeted under, into the cold wet. I was knocked around, and then hurled into a somersault. I tensed, hoping I wouldn't hit the reef. Then I remembered to relax and let the ocean move me. I kicked my feet to help propel myself toward the light—and surfaced. My colorful Easter Egg board was being carried away towards shore by the whitewash. *My leash must have broken*, I realized. I swam toward it and finally grasped it, riding the whitewash towards shore. I stepped carefully over rocks, leaning on my board for balance, as Jen rode the next wave in.

"Are you okay?" she asked, out of breath. She'd gotten to me as quickly as possible.

"Yeah, my leash broke."

"Oh." She sounded relieved. "Did you get barreled?"

"It wasn't completely covering me, but it was up top like this." I motioned with my hand above my head.

"Oh wow! It looked like a good one!" She gave me a radiant smile.

"Yeah, it was fun." I took a deep breath, my heartbeat quickening, recalling the feeling of flying I'd had riding it, my fingers touching the water wall. Jen put her board down and started to undo her leash.

"You can have mine," she offered.

"Oh, that's okay, I can swim for it."

"But you don't need to," she said matter-of-factly. "Here you go." She was already undoing mine and attaching hers to it. She always seemed to think of me before herself.

"Thanks," I said.

She beamed. "What do you say we get back out there and catch some more fun ones?"

I nodded. "Sounds good."

We were all smiles when Charlie paddled out to join us. He got the very best set waves on his longboard. On one wave, he took off with the board backwards, the fin in front. When he was back up top at the crest, he walked to the front (which was now the tail) and spun the board back around while walking back. He called it a "fin-first take-off."

"They just didn't know what hit them," Uncle Charlie said later over tacos. "Three girls, totally ripping, getting tubed—at Lowers! And I was the lucky guy with all three girls. Woo-hoo! Tah-wee!"

It felt like a milestone in surfing for me to have surfed Lowers. I was so relieved to be on break from school and to not have to deal with Bonnie's stupid group. My arms were noodles. Chris looked beat, too. It was good to eat. I hadn't realized I was so hungry. With full bellies, Chris and I fell asleep in the back of the van on the ride home to Charlie whistling along to "Wipe Out" by the Surfaris.

During the break, since I was home with Mom before she left for work, I noticed she was drinking more. She didn't think I knew that her "water glass" was actually filled with vodka. She asked me about school, and I lied and said it was better this year. After meeting Aisha, she was pleased I'd made a friend, and had no reason to think everything wasn't okay.

Aisha and I explored around Manhattan Beach on our skateboards, taking the Strand to downtown. It was so small and quaint compared to the real Manhattan I grew up in. I felt at ease, not having to use my street smarts all the time to stay safe. It felt like a weight was lifted off me. And it was so uncrowded, compared to what I was used to, that it almost seemed empty. People here weren't rushing by in a hurry. They took their time walking, took a breath now and then, and said hi to everyone they passed by. The streets were clean, and so was the beach.

At Jo's Candy Cottage, we'd buy a bag of chocolates and honeycomb to share. Then we'd wander down Manhattan Avenue to Fireline Surf Shop on Tenth Street, owned by the local pros, Benny and Barela. Once, while I was studying the new Brian Bulkley "3-4 set-ups" that you could use as a tri-fin or quad, a friendly female surfer who worked there gave us Fireline stickers.

Aisha and I usually ended up at the Kettle, the diner on the corner where Charlie had taken me. We'd sit in the back and share an order of French fries, and Aisha would order coffee. They were open all night, so she got lots of refills. Sometimes we hung out in my aunt and uncle's garden, or Aisha read a book on the beach while I surfed.

That week, I'd paddled out with Chris one morning to a left that was breaking nicely out front. We caught a few good ones.

"Yesterday there were a lot of dolphins out," Chris said.

"Yeah, I hope they come today."

"Are you gonna call them?" she asked me.

"Yeah." I began to rub the side of my shortboard.

"They're over there!" Chris shouted, pointing to my right. I saw some gray fins, and lots of seagulls and birds were flying around in circles. I guessed they were probably feeding. I kept rubbing my board, and a little seal swam over to us. It was so cute—it must've been a pup. Its big brown eyes looked into mine.

"Hello," I said. *It's so close to us!* Suddenly, to our surprise, it hopped on top of Chris's board. She immediately put her hands up, afraid that it would bite her.

My heart was beating fast, but I blurted out, "I want to pet it!" I reached out and gently pet its back. It was smooth, warm, and fuzzy, like a wet cat curled up.

"She's a board hugger," Chris said.

"Board Hugger needs a name," I said.

The seal looked up at me with her big, soulful eyes. I studied her shiny brown coat, and her front and hind flippers. She had a cute darker mug with whiskers. *You're beautiful!* I asked Chris, "Why don't we name her Lucy?"

"Sure, that's a good name." We were too enchanted with Lucy to focus on the waves. When a set came and we were too far inside, Lucy bailed the board, diving under, and Chris and I duck-dove. Surfacing up ahead, Lucy looked back at me as if to say, "*How come you can't do it as well as I do?*"

Then Lucy got up onto my board and rested the side of her head against it, her mouth under water. I rested my head against her back. She was relaxed and motionless.

"Chris, I think she's sleeping."

"Yeah," she giggled. "She is."

We floated there with her until a wave tipped her over, waking her. She came up under my board, rubbing her belly on the bottom of it.

I slipped into the water to let her have the board. Lucy popped up and onto my board, her cute mug in my face. We gazed into each other's eyes. Then I couldn't help it—I kissed her smack on the snout, just like I kissed Zuzu, against the whiskers.

"Ah!" I shrieked. We both were taken by surprise. Lucy swam away.

"She's scared," Chris said. "No, she's excited. She's gone to tell her friends—'I kissed a human!'"

"Oh my God, I kissed a seal!"

"Is that your first kiss?"

"No." I thought about it. "My first kiss in California was a seal. I'd rather it be a boy."

"Girls are more fun," Chris said, smiling.

"Does your girlfriend surf?"

"No. But, she's really into soccer. I'm sure you'll meet her soon."

"I'd like that."

"Thinking of kissing anyone in particular?" Chris said with a side smile.

"No!" I answered, but I couldn't help but think of Nick. He was so fun to surf with. And the sight of him sent sparks through me.

Lucy popped her head up from far out past the lineup. "Goodbye, Lucy!" I called out. "Thanks for visiting us!" I caught a wave all the way in to shore. Soon after, Chris did the same. We stood on the beach, stunned, in awe of what had just happened. Lucy was still out there, staring at us, her little head bobbing up above the surf.

"That was mad outrageous," said Chris.

"Yeah," I said, "unbelievable."

There was much animated discussion in the cottage that night about Lucy. Uncle Charlie said that I must be a selkie. A selkie was a mythical being, a seal who could transform into a human by shedding its sealskin, according to the Celtic folklore of Scotland, where his father was from. He said the seal had recognized one of her own kind, "selkie-folk." Aunt Jen took in my story, her eyes twinkling.

"I've heard of Lucy before," she said.

"Really?"

"One of the guys from Twenty-Sixth Street said a baby seal or sea lion hopped onto his board about two weeks ago."

"I bet it was Lucy," I said. "I hope I get to see her again."

"It's probably a sea lion, because seals are usually very shy of humans. Ellie, you want to make sure you're doing the right thing by her. It's magical what happened today. Like out of a fairy-tale. But human interaction isn't usually the best thing for wild animals."

"But maybe she's lost her mom and is all alone." *Like me*, I thought, thinking of Dad and how Mom was never around.

My mom was passed out all the next morning. I was dying to tell her about Lucy. When she finally surfaced and slowly made her way into the kitchen, I told her.

"It could've bitten your nose off!" she scolded. "That's a wild animal, not a dog like Zuzu!"

"It wasn't going to *bite* me! We had a connection. We were playing together."

"How can you be so naive? Those are wild animals. They have sharp teeth. Next thing you're going to say you're friends with a shark."

"I'm not afraid of sharks."

She scowled. "You should be afraid. Big sharks can bite you in half."

Mom didn't get me at all. I watched her fumble with her coffee, ripping open a small pink packet, pouring in the white powder, and stirring it.

"What is that?" I asked.

"Just some pills for my headache."

I hadn't noticed the pills. "No, the pink packets."

"Oh, that's a sweetener."

"Why don't you just use sugar?"

"This doesn't have calories, it doesn't make you fat."

"Mom, you don't need to worry about that," I said. She was so skinny, it didn't make sense that she was worried about her weight.

"I need to look good so I can wear fashionable clothes well," she stated. "No one would buy art from me if I looked like my sister, for instance. Sloppy clothes, sand in her hair."

Aunt Jen walked into the kitchen just then, and I thought she must have heard Mom. *Why does she have to make such mean comments?* Jen pretended she hadn't heard anything. I ran to my room and slammed the door.

The next day, as the sun was setting, I was out walking Zuzu. Above the silver-blue horizon, the tangerine sky blended into blue, with bands of lavender and peach clouds. I saw a brown head pop up out of the water. *Is it Lucy?* It dove in and out of the rippled surface, following me while I walked down the beach, past two lifeguard towers.

"Aunt Jen!" I yelled as I flung the back door open. "I saw Lucy again!" My aunt was in the kitchen, chopping vegetables. "She was following me."

"Wow." She looked up from stirring the pot. "But how can you be sure it was Lucy?"

"I just know. I saw her looking at me! I should get my wet-suit and swim out there."

Jen shook her head, "I don't think that's a good idea, Ellie. Those animals are wild. We need to stay our distance. If that was a baby, you need to be careful not to look into its eyes."

"Why?"

"Because you can imprint it like a mother sea lion does."

"What does that mean?"

"The sea lion would form an attachment to you, and then

you'd leave it to go have dinner, or go to school. And then what about the poor sea lion? It would need you."

"Oh." I hadn't thought about it that way.

That night, Jen and I had pasta with veggie sauce. Uncle Charlie was at the firehouse for a few days. I missed his funny remarks. My mom was working late, as usual.

The wind picked up outside. The trees were swaying, branches hitting the windowpanes. Aunt Jen went to take the laundry off the line because it was about to blow away. I stepped outside with her. Over the houses, down towards the ocean, there was a sliver of pink in the sky. Twilight cast a violet glow on the garden foliage.

"Can I help?" I asked.

"I've got it," she said, holding the basket. "How about some tea?"

"Okay."

A few minutes later, we were sitting in the living room with our tea, staring into the fire, all cozy with blankets covering us. Zuzu lay at my feet.

"Do you think I was imprinted?" I asked Jen.

"Huh?"

"As a baby, do you think I was imprinted like the sea lion . . . by Dad?"

"Sure, you were," Jen said, sipping her tea, "and by your mom, too."

"But Dad's gone." I said it so easily now. Too easily. I had accepted the fact, though when I thought about Dad, my heart felt just as raw as the day I'd found out nine months ago.

Aunt Jen nodded. "But your mom's here."

"Barely," I said. "She's never home." I clenched the blanket.

"Yes, but she's trying hard to make it work here. It's not easy in the art world. She knew she'd have to put time in, and she knew I was home a lot, so that's how we figured it could work."

"I don't even want her around," I spat out. "She's embarrassing!"

Aunt Jen gaped at me. "Do you really mean that?"

"The way she looks, how she dresses."

"She's creative with her clothes—there's nothing wrong with that," Jen said.

"All black and high heels, her crazy hair and makeup—please! Kids give me looks. They say she's trashy. I nearly died when she came to school."

"It shouldn't matter what other kids think. She's your mom."

"They called her a blonde Elvira!"

Jen couldn't help but chuckle at that. "Your mom definitely does look very New York, but that goes with her job, and that's who she is."

"But it's not just how she looks, it's how she acts. She gets annoyed at everyone for not doing things the way they're done in New York City—no one's fast enough or smart enough here. It's embarrassing."

"Are you feeling sorry for yourself?" Jen asked.

"I *am* sorry! I'm not like her. I never liked New York, and I don't want to go back there."

Jen's brow furrowed. "Did she say she wanted to?"

"She doesn't have to say it. I can tell she wants to."

"Well, I hope not. I like having you here." Jen patted my leg with a radiant smile.

"Me too."

"You know you can't change your mom," Jen said. "I can't, nobody can. It might be best to try and accept her the way she is." The warm glow of the fire cast light onto her shining, olive-green eyes.

I sighed.

"Or don't take her so seriously," she continued. "Make jokes about it like Charlie does."

"Heels?"

Jen cracked up. "Ha! Yeah, Heels. My sister's a trip, but I love her. There's nobody else like her."

"Yeah, for sure," I said, feeling a little guilty that it was so hard for me to be her daughter.

Aunt Jen put *The Endless Summer* into the VCR player. I fell asleep with visions of surfing in my head.

SIXTEEN

Charger

When a winter swell made the waves line up in a big wall with no corners and no one else dared paddle out, I did. *I've got to make it out*, I'd say to myself. After trying and failing, I'd try again.

I finally made it out one morning. I started into a wave that I thought had a corner, when it abruptly met with itself to form a wall as tall as a two-story building. There was no wave under me to go on. After about an hour, I caught a wave and made the bottom turn, but then it threw me off when it closed out.

When I got to shore and walked past the parking lot, Wilkies' friend Steve came up to me and yelled, "Hey just what are you trying to prove? You scared me to death, watching you out there!"

I shrugged. When Charlie heard about it, he chided me, too. "Next time the swell's big and walled up like that, we'll go to the cove," he said.

The next morning, the surf was pounding out front with those same two-story-high walls. Jen had left early to work on a garden, so it was just me and Charlie.

"It's hairball out there!" he announced. "Let's go to the cove."

"Okay," I said right away, but then I thought out loud, "What about school?"

"This *is* school!" he replied.

My eyes opened wide. "What will Mom say?"

"Heels doesn't need to know what Heels doesn't need to know." He raised one eyebrow as the corner of his mouth curled up.

He is serious, I realized. I was game. I grinned back at him.

I tossed my wetsuit and towel into the yellow VW bus along with the Easter Egg board. We drove south along the coast and, as usual, Charlie had the Beach Boys playing in the eight-track player. As they harmonized "Surfin' Safari," the road began to go up in elevation, above sea level. Looking down to my right, the ocean peeked out at me, an expanse of light-blue sky above it.

Uncle Charlie pulled over and parked, and we got out and walked to the edge of the cliff. It swept down four hundred feet below to a rocky beach. The cove was breathtaking; raw nature, no human-built structures in sight. An expanse of open sky before me, with the infinite ocean below. There were lines on the horizon, swells moving in, as far as I could see.

"Corduroy!" I burst out loud.

"Sure is!" said Charlie, lines crinkling at the corners of his bright eyes.

As the sunlight hit the ocean waves, it bounced reflected light around in patches. The ocean was luminescent, glistening blue-green. The ripples on the surface looked like the ridges in corduroy fabric, shiny velveteen fibers. Millions of tiny molecules of water were vibrating, pulsating. Wind blew from a storm far across the Pacific, transferring its energy into water, surging toward us.

Uncle Charlie began hopping from one foot to the other.

"Let's get out there . . . tah-wee, Ellie!" he sang, grinning while raising his arms in the air. I giggled.

We carried our boards, towels, and wetsuits down a descending dirt path at the cliff's edge.

"We used to be able to drive down this road to the beach," Charlie said. "Now we gotta hike it."

When we got down to the bottom of the cliff, there was no sand; it was all rocks. We put on our wetsuits. Charlie wrapped a towel around his waist for cover while changing, because guys didn't wear swim trunks under their wetsuits. I had my suit on under my clothes, so I didn't need to use a towel to change.

"See that over on the left?" he said, pointing out. "That's Boneyards, a bunch of rocks. We'll steer clear of it."

"Uh-huh." I nodded, wide-eyed. The surf looked much bigger from down here.

After we waxed our boards, Charlie asked, "Ready?"

"Yup." I swallowed against the butterflies swarming in my stomach. I followed him, being careful with every step my trembling legs took, gripping the rocks with my feet. Charlie timed his entry between whitewater swells, and I followed. He put his board on the water's surface with the fin up, like Jen did at Trestles. It was shallow here, and rocky. I copied him.

I leaned onto the shortboard as I walked on top of rocks through the swaying incoming surges. We paddled through massive clumps of thick seaweed that looked like it was from the time of dinosaurs. I followed Charlie close. It was a long paddle already, and we weren't even halfway out. The impact zone was flooded with violent bursts of monstrous whitewash. Even though I was with Charlie, I was keenly aware that in surfing, you are on your own. No one is holding your hand. My fear fueled me to put everything I had into getting out as quick as possible. I paddled hard and dug deep, my arms aching. I had to duck-dive a dozen big waves. Finally, I made it to the outside, just behind Charlie, trying to catch my breath.

We continued to paddle over to the middle of the bay. A line of swell was swiftly approaching. Charlie picked up his speed, paddling towards it, and I strained to keep up with him. The base of the impending wave grew a darker teal, the ominous sign that it was about to break. *We aren't going to make it— it's going to break on us!* I panicked, paddling with all my strength. My heart sank as it came crashing down in a waterfall, spouts spurting white foam at me. I dove under, but my board broke free from my grasp and I was hurled below into somersaults and held under. Finally let free, I came up for air.

Charlie shouted, "Are you okay?"

"Yeah, my board got torn from me," I said, gasping for air.

"Pull your leash," he advised. "Let's go out further. There are some sets breaking way outside."

I pulled my board to me with my leash, got back on, and kept paddling, praying another wave wouldn't break on me. As if answering my plea, there was a lull; the ocean turned calm like a lake, a glass mirror reflecting the blue sky. Now that I was way outside, I was able to enjoy just sitting next to Charlie. It was breathtakingly beautiful. The pink cliffs stood high above us, raw earth framing the endless open sea. Shiny patches of seaweed glistened in amber stripes along the shoreline. Brown boulders emerged out of the cobalt blue.

"Is that Catalina?" I asked, pointing straight out beyond the swell lines to a barely visible lavender outline.

"Yup," he said.

In front of Catalina, a blue line was getting darker, growing and moving towards us. It swung out to our left, forming a big right. A longboarder caught it, gliding at an angle down the line, his head covered by the back of the wave.

"Woo-hoo!" Charlie hooted. "You ready, Ellie?"

I nodded. With all that energy build-up exploding into big waves, there was excitement in the air. Another one was coming, this one a left. Charlie moved further out to meet it. As he began to paddle into it, he stopped and shouted, "Go Ellie!"

I scratched, digging deep to catch up to its speed. When I felt its momentum, I pushed myself up, my feet clamped to the board underneath me. I soared as my board cut a line through the glassy wave face, swooping down. I turned towards the left more, moving up the next slope to the crest, then swooped back down again. Such a strong feeling of elation overcame me, the adrenaline pumping through my veins as I carved up the open surface of the wave, back up to the top and down, over and over. As the wave petered out, I kicked out and gracefully lay back on my board the way I'd been practicing. I paddled back out with the extra energy boost the wave had given me.

As I approached the lineup, Charlie shouted out, "Wow, great wave!"

"Thanks," I replied. "I can't believe it."

"You're ripping," Charlie said.

"It was such a good wave!" I shouted back.

"Yeah, it was. Now let's get you some more."

Some guys were looking at us with mouths agape. "This is my niece, Ellie," Charlie said proudly. "She's a charger."

A few of the guys waved and said hi to me. "Hi," I said back.

Charlie and I both got so many good waves that morning. We stayed out way past noon, and my arms became noodles. Before we left, I spotted Nick out there. My heart skipped a beat. He beamed when he saw me, waved, and called out, "Hi." I smiled and waved back, hoping he'd seen me on my really good wave.

It was the best day ever. Uncle Charlie promised not to tell Heels about skipping school. He said that the conditions were just right for the cove that day, so we had to take advantage of that and go. *Nick seemed to agree,* I mused.

Later that afternoon, I took Zuzu for a walk. As I passed the beach parking lot, Wilkies shouted out to me, "Hey Charger, I hear you've been going on big waves." I smiled, hoping this meant I'd earned a new nickname.

"Hi," I said, strolling up to him.

"Hear your uncle took you to the cove."

"Yeah."

"It's nice out there, huh?"

"It's beautiful."

I smiled to myself throughout the walk and on the way home, thinking about that wave at the cove and how Wilkies had just called me Charger. *I'm not Calamity Jane anymore!*

As I entered homeroom the next morning, April pretended to cough as she said "Freak!" into her cupped hands. When I took my seat, Tiffany said loudly, "Like, have you seen Poser's mom?"

"Yeah, it's like Elvira meets Madonna," said Brooke to Bonnie, who responded just as audibly, "She's a trashy Madonna wannabe!" They cackled.

"She's a whore," stated Bonnie.

Against the barrage of insults Bonnie's group slung at Mom and me, I held my new nickname, Charger, close to my heart. They couldn't tarnish the treasure it was to me.

One day after school, the surf was up out front. Chris and I paddled out together. While paddling into a wave, I checked to see if anyone was deeper first. No one was, so I committed and paddled hard. After my bottom turn, I was going back up towards the top when, out of my peripheral vision, I saw a guy heading straight for me. I glanced back, doing a quick maneuver so I didn't hit him. Because of that, I ended up getting worked and my board hit me in the shin. The guy had seen me going when he was way outside and had back-paddled me, after I'd already stood up.

Chris paddled up to me, and said, "What a bogus move! I hate when guys back-paddle. Are you okay?" The sting of my shin pierced me with pain.

"I hurt my leg," I said. "I'm gonna go in."

I took the whitewater in and sat on the beach, waiting for the pain to subside. I wanted to paddle out again, but my shin was throbbing. I clenched my fists. Back-paddling was a regular occurrence amongst wave-zealous, macho guys.

"It's like they're so sure I won't make the wave that's coming to me," I told Charlie that night at dinner. "It's insulting. Why can't they be nice like you?"

"Oh, I bet when they see you on a wave, they'll change their tune," he said, his eyebrows raised.

"Well, yeah, but—"

"Uh-huh," he affirmed with a smile.

"But it isn't right," Jen chimed in. "Guys will do that around here."

"Yeah, I don't know what's wrong with these guys," Charlie said. "I'm happy to surf with women . . . they're so fun to surf with!" He put his arms around Jen and kissed her cheek.

"Ah, Charlie!" Jen sighed.

Most guys never gave away any waves like Uncle Charlie did. They never made it easier for me. In fact, they made it harder.

There was the occasional exception, like Nick, but for the most part, guys didn't seem to like a girl in the water. Aunt Jen called it sexism.

Sally said sexism was rampant in professional surfing, too. Guys would scream and curse at her to get out of the water. "What do you think you're doing here?" they'd shout. At contests, if the waves were good and the women were scheduled to surf, they'd change it and have the men surf first. Then, when the tide was wrong and the wind was on it—meaning the waves were bad—they'd have the women go. Sally said one time, at Pipeline, the waves were pumping and they were scheduled to surf but all the judges were somewhere else watching a men's contest. She added that the women's contest winnings were nothing compared to the men's, a token amount. She couldn't get by on her surfing winnings, but guys she knew could live off being pro.

Most guys acted like it was a given that I wouldn't be able to make a wave when it came, and on the off-chance that I did, I certainly wouldn't be able to surf it. I liked to prove them wrong each time. Most of the time, when I did make it into waves and rode them well, guys would respect me and not snake or back-paddle me. But before I showed what I could do, they always assumed the worst—the stereotype that girls couldn't surf. Snakers liked to burn me on lefts, not looking to their right to see that I'd caught the wave deeper. Being that I had the right of way, that it was my wave and not theirs, I would just go, even though it was dangerous. With the force of the ocean, if boards collided upon bodies, especially fins, someone was going to get hurt. I took that chance because I was sick and tired of the constant back-paddling and snaking. I was determined to go every time I was in priority position, so watch out! *Maybe next time they won't snake me*, I thought. *Yes, I'm a girl, but I actually* can *paddle and I actually* can *surf! Here I come, watch out!* Some people shouted or whistled when they got a wave to warn others that they were behind them. I found that hard to do, and I couldn't whistle well.

The next morning, it was a breath of fresh air to surf with Nick. He hooted and hollered for whoever was about to catch a wave. "Woo-woo!" he shouted as the Duke paddled his board into a nice little corner. I gazed back at Nick. *He's so nice!* Then a left was coming in, and he called out, "Yeah!" as another guy paddled and made it.

I turned to him and asked, "Do you know that guy?"

"No," he said, grinning ear to ear. "I'm just excited for everyone." His smile pierced my heart, my body filling with his contagious happy-go-lucky energy. *He'd never back-paddle me to catch a wave,* I mused. In fact, later I was sitting out there next to him, when a nice-sized left rolled in. He was deeper and I was on the shoulder, so he had the right of way. But he shouted, "Go, Ellie!"

"It's your wave," I said.

But he didn't paddle for it. "Go!" he called out again.

I went, because otherwise it would've been a wasted wave with no one on it. When I paddled back out, he asked, "How was it?"

"Well, I think I got too excited because I dug my rail on it, but then I kind of got a mini-barrel."

"Oh, I've done that," he beamed. "It slows you down, and then you're in the perfect pocket."

"Yeah." I smiled back at him. *Gosh, maybe I need to just relax and have more fun in the water.* I was always so focused on trying to be a better surfer.

At school, Bonnie's group continued to call me and my mom mean names every chance they got, but thankfully I had Aisha. And Liam had started sitting at our lunch table, along with some other boys. Danny Wen, one of Liam's friends, was really nice, and he surfed too. His skin was so brown from the sun that he looked Hawaiian, though he was Chinese. Sometimes I saw Liam out surfing, often with Danny or another boy who preferred to boogie board, wearing fins to the catch waves easier.

Aisha and I liked to skate down the Strand and explore Hermosa Beach. Hermosa was less fuddy-duddy, less uptight, and a little seedy. It reminded me of the Village in New York City. Hermosa had the vibe of Venice Beach, but less urban. It was fun to walk around and people-watch; there were hippies, beatniks, surfers, roller skaters, and biker gangs. It was a much different crowd than the working moms and dads that made up Manhattan Beach.

Other than surfers, my aunt and uncle's friends were firemen like Charlie, or lifeguards, or police. Some worked at the mill yard or at the Standard Oil refinery. Liam's dad was an electrician. Caitlyn's parents, like many others at school, were pilots and flight attendants. Aisha's dad worked for Hughes Aircraft, and her mom was a teacher. No one seemed to have a job in Hermosa; they were all just hanging out.

Hermosa Avenue in particular reminded me of Eighth Street in the Village. Restyle was a cool punk store we liked to browse in, next to the Bijou, an old movie theater built in the twenties. The Bijou reminded me of the Eighth Street Playhouse, which also had midnight screenings of movies like *The Rocky Horror Picture Show*. Sayen and I had gone to see the show in New York together. I told Aisha about it, so we planned to go one day.

Greekos was a sandal shop that sold rock posters and silver earrings. The Scorpio Shoppe was full of bins of all sorts of weird stuff like shells, jewelry parts, and patches. In Either/Or Bookstore on Pier Avenue, we sat on the floor next to a friendly black cat named Justine and looked through books until we got really hungry. Then we'd hang out at the communal tables at Lee's Surfboarder at Fourteenth Street and eat steel-cut oatmeal with raisins and brown sugar and toast. It was cheap and filling. I noticed they had pictures of Benny and other local pros on the walls.

I wanted to look at records, so we skated up to Recycled Records at the intersection of Pacific Coast Highway and Eighth Street. I bought X's new album, *More Fun in the New World*, on tape so I could play it in my Walkman. From there, we crossed PCH to go to ET Surf, where Aisha bought new bushings for the trucks on her skateboard, and I lovingly ran my palm across the new, smooth surfboard rails in rows.

Almost every afternoon I went surfing with Chris. It was nice to have a surf buddy who was a girl. We both understood what it felt like to not be wanted in the water, and to have to prove yourself all the time. Because we were together, it was easier not to let the guys' attitudes affect us.

One Saturday morning, Chris wanted to surf Hermosa Pier, so I skated down early to meet her. I hoped we'd run into the pros that surfed there, like Benny and his sister, but Chris said they were on tour in Japan.

After surfing, Aisha and Chris's girlfriend, Trini, met us at the north side of the pier. We avoided the south side, which was where the seedy characters or thugs who might steal your stuff would hang out. We went to Winchell's Donuts, where we ordered half and halfs—half hot chocolate and half coffee. Chris wanted to check out the swimsuits at Beach B's, so we strolled up to Fourteenth Street. Soon we got hungry, so we went to the Surfboarder for our usual oatmeal. Aisha always wanted to look for books, so we ended up at the bookstore on Pier Avenue.

During one after-school surf session, Chris, Liam, Danny, and I stayed in the water until sunset while Aisha read on the beach. The wind had come up, and it was really blowing; it was so cold. I invited everyone back to my house for hot cocoa to warm up. Aunt Jen had muffins for us, which we gobbled up. Looking around at everyone, it suddenly hit me—these were my friends. I wasn't alone anymore.

SEVENTEEN

Christmastime in California

The dolphins are here! Seeing their large, wave-shaped dorsal fins jolted my heartbeat to quicken.

They weren't the only things that made my heart pound. When Nick joined me and Chris while we were out surfing, I thought it would pop out of my chest. He brought his contagious, happy-go-lucky energy and his friend, Toma. I learned later that Toma was his last name; his family was Okinawan. Everybody called him Toma because he preferred it to his first name, which I didn't know because he never used it. He was a really good surfer, but unlike Nick, he was quiet and calm. But they both shared a gentleness, and were kind in the way they shared waves with us girls. I could tell Toma loved surfing just as much as we did. With every wave, his face lit up with a genuine smile. The four of us traded waves and split peaks, and there was a jolly atmosphere all around.

I went on a steep left and stalled—a tunnel of water formed over and around me. I was in the revered green room. All of a sudden, a dolphin burst up in front of me. Together we sped through the wave for what must have only been two seconds, but it was as if time stood still in the tunnel of water. In harmony and rapture, I was transported to a place of communion with the ocean and the dolphin. Then it was over, and

I was falling in and under water.

What had just happened sunk in: *I was in a barrel with a dolphin!* When I surfaced, I screamed, "Oh my God! Did you see that?"

"The dolphin snaked you!" Chris shouted.

"Oh my God, I was snaked by a dolphin! Woo-hoo!"

"It totally burned you!" she yelled.

"Bitchin'!" Nick hollered from the right peak. "Radical!"

"That was awesome!" exclaimed Toma, who was right next to him.

"Like, totally," Chris agreed.

"I can't believe it." I was stunned.

"That was epic!" Nick shouted back, beaming. He threw his head back, let out a big belly laugh, and then we all burst out laughing. The energy was palpable. We were all in awe of what had just happened.

Closing my eyes to sleep that night, I relived the amazing moment of being barreled with the dolphin. Then I pictured Nick and my chest got tight, like something was trapped inside and wanted out. *Was I so bowled over by the experience of being tubed with a dolphin, or was the feeling intensified because Nick was there?* I was beginning to hope I'd see Nick in the water every time I paddled out, and I felt disappointed if he wasn't there. My hands were sweating, resting against my fast-beating heart. *Do I have a crush on him?*

I grabbed my Walkman. "Wishing (If I had a Photograph of You)" by A Flock of Seagulls was playing on Rodney on the ROQ. I sighed. *Maybe it's just the excitement I always feel at Christmastime.* What would Christmas be like here? I wished I still believed in the magic of things. I remembered when I was little—staring at the half-empty glass of milk in the cold morning. The night before, it'd been full, and the plate that once had five cookies on it now only held crumbs. It was solid proof. Santa had been at my house!

My thoughts went to last Christmas. It had been my worst, with Dad in the hospital. But I didn't cry. Instead, I thought about Dad being happy for me that I was surfing. Maybe it was my enthusiasm for Nick or for getting barreled with a dolphin that overrode that sad memory. The stars were beaming through the trees, their rays of light reaching out to me. *Misiek, are you up there, watching over me?*

That December, the beach was still so hot that the sand burned your feet. People wore t-shirts and shorts in dayglow colors. Girls wore mirrored sunglasses with neon frames, their high-cut swimsuits showing their hipbones.

This was funny to me. Christmastime was supposed to be cold, with snow. Here the sun was always so bright. The amount of light in New York was about a tenth of what it was here. The city light was dim, thin, and cold. The buildings were gray, and even the light seemed grayish. When the snow fell, it brightened things up for a day or two until the snow turned gray and brown from soot and dirt. The Decembers I'd known in New York were such a sharp contrast to what it was like here. Bright, colorful hummingbirds darted about in greenery that glistened in the shining sun. Flowers continued to bloom profusely, unaware of any season change.

On the last day of school before Christmas break, Bonnie came up to me, pointed to my leg, and shouted, "Eww, your tampon is leaking!" The other girls gathered in a clump, snickering and pointing.

There was a trickle of blood making its way down the back of my leg. But it wasn't due to my period, as I first thought in a panic. There was a thumbtack stuck in the back of my upper thigh. I hadn't even felt it. When I pulled it out, it stung.

"You did this, didn't you?" I shouted at Bonnie, holding up the tack. I trembled, realizing that I'd just shouted at her. That wasn't like me.

"I don't know what you're talking about," she replied with a smirk. I looked back at my seat and saw that it was covered in metal tacks, all pointing upwards. It made my blood boil. I trudged up to the teacher, the pain piercing my leg.

"Ms. Mathews!" I said, quivering. "Look, Bonnie put tacks on my seat."

"Ellie! Raise your hand if . . ." She stopped when she noticed my leg, and whispered in my ear, "I think you should excuse yourself to the ladies' room."

"No, you don't understand," I pleaded. "I'm bleeding from thumbtacks—those girls put them on my chair."

She looked clueless.

"Look, I'll show you," I turned to lead her towards my chair, and she reluctantly followed. When we got there, the tacks were gone. "They were right here," I said, "all over the seat."

"I think it's time you went to the office to see the nurse," she stated.

I couldn't believe it. Even Ms. Mathews was on their side. I bit back my anger. As I left the room, the girls broke out in a fit of derisive laughter.

I stayed in the office, stewing. When the bell rang, I wanted to shout for joy—no school for two weeks!

I was turning down the hall toward the lockers when I saw him. *It's Nick!* My heart started beating a thousand times per minute as energy exploded like fireworks throughout my body.

"Ellie!" he shouted. The hallway around us was filled with students like schools of fish, swarming in packs.

"Nick! What are you doing here?"

"I was just in the auto shop," he said as he ran up to me. "Dude, how are you?" He glanced at my leg, then quickly looked up at my face. I looked down. Blood had started to run down my leg again, which was now trembling. The band-aid had failed. My stomach sank.

"Tacks!" I blurted out. "It's not what it looks like. I sat on some tacks."

"What?" he said, looking confused. Then, thankfully, he changed the subject. "You go to school here?"

"Yes, are you a senior? I've never seen you here."

"Yeah, I basically live in the auto shop. I never leave, even during lunch."

"Oh." *Oh my God! He goes to my school!* I was in shock, but I rambled on, "No one believed me, not even the teacher . . . about the tacks."

"Well, I believe you," he said, fixing his soft eyes on mine. They were so green, and his tender gaze shook me to my core. My heart was pounding so hard, I thought it would burst out of my chest.

"They were in my s-seat," I stammered. "My seat at my desk. But I didn't see them." My face suddenly grew hot. I looked down at the floor, ashamed that I hadn't seen them and had sat on them.

"Gnarly—how did they get there?" he asked, tilting his head to one side.

"Ah . . . you don't want to know. It's nothing."

"Dude, I want to know." He leaned in closer to me. "And it's not nothing." His scent was so good. *Like fresh citrus and . . . gasoline!* It made me weak in the knees. I dared to meet his eyes again and when they sparkled, a warmth rushed through me and my heart melted. I was buzzing.

Just then, those girls walked by. Normally, they would have spewed insults at me like "beach trash" and "poser," but they were dumbstruck that Nick was with me. Someone from the clump couldn't help but shout, "Your tampon is leaking!" They laughed at me.

I was dying from embarrassment. Nick gave them a hard stare.

"Can we get out of here?" I burst out. "I need to go surf."

He broke into a smile. "For sure—want a ride?"

"You . . . you have a car?" I stammered, not sure whether to believe this was really happening.

"Yeah. Well, it's a work in progress."

I smiled back at him. "Um, I just need to get my bag from my locker." I pointed towards it.

"Okay, I'm not going anywhere." He leaned on the lockers next to him and smiled.

I dashed down the hall a few yards to my locker. I could feel his eyes following me. I glanced back at him while I got my stuff. He gave me a sheepish grin as I approached him. He looked even more tall, dark, and handsome dry and out of the water. Though, as I let him lead me to the parking lot, I imagined his hair wet and glistening black, his wetsuit tight to his chest, bobbing in the water on his shortboard.

"I need to grab my board," I said, darting towards the bushes.

"Your surfboard?" Nick asked, waiting at the stairs.

I held up my skateboard for him to see.

He smiled and when I caught up to him, we proceeded down the stairs to the parking lot.

I held my breath. Bonnie and the rest of the No Beach Trash Club were hanging out around a white Mercedes-Benz. I quickly looked away, but when we crossed the lot to his car, I glanced over just in time to see their mouths agape.

"Here she is," Nick announced proudly as we approached what looked like a Volkswagen bug from the front, but a vintage van with wood-lined windows in the back.

"I've never seen one before," I said. "It's so pretty. What is it?"

"*She's* a 1959 Morris Minor Traveller," he beamed.

"She." I nodded approvingly. "I like her, she's a happy green."

"Yeah, she's bright all right. When I first got her, I wasn't sure I liked the color, but it's grown on me." It was fitting he had a green car, given his beautiful green eyes. He opened the passenger door for me and said, "Hop in." As he stretched his arm out to hold the door for me, his developed pectoral muscles peeked out from under his white t-shirt. It was probably from all that paddling.

"Thanks." As I got in, I noticed there were shortboards in the back. I was relieved that the seats were black vinyl: I didn't want to ruin a cloth seat by bleeding on it. I checked my leg, and thankfully the bleeding had stopped.

Quick as a wink, Nick plopped himself in the seat next to me. *We're so close.* As he leaned in to turn the key in the ignition and pull the starter knob, a dark strand of hair let loose, falling onto his forehead. The car sputtered and putted.

"She needs a new distributor," he said.

"Does she have a name?" I asked.

He smiled as he backed out of the spot and switched gears, lurching us forward. "No. Not yet. Do you want to name her?"

"Me?"

"Yeah."

"Oh no," I said out loud, realizing we were headed towards Bonnie's group.

"No?"

I tried to duck in my seat. "Oh no, it's just . . . I don't want to run into them again," I said.

"Hang on," he said, turning the wheel. He drove diagonally across empty parking spaces, toward the exit, to avoid Bonnie's group.

"You okay?" he asked me.

I took a deep breath. "Yeah. Thanks."

"Like, no way," he chuckled. "There's Danny getting out from under his car cover—duh."

"What—why would he do that?"

"He puts it on so he can smoke pot under there without getting caught. He's such a goober."

"Really?" I started cracking up, and then we both were.

When the ocean horizon came into view as we crossed Sepulveda, he asked, "So, what do you want to name her?"

"Oh, gosh, I don't know. She sure is a bright green . . . and she's pretty awesome."

"Yeah, she's pretty wizard."

"Wizard!" I exclaimed. "But it's not very feminine."

"Wizard is perfect." He beamed, the glint in his eye flashing.

He pressed play on his tape deck, and a punk band I'd never heard sounded over the car stereo. As the fervent drumming pulsed with my beating heart, I asked, "What song is this?"

He blushed. "'Marriage' by the Descendents." Just then, I got why he blushed. The lyrics sounded like a marriage proposal.

"I like it."

"Me too, one of my faves," he said. "They're a local band. They went to our high school."

"Really?"

"Yeah."

"Cool."

We drove to Marine Avenue, stopping to check the surf at the turnaround above the lifeguard station. From here, it was the best unobstructed view of the stretch of beach from the pier to El Porto. The ocean looked a lot like it had that morning. The wind hadn't picked up much. It was a north-west wind swell and south swell combo, about three feet. I was anxious to get my board.

"Tide's going down," I said.

"Yeah, let's get out there before it's too low," he said. "Let's get you your board. Where do you live?"

"Twenty-Eighth Street."

"Wow, you're close to me. I live here." He moved the car forward.

"Here?"

"Yeah. Right there." He pointed to a little house in from the corner of Ocean and Twenty-Third Street.

As he headed north on Manhattan Avenue, I told him to make a right in the alley after Twenty-Seventh and pointed out my aunt's house. He parked in the alley behind the garden. I ran inside, changed into my wetsuit, grabbed my shortboard, and was back out in no time. My heart leapt at the sight of him already in his wetsuit.

"Is it okay to leave her here?" he said, patting the car's hood.

"Sure, let's get in the water." I took off running towards the beach, and he joined me, passing me. I was laughing while running, the weight of the drama from Bonnie's group lifting off me. As each breath of fresh sea air filled my lungs, my heart grew elated. Nick reached the shore before me and dove in. I jumped in after him.

I thought Nick had forgotten about the tacks, but as we waited for a set, he brought it up again. "So, how exactly did tacks get on your chair?"

I sighed. "Someone put them there on purpose."

"Who'd do that?"

"The No Beach Trash Club," I said.

"The what?"

"Those girls you saw who walked by us. The girls by the white Mercedes. All the girls in my homeroom, except for Aisha, are part of it. They hate me. They call me beach trash."

"What? Because you surf?"

"No, because I don't wear designer clothes and dress preppy like they do."

"What a bunch of stuck-up yuppie wannabes. They're so lame." He looked outraged.

"Yeah, they've called me 'homeless' before."

"What? Heavy. They sound like heinous losers to me." Nick's expression changed to disgust.

"They call me a poser. They don't think I surf."

"Well, that's a bunch a bunk! You are like the raddest, most awesome surfer girl ever, which is major. Way cool."

As his kind words flooded me like sunshine, I broke into a smile. "Thanks."

He beamed back at me. I was certain I blushed.

"Just don't tell my mom," I said. "I don't want her moving us back to New York."

"No way. She'd do that?"

"Uh-huh."

"No worries, I won't . . . I've never seen your mom, I don't think. Does she surf?"

"No. No, that's my Aunt Jen. You probably won't ever see my mom. She doesn't like the beach. She doesn't like me surfing, either."

"Why? Surfing's bitchin'."

I agreed.

During Christmas break, Mom went back to New York for a week to work. Even if she'd invited me, I wouldn't have wanted to go and miss the surfing. In the winter, the surf was the biggest. I was excited to surf overhead sets, even double overhead, though it meant getting held under longer when I ate it. I'd been training, holding my breath in the bathtub and running on the beach to build stamina.

Then, sure enough, a winter storm came in a few days after Mom left. I awoke to the pitter-patter of raindrops falling on the leaves, on the paved stones, on the roof, down the rain gutters, and on top of surfboards. It was a cacophony of sounds. A song of release. All the plants in the garden had their longings answered. I was relieved to experience rain after so long without it. I hadn't realized that Southern California was a desert.

As it showered hard, I burst out of the house and danced around in circles in the lush backyard garden, getting wet. I didn't care; it wasn't cold. All the plants in the garden and the whole neighborhood seemed happy, glistening. Flowers popped their brightest in the diffused light. I had always enjoyed the rain back home. Any kind of nature imposing itself on me in the city was welcome.

I decided to take Zuzu out for a walk. She liked the rain, too; it brought out the scents of earth. The Strand and the beach were deserted. It was as if all the people here were afraid of a little rain—that seemed funny to me. I watched the surf. *Peaks—there are little peaks!*

I rushed back to the house to get my board and paddled out. *What does it matter if rain falls on you while surfing? You're already wet.* Nick seemed to agree—he was out there, hooting and hollering and having a ball. My heart skipped a beat when I saw him. We had all the waves we wanted, all to ourselves. After I got a long left, he complimented me: "Nice wave, Ellie."

I was beaming, sitting in the ocean in the heavy rain, soaking in his compliment. But something more was happening inside me—a yearning, a tug at my heartstrings. Yes, I had a soft spot for Nick.

The storm continued for a few days. On the rainy nights, I sat by the fire with Zuzu at my feet. Aunt Jen and I drank lots of tea. The kettle was always on the stove. I would read my aunt and uncle's surfing magazines while lounging on the couch. I was reading the December 1983 issue of *U.S. Surf,* and Benny was featured in the article "Why the Winners Win," a two-page photo spread all to himself.

It was then that I realized it—I was cozy. This was something I'd never felt back home in the cold, drafty loft, high above an entire island covered in pavement. Maybe that's why I'd build a bear cave out of sheets for Dad and me. When Dad was gone, I'd been isolated there, like in a prison cell. I had no interaction with the elements of the natural world in the city, except when Dad had taken me on hikes up north in the country. There was no ocean surf, and the skies were gray, smog blocking out the stars. There was hardly any warmth from the sun there. The sunlight had a dirty-gray filter over it, an artificial fog. Life back in the city was beginning to seem like a bad dream, one that I was forgetting.

The week before Christmas, after surfing one morning with

Chris, I went with Uncle Charlie to pick out a tree. He let me choose it—a little lopsided pine that I thought looked lonely. He strapped it to the top of the yellow VW bus with some rope. Aunt Jen said this was the first Christmas that Charlie had bought a tree, and that he'd done it for me.

Inside the little cottage, the tree took up most of the living room. Jen didn't have any ornaments, so we made them. We collected shells on the beach and strung them up. We folded and cut out paper angels and painted them. Then we decided that it needed more, so we went and bought some colorful balls and Christmas lights. With those additions, it sparkled, looking glorious and proud to be our tree.

On Christmas Eve, Jen and I were alone since Mom was in New York and Charlie was at the fire station. We went for a surf, ate a yummy vegetarian dinner, and watched *It's a Wonderful Life* on TV together. Now I knew where Jen got the name Zuzu for her dog. I cried. The movie made me think about Dad; he didn't have that second chance Jimmy Stewart's character had. At the same time, I realized that this was my life to live fully now, even though things weren't perfect. I was grateful for what I had: Mom, Jen, Charlie, Zuzu, my friends, and surfing.

On Christmas day, I awoke early and went straight outside with Jen's Easter Egg board to surf at dawn. I was the only one out until my aunt joined me.

Paddling up to me, she asked, "Did you even look at the tree?"

"No."

"Well, you might want to," she said, her eyes wide with a radiant smile.

"I'll go and look," I said.

Back at the house, I put the board down and went in to see

the tree. There was something long and neon-green wedged between the tree and the wall. My frozen feet could hardly feel the floor as I hobbled closer to it. *A surfboard!* I reached out to it, running my fingers along the smooth rail. I got a grip on it and pulled the nose out a little. It was pointy, but the tip was smoothed out. The top was sky-blue, with a Japanese-style ink painting of a dolphin on it.

I lifted it, pulling it out from behind the tree, and held it with both hands, resting the rounded pin tail on my toes. *It's just like Jen's thruster!* I took in a deep breath. I'd been holding my breath in shock. The width looked perfect, like it'd been made for me. I turned it around and laid it over my lap as I sat down. It was a tri-fin. *The new thruster!* My hand glided down its smooth surface, my fingertips lovingly sliding into the carved channels down to another brushstroke painting of a seal. I looked closely at the writing along the stringer. It read in pencil marks: "for Ellie 'Charger'." The dedication was followed by a bunch of numbers and then a signature starting with "Don." It began to soak in. The board had been custom-made for me by the shaper Don Kadowaki.

Wow! It's from Jen and Charlie! It was all so much. Zuzu woke up and came over to me, nudging me with her wet nose. I started to cry, overwhelmed by such a big gift that was so personal and so precious. Hunched over the board, I shuddered and let it all out. Zuzu licked the tears off my face. Dad wasn't here this Christmas, but I had surfing, and now—I had a beautiful new board.

I couldn't wait to try it. I put a basecoat of wax on it, then a topcoat, and I was off to the beach for a second session. Chris, Liam, and Danny were out, too. Then I saw Nick. My heart started pounding wildly in my chest. I was thinking that it was all too much—that things couldn't get any better—when

I spotted curved gray fins on the horizon. *The dolphins are here!* We had a party out there, all of us that Christmas morning, playing in the waves.

My new board paddled well, but I wondered: *How will it ride? How will it handle turns?* I paddled into a four-foot left. Feeling the force of the wave, I grabbed onto my rails and stood up. It glided and swept—I was flying. Bending my knees in unison with the wave rising under me, I turned back up towards the crest with ease, went off the top, then flew back down the face until it closed out.

"Woo-hoo!" I hollered. *It turns great!*

"You like it?" Jen called out to me.

"Yeah," I replied. "Thank you *so* much!"

"Thank your mom," she said, paddling up to me.

"What?"

"Yeah, your mom paid for it."

"Really?"

"Yup, she insisted."

"Wow." It was as if a weight lifted from my soul. *Am I wrong about Mom not liking me surfing?* I took a deep breath. "Who did the painting on it?"

Jen had a twinkle in her eyes, along with a smile about to burst.

"You did?"

"Yup," she said, grinning ear to ear.

"Oh—I love it!" I reached out across the water and hugged her.

That Christmas, I scored. First on good waves, and second on good times with my friends, my aunt included. Lastly, I scored on the best present I'd ever received. A surfboard from Mom—who would've thought? And with paintings of a dolphin and seal on it by Jen. It was priceless.

When Charlie got back from the station, he jokingly blamed me for there being no surf. It was flat with north winds on it, all blown out. "Oh great, now there's no waves," he said, "'cause Ellie Bo-Belly's got herself a new board!" He explained to me that it was a well-known surfers curse; whenever you got a new board, there were no waves.

But when the moonlight met the pink of the early dawn the next day, I paddled out on my new board anyway. I paddled fifteen blocks and back. I needed paddling practice, after all. When Charlie found out that I'd gone paddling, he chuckled with pride.

"You've got the sea in your bones, Charger," he said, tinkering on his VW bus. I held my hand up to shield my eyes against the sun and peered at him.

"I guess so, Shaggy," I replied. "I mean, Richie."

"Ha! That's right, I sure am funny lookin'," he stuck out his tongue and went cross-eyed.

I laughed and started to walk Zuzu.

"Hey, Ellie Bo-Belly!" Charlie shouted. "Do me a favor and pull my finger." He held his pointer finger out to me.

"Oh no," I said, rolling my eyes and continuing to walk away.

"No, no, really, look!" he shouted. I turned back to look at him. He raised his hand with his thumb now up, his finger pointed at me like a gun. Then he closed his thumb down onto his outstretched pointer finger like he shot the gun, while at the same time blowing a loud raspberry. I shook my head, and he chuckled.

As Zuzu and I crossed through the surfers' parking lot, Wilkies called out, "Merry Christmas, Charger!"

Stoked that he'd called me "Charger" and not my previous nickname, I called back, "Merry Christmas, Wilkies!"

On New Year's Eve, I fell asleep by the fire, trying to stay up until midnight. Mom was back from her trip, and we'd watched the ball drop at Times Square on television, when the clock struck twelve in New York City. Here it was only nine o'clock, at which point Mom excused herself. She said she had to go to some parties for work. She kissed me on my cheek, marking it with her bright-red lipstick. The stench of her too-strong perfume wafted over me.

"Happy New Year, beautiful darling girl," Mom said.

"Happy New Year, Mom!"

Then click, click, click, off she went in her shiny black patent-leather heels.

"Heels is on a mission," Charlie commented.

"Uh!" Mom shouted from the yard, then hollered out some curse words.

Charlie chuckled, "Ha! She must've gotten stuck between pavers."

I giggled. "Uh-huh."

"Stop, you two!" Jen scolded.

The next day, I paddled out at first light on my new board. No one was out. Maybe people had partied too much the night before, drinking too much like my mom must've done. I hadn't seen her since the night before.

Out here on my new custom board, it was peaceful and quiet, the ocean a sheet of blue-gray glass. Suddenly a dolphin popped up next to me. I shrieked in shock; it was so close.

"Hello!" I said out loud. I was shaking with excitement. The rush of being so close to a wild dolphin always did that to me. Quick as she'd snuck up on me, she leapt away. "And Happy New Year to you, too," I said.

Soon Chris joined me in the lineup, and Charlie and Jen shortly after, along with seemingly all of their friends. Later that afternoon, there was a big potluck party at my aunt and uncle's friend Eddie's house. I wanted Mom to come to the party with us, but she had one of her headaches.

All the surfers were there. I nearly died when I saw Nick. He was there with Toma and someone who looked like he might be Nick's dad. I was sure I was blushing. Nick looked handsome in his t-shirt and shorts. My uncle made a beeline straight to him, with a big "How ya doin'!" I thought I'd die.

It turned out that Uncle Charlie was friends with Nick's dad, Captain Cruz, who was a lifeguard stationed in the next town, Hermosa Beach.

While Charlie and Jen were in conversation with Nick's dad, Nick asked me, "Did you surf today?"

"Yeah. Early."

"Us too," said Toma.

"I didn't see you guys," I said.

"We surfed Hermosa," said Nick. "I stayed over at Toma's house there."

"Oh . . . do you go to a different high school, then?" I asked Toma.

"Yeah, Redondo," said Toma.

"Hey, do you want to get a drink?" Nick asked me.

"Sure."

He led me and Toma to a table with a big pitcher and poured me some lemonade, then some for Toma and himself.

"Thanks," I said. "It's good." It tasted perfectly sour and sweet.

Nick leaned in and said softly, "We're going on a surf trip

down south to Baja, Mexico."

"Oh wow. Just you guys?"

"Us and a few friends," said Toma. "We're telling the parents we're goin' to camp in San Diego, but we'll just keep going."

"I'm so stoked," said Nick. "Baja's so rad."

"Our New Year's resolution—getting tubed!" added Toma.

They went on talking excitedly about their adventure. I wanted to go, but Nick didn't invite me. *Maybe he thought I wasn't a good enough surfer, or he wouldn't want to invite a girl, or he wasn't into me. Maybe other girls were going.* Those thoughts upset me; I wanted him to like me the way I liked him. I excused myself and wandered over to Jen.

"I wish your mom could be here," Jen said.

"Maybe her headache's gone. I'll go see if she wants to come."

"Okay, yeah, good idea," Jen replied. "I hope so."

I walked out from the backyard to the street and started heading home when a familiar voice rang out.

"Hey—where ya going?" I turned around. It was Nick. My heart pounded and my knees got wobbly.

"I'm going to get my mom," I said.

"Would you like company?" he asked.

"Sure." I couldn't believe he wanted to come with me.

"Baja sounds so amazing," I blurted out.

"You'd love it!" he said, bouncing along with my quick pace.

"Yeah?" I met his gaze. The sparkle in his eyes lit a flame in my chest.

"It's got bitchin' reef-breaks, rad lefts and rights. But the water's colder."

"I like it cold," I said.

He raised an eyebrow. "Yeah, like you never want to get outta the water, do you?"

"Nope."

He cracked a smile and I beamed back at him, feeling wonderfully alive and like I was floating.

The harsh, loud barks of a dog echoed as we approached the alley leading to the garden.

"Is that Zuzu?" I said. "She never barks." As I unlatched the gate, the deep, full barks of a German shepherd bellowed from inside the house. She burst out to greet me but kept barking urgently.

"Zuzu, it's just Nick," I said, thinking she was barking at him. But Zuzu went right back inside the house. We followed.

That's when I saw Mom lying on the rug, passed out. My stomach twisted in dread. I ran to her and shouted, "Mom! Mom!" I tried to pick her up. She didn't wake up. A bolt of panic hit me. The rug was smoking. I could see that a cigarette was burning it. Adrenaline stormed through me as I dashed to the kitchen, filled up a glass of water, and doused the rug. Only then did Zuzu stop barking. It would've been a fire if I hadn't come when I did.

I pressed my fingers against Mom's neck. I felt a heartbeat.

"Call 911," Nick said.

"Should I get Jen and Charlie? I could skateboard over there real fast."

"No, you call, I'll go get them."

"Take my skateboard," I said, as I grabbed the phone off the hook and dialed 911. I couldn't lose Mom. *What if she hit her head when she fell?* Needles crept up my spine.

The fire department showed up in no time. Two medics went over to Mom right away, while one of them came over to me. Zuzu stayed by my side.

"You're Charlie's niece, aren't you?" he said. He was a big, beefy guy who exuded safety.

"Yeah."

"Where is he?" he asked.

"He's at a party with Jen, a few blocks away," I said. "My friend's getting them."

"Okay, don't you worry, your mom's going to be all right. You did the right thing, calling us." His brown eyes were full of empathy, his dark, furrowed brow standing out against his tanned skin. He gave me a little reassuring squeeze on my shoulder as the loud siren of an ambulance rang out.

They took Mom away in the ambulance. I wanted to go with her, but they said I couldn't go because I wasn't eighteen yet.

Then Charlie bolted in. "They took Mom in an ambulance," I said as he gave me a big hug.

"Is she okay?" Charlie asked the captain.

"Yeah, she'll be all right. This one's quite the firefighter herself. Put a fire out in your own house."

"Wha—Ellie?"

"Zuzu warned me," I said. Charlie had a stunned look on his face.

Jen almost smothered me when she came in through the door; her embrace was too tight, like Mom's. She only released me when I assured her that I was okay. Then she joined Charlie and the captain at the front door to inquire about Mom.

"Are you okay?" Nick asked me, his tender eyes searching mine.

"Yeah," I said. But I was spinning. Everything was falling apart all over again. "Thanks for getting my aunt and uncle so quick," I managed.

"No problem, glad to help." He tilted his head and leaned

in closer to me. "I hope your mom's okay."

"Thanks." I dared to glance into his eyes again, my heart pounding against a rising queasiness.

"Ellie," my aunt called out, her voice strained. "We gotta go."

Jen, Charlie, and I got into the VW bus and headed for the hospital. At first, no one said anything. My stomach was flipping somersaults, like I was getting worked by a giant wave.

"Don't worry, your sister will be okay," Uncle Charlie reassured Jen. "She's a tough cookie."

"She seems that way, but on the inside she's fragile," Jen said, her voice taut.

"We have Ellie to thank that the house didn't burn down," Charlie said.

"Can we please not talk about this right now? I don't want to stress Ellie out more than she already is."

"You're the one stressed out," he said. "Do you hear how you're talking to me right now?"

Jen grimaced. "I'm sorry." She turned to me in the back seat. "I'm sorry, Ellie."

"It's okay," I said.

Charlie sped down the road. The green and red street lights started to blur as tears flooded my eyes. My churning stomach became a tangle of knots at the thought of Mom dying.

Charlie pulled up to the hospital entrance to let Jen out, so she could see Mom as soon as possible. He explained that they only let one family member in at a time, and only an adult. Then Charlie parked in the lot and we went inside. He spoke to the nurse at the desk, and she let us wait in the hall.

"She's gonna be okay," Charlie said to me as we sat down.

"What happened to her?"

His face looked pained, like he wanted to tell me but he couldn't. "Not sure, but we'll find out soon."

"I'm not a little girl anymore. I need to know the truth."

Charlie let loose a breath. "I'm not gonna sugarcoat anything. We need to talk to a doctor first, but from what the captain said, seems like she drank too much and passed out. Ellie Bo-Belly . . . your mom's gonna be just fine." Crow's feet crinkled around his eyes, bright with sincerity.

We sat and waited for a long time. The empty hallway's too-bright fluorescent lights brought every detail into focus—the beige vinyl seat-bench and every particle of dust in the corner.

When Jen came back, she said they weren't allowing anyone to see Mom and that Charlie should take me home. But I insisted on staying, too, so she let me. Charlie had to go in to work early, so he left. Tired and drained from the drama of the day, I fell asleep waiting.

Later that night, when I awoke, Jen was asleep beside me on the bench. I crept down the empty hall and found Mom's room. Her hospital robe and the sheets were white. She looked pale, like a marble statue. Her white hair blended into her skin, her features undefined without makeup. I approached her, found her hand, and grasped it tight.

EIGHTEEN

The Raddest Most Epic Surf Trip Ever

I washed the hospital off in the surf as soon as I got home the next day. After paddling far out passed the lineup, I plunged off my board into the salty blue-green water and held my breath. The swish of swirling water hummed its song around me. Surfacing to breathe, I lay on my back to float, the comforting white noise of ocean filling my ears. Supported by saltwater, I let go and let the ocean cleanse me of my worries.

Mom was home and resting. Earlier, I'd stayed with her in the hospital while Jen went back to the house to pick up her truck and then brought us home. There was no school for a few more days, so I could relax. Mom had promised not to drink too much again. *Soon everything will be back to normal.*

A pelican flew only a few feet above, so close that its large wings fanned the air into me. I treaded water and watched the incoming surge get closer and closer, then pass me and crash into foamy soup towards shore.

There are waves! They were a good size, so a few hours of surfing flew by like nothing.

I saw them as I came out of the water—all the blonde preppy girls from Bonnie's group had shown up at the beach. They lay out on colorful towels in their high-cut bikinis. Their big hair looked blow-dried, and they were wearing makeup.

I was readying myself to pass by them when Nick appeared, running towards me.

"Ellie!" he shouted. "It is you! How are you? How's your mom?"

"She's okay," I said, my heart racing. "She's back home."

He dropped his board down and picked up both me and my board, lifting me up by my hips and shouting, "Yeah— Charger's back!"

I laughed and shrieked, "Put me down!" As my nose brushed against his hair, I inhaled his heady scent. *He smells like orange blossoms!* When he put me down, I was so close to him that our cheeks touched. His felt warm. I was shaking.

"Shouldn't you be in Baja?" I asked, stepping back.

"Yeah, but I was worried about you," he said, tilting his head and leaning in close. "Toma and I can go later this week, before Christmas break is over."

When I met his shining gaze, a thrill shot through me. "Um . . . thanks for helping out the other day," I stammered.

"I didn't do anything," he said. "You saved the day, fire-fighter. But I'm here for you—any time, night or day. Sunshine or rain." He spread his arms out at "sunshine" and mimed "rain" by wiggling his fingers above his head and swooping down to his waist. "Happy or sad," he continued, pushing his cheeks up with his fingers into an exaggerated smile, and then making a melodramatic pouty face.

I couldn't help but break into giggles at his antics. He flashed me a warm smile.

He had gotten the attention of the No Beach Trash Club. They saw and heard every word. Their mouths were open in shock.

I started to tell Nick I was going to get some lunch when he blurted out, "Come surf some waves with me. It looks killer out there. John and Toma are comin' down, too."

"Okay." I couldn't say no to him, and any trace of hunger had left me.

"Hey, you wanna come to Baja with me and Toma?"

I thought my heart would explode, it was pounding so forcefully. I was too shocked to answer right away.

"You could bring a friend, too, if you want," he added.

"Yeah, sure, I'd love to! I'll ask my friend Chris. You know her, we've all surfed together."

"Oh yeah—Ripper!"

"Yeah!" Recharged by his amazing invitation, I paddled back out with Nick and his friends and we traded off waves for another two hours. I was on fire. I really enjoyed showing the No Beach Trash Club how well I could surf, and that I wasn't by any means a "poser." By the time I went in, all the girls had gone.

During our surf session, Nick had invited me and Chris to join him and Toma at the Kettle that night. Over coffee and root beer floats, Toma told us there was a south swell coming. He'd listened to the report on his dad's NOAA weather radio. We decided to leave early the next morning for Baja. We had two more days of vacation before school started. Chris would stay over at my house and Toma at Nick's, so Nick could pick us up in Wizard and we could "book" early, according to Nick. Even though they'd gone by themselves before, Toma, Nick, and Chris insisted that we keep our destination a secret from our parents. They said if they knew we were going to Baja alone, they wouldn't give us permission, or they'd worry too much. So we decided to tell them we were going to camp down in San Diego, which is what they'd said last time. I felt bad lying to Aunt Jen, but I figured a little white lie was okay.

At four o'clock in the morning, we strapped our boards to Wizard's roof and piled in. Chris and Toma took the back, and I got to sit in the front next to Nick. I almost had to pinch myself. *We're going on a surf trip to Baja! Just us, no aunt or uncle, no parents. We can roam wild and free!* This was really happening.

Everything was quiet in the dark, pre-dawn morning, except for the hum of the motor on the freeway and my beating heart. Nick slipped his hand in mine and shot me a warm smile, a sparkle in his green eyes. I melted. *Will we kiss? Will we sleep next to each other in the tent?*

Toma tapped me on the shoulder. "Dude, can you put this in the stereo?" He handed me a blank cassette tape.

"Chee-uh!" said Nick. "Most definitely! We made the tape last night, especially for this surf trip."

I opened the sleeve. "Cowabunga" was written in black pen on the label. I put it into Wizard's stereo cassette. The Plugz's "El Clavo Y La Cruz" blasted from the car speakers in Spanish. Toma and Chris talked excitedly about Baja. Everyone had surfed there before except me. I soaked it all up. It was colder there, with more nature and less houses. Lots of reef breaks, mostly rights.

As we crossed the border, two hawks circled above us in the pale sky of the early dawn, riding the wind, doing figure eights. *It's like me and you up there, Dad.* I felt his spirit with me. It was a good sign to see the hawks. Everything felt so right.

The sun was rising. The song changed to "I Melt With You" by Modern English. A shaft of sunlight touched the side of Nick's face, illuminating his beautiful gaze as he turned towards me. My heart skipped a beat; it hit me that Nick may have picked this love song on the mixtape for me.

I was overcome with the thrill of the adventure we were

on. We were in Mexico, on a highway road traveling through a run-down city that reminded me of New York City, except all the signs on the sides of buildings were in Spanish.

From Federal Highway One, what started as a speck of ocean expanded into a blue horizon above colorful cement houses. We kept driving south, then peeled off the highway down a dirt road with the sea to our right. At a tin shack, we turned onto an empty bluff, an expanse of sea and sky before us.

"Where are we?" I asked.

"K-38," said Toma.

"Why 'K'?"

"Kilometers," he said. "Everything here is measured in how many kilometers south of the border it is. Las Gaviotas is K-41 just south of here. K-58 is La Fonda."

"Does K-38 have a name, too?" I asked.

"It's just K-38, isn't it?" said Chris.

"Yeah, but K-87 has a good name," Nick said.

"What is it?" I asked.

"Salsipuedes," he said as he parked Wizard on a deserted dirt cliff overlooking the ocean. There were no houses around. "It means 'leave if you can'," he added, smiling. "It's a dirt road, crazy steep. If it rains, good luck getting out."

"No way, we're stoked," said Toma, nodding to the surf.

"Trippendicular!" Nick exclaimed, swinging his door open.

I jumped out and ran to the edge of the cliff. Excitement pulsed through me as I took in the lines of surf rolling in.

"Corduroy," I said, inhaling the ocean's fresh scent as Nick, Chris, and Toma arrived by my side.

"Major!" said Nick. "It's stellar."

"Whoa—there's some swell," Chris pointed out. A huge right swept across, from the point past a big black rock, and extended far down the beach, south. It looked scary. "Mint!" she said.

"Get out, that's like double overhead," said Toma.

"Are you close to that rock out there?" I asked.

"Don't worry about the rock, you'll pass clear of it riding the wave," Nick said.

"Unless you fall on your take-off," I said.

"You won't be as close to the rocks as it looks," Chris said. "You'll be fine, for sure."

"Just don't sit too deep," added Toma.

That meant don't sit too far to the left of the rock when the wave came in, a sweeping right.

"Woo-hoo, come on, what are you waitin' for? Let's get out there!" Nick exploded with glee, extending his arms up in the air. "It's, like, major radical!"

Nick, Toma, and Chris continued to celebrate our good fortune in having awesome waves to surf as we busied ourselves with putting on wetsuits and waxing boards. Along with her new thruster by Gumby from ET, Chris had brought her wetsuit to Baja; the water was colder here.

Though their stoke was contagious, my stomach started turning backflips. The surf was massive. I feared colliding with that big rock.

On the north side of the bluff, there was a steep trail down to a rocky beach. I followed Chris carefully, clutching my new thruster, Nick and Toma behind me. When we got to the shore, Chris pointed out a rip we could paddle out in, far to the right of the rocks, away from where the point was breaking. I braced myself. The surf was substantial. I wanted to make it out without getting worked or hurled into the rocks by masses of whitewater. Chris jumped in first, and I followed with Nick and Toma.

Against the freezing gush, I focused on paddling as hard as I could. *I've got to make it out as fast as possible!* Big kelp floated all around. I didn't want to get tangled in it. I duck-dove the torrential whitewater, and then the sizable waves. The adrenaline rush accelerated my paddling.

I was relieved when I finally made it out. Toma and Nick were in the lineup, and Chris was already on a wave. She was shredding.

Nick sat up on his board. "There are some sets—it's goin' off!"

"I'm stoked," I said, smiling.

"Totally—we're so lucky, could've been skunked." Nick turned to the incoming waves, a cheerful grin on his face.

I was so lucky to be here, surfing Baja with Nick, Chris, and Toma, my surf buddies. There were solid waves, and I'd made it out without getting worked. I was shaking, but my heart was open. *Anything is possible.* I could surf a double overhead set backside without falling on take-off; I'd done it plenty of times in California. I wouldn't hit the rocks. *I can do this.*

Toma took off on the next set. It looked ominous as it rose and towered above.

"Charger, you got this," Nick said, accentuating his words with a wink. He surprised me. He knew intuitively that I was doubting myself.

"Thanks," I mumbled.

Toma was ripping up his wave. *If he can do it, I can.*

As Chris paddled back to the lineup, Nick called out, "You ripped that wave to shreds!"

"Thanks, I can't believe how awesome it is out here!" she replied.

"Go Ripper!" I added, smiling at her. She returned my smile, sitting on her board next to me.

As the set continued to loom toward us, I decided to wait in the wings inside of the peak and let Nick, Chris, and Toma, who were sitting deeper, have them. But when it was Nick's turn, he said, "Go Ellie!" He was backing out, so I had to go for it or it would be a wasted wave. Chris was cheering me on: "Go Charger!"

I had no time to hesitate. I scrambled, digging deep. When I felt the force of the wave beneath me, I popped up and crouched low, my weight in my feet, toes clutching the top of my board. The waves' glass-like surface reflected the light-blue sky. Doing a bottom turn and angling up toward the crest, I went off the top and into the force of the wave, focusing on carving a line through it. The pulsing ocean behind me surged, pushing me on. I snapped back to attack the lip and re-enter the power, again and again, carving it up. My heart soared as I sped through. I shouted out, "Woo-hoo!" as it petered out and I fell off.

When I surfaced, everyone was cheering. I shot my arms up in celebration. That euphoric, frenzied rush of riding an awesome big wave surged through me. I was facing my fear and going for it, even though I was scared.

Paddling back out was much easier this time. Pumped up, I felt invincible. I paddled around the perimeter of where the waves were breaking, far south of the point. I had a great view of Nick on a set. He flew down the line with such fluidity and style, and, as if emphasizing the joy that he felt, he executed a three-hundred-and-sixty-degree spin. His joy was contagious—we all cheered enthusiastically.

Back in the lineup, everyone praised me.

"That was incredible!" Chris said, patting me on the back. "You're ripping!"

"Nice wave," said Toma, smiling at me.

When Nick paddled back out he congratulated me, too. "Your wave was bitchin'!" he said as his beautiful eyes lit up.

I beamed. "Thanks, it was a nice wave." I tilted my head down in a shy smile. *After all, he gave me his wave, he told me to go, and it was the wave that was great, not me.*

"Yeah it was," Toma piped in.

"That thing had your name all over it," Nick affirmed. "You had to have it."

I smiled at him before turning to face the incoming sets. We surfed for a few hours, taking turns. It was so much fun to only surf with friends and to have it all to ourselves. No old guys calling me a kook.

There was a long lull. As I sat on my board, talking to Chris, I forgot about my fear of the rocks. Then, before there was time for anyone to shout "outside," a wave grew rapidly, much faster than all the other sets. I scrambled, paddling as fast as I could further outside. But it was no use. Gripped with fear, I pleaded, *Please don't break on me!* Then, like a towering building exploding, its colossal mass broke right in front of me. Pure fear shot through me. I tried to duck-dive, but it was a joke. My board ripped from my grasp as I plummeted to the depths, tossed this way and that like a rag doll.

Abruptly, I was whipped around and then—wham! The clunk resounded in my ears. My head hit something hard. *A rock!* It hurt. I started to panic. I didn't know which way was up. I was being held under by the force of the wave and I couldn't hold my breath any longer. *I might die. I need to breathe!* But I forced myself not to breathe underwater.

I flailed my arms and legs, desperately hoping to propel to the surface. I could see light and scratched towards it. I made it and surfaced, but only had a few seconds to breathe air. I had just realized I'd drifted into the reef and was surrounded by big rocks when another forceful set came crashing down on me. While being pummeled, I prayed I could hold my breath long enough, and that I didn't hit another rock. At one point, my foot pushed off on one. I knew I shouldn't panic to save energy, but I couldn't help it. I was fighting for my life.

When I finally surfaced again, it was the instant that another set was breaking. I hadn't managed to breathe much air before it brought me down again. Groggy with the heavy weight of the ocean upon me and tired from struggling against it, all I could manage was to protect my head with my arms. Dad's face flashed before me—his last desperate look full of all his devotion for me. Then something miraculous happened. Though my eyes were shut, I saw golden-white light. The warmth of being cradled in Dad's arms filled me as fear instantly left me, replaced by a oneness, a connectedness between my spirit and the ocean. My body performed automatically, surfacing up to breathe, grabbing onto my board, duck-diving whitewater, and paddling out of the kill zone.

"Are you okay?" Nick shouted out.

"No," I cried, without a break in my paddling. I finally reached shore, dragging my weary self out of the water. Nick wasn't far behind me.

"Ellie!" he shouted.

Dizzy, I sat down on a pebbly bank and felt my head where it ached. There was a lump.

Nick was running through the whitewater to me. "Did you hit your head?" he asked, kneeling.

"Yeah, on a rock. There's a lump." He put his board down next to mine and gently took my hand from on top of my head and turned it palm-up. My hand was trembling.

"Doesn't look like it's bleeding," he said. "You're okay, just a shock, I'd say. That was some rogue set wave! Came outta nowhere! That thing was mega, twice the size of the others." His sea-green eyes lit up with sincerity in the morning sun. He would've swept me off my feet if I'd been standing. Thankfully I was not.

"Yeah," I said. "Thanks." I gulped back tears. He was still holding my hand. My heart fluttered. He flashed me a warm smile and my face began to feel warm, which didn't make sense because the water was cold and I was trembling. *I must be blushing.*

"You're shivering," he said, leaning into me. He put his arm around me. A craving stirred deep within me. He was so close. He was so sweet. I couldn't help myself. I leaned into him impulsively and kissed him on the lips. Tenderly, he kissed me back.

Everything else ceased to be. Time stopped. Even the thunderous crashing surf and the song it sang silenced as it receded over the rocky shore. Our lips pressed against each other gently, and then passionately.

Our dreamy moment was interrupted by Chris and Toma, who came in to see if I was okay. Nick jumped up, blushing. Then he had me do the concussion test. I followed his finger with my eyes as he held it to my left and then my right, across my field of vision. He'd learned it from his dad. I guess I passed.

"You're okay," he assured me.

"No one saw *that* one comin'!" said Toma.

Chris suggested I rest awhile. Normally I would paddle back out, no matter what. I always liked to have a good last wave in. But right then, I felt ragged and worn. I'd just run the gamut of emotions, from the shock of hitting my head on a rock, to fear of drowning, to desiring Nick.

"You should get some ice on it," Toma suggested.

"We've got some in the cooler," Nick said. "I'll get it."

"Yeah, ice'll be good," Chris said, giving him an approving nod. "You should also have one of your aunt's famous muffins," she added. "I bet they're still warm."

"Yeah," I said. Jen had packed them in tin foil early that morning.

Chris and Toma paddled back out for more waves only once they were sure I was okay.

Nick insisted on carrying my board, and I actually let him. The two of us hiked back up the trail.

When we got up to the bluff, Nick brought over some ice he'd wrapped in his t-shirt and pressed it to my head. I took over the job of holding the ice to my head, and he handed me one of Aunt Jen's muffins. "Here, this'll make you feel better."

"Thanks. You should get back out there." I gestured to the waves with my free hand.

"I'm good right here," he said, taking me in with a heartfelt smile that tugged at my soul. He unzipped his wetsuit and pulled it down and off his arms to below his waist, revealing his sculpted bare chest and torso. A rush of passion coursed through me. He was so handsome. And kind, to keep me company when the surf was going off.

We had the perfect vantage point from up on the bluff to watch Chris and Toma. I unwrapped the muffin Nick gave me and took a bite. It *was* still warm, and it was blueberry, my favorite. Right then it tasted so good. The shock of what had happened began to wear off. With some food in my belly, I started to feel grounded.

Chris caught the next one. After a powerful bottom turn, she cut back up to the lip and then rotated her torso in the opposite direction of her board, stretching her arm back and seemingly laying back on the wave face before going back off the lip.

"What's she doing?" I asked.

"A layback snap!" said Nick. "Whoa, rad!" He chuckled.

"Yeah," I agreed, "Ripper rips."

Toma got the next set. He paddled in at the peak, stayed there for the long drop, and stalled. He got barreled and when he shot out, he carved up the rest of the wave, speeding down the line in a frenzy and finishing with a floater.

"He got shacked—floater, righteous!" Nick said, clapping his hands together.

"Whoa . . . he's awesome."

"Most definitely, he's ace." Nick turned to me. "Dude, we should camp at Shipwrecks tonight. It's the raddest thing you've ever seen. A big sunken freighter ship, half out of the water, near the take-off point. The right peels a hundred yards down the beach, and there's a left for you."

"That sounds really cool," I said. "I'd like to go see it . . . I wonder what happened to the ship?"

"My dad said it appeared like that out of the mist after a hurricane two years ago. He calls the spot 'Freighters.' Toma and I surfed it a few months ago. It was overhead and bitchin'."

I was amped. This was my dream come true, except I hadn't even thought about actually being in Mexico with Nick because I never thought it would happen. Also, I was just giddy about being alive and well—after my near-death experience with the rocks.

When Chris and Toma got out of the water, Toma suggested we stop in the next town, Ensenada. "They've got the most excellent fish tacos there," he said.

"I could go for some grindage—mmm-mmm," Nick agreed.

"I could go for a bean and cheese burrito," Chris said.

"Me too," I said.

"Sweet, let's book," said Nick.

We set off with a jolt of energy from Bad Brains' "Attitude." Ensenada was an hour away. Shipwrecks would be another two hours south. As we drove down the coast, Chris, Nick, and Toma pointed out different surf spots: Las Gaviotas, a reef with rights and lefts, then La Fonda, which was K-58, a big, wide beach break. Further south, Toma pointed at the "leave if you can" entrance to the road down to Salsipuedes.

Next was San Miguel, which Nick said was an amazing right he and Toma surfed one day when you could ride all the way past the jetty. Chris said the right seemed to "always hold up and not close out." South of San Miguel, as we passed a fish-canning plant, Bob Marley's "Three Little Birds" played, my heartbeat in rhythm with the reggae beat. We saw fishing boats before arriving in Ensenada.

We pulled over to the side of the road, stopping by a bright-pink building. I guessed it must be Toma's favorite taco place. We piled out, sandy and hungry. Toma went up to the counter and started to order in English, but Chris interrupted him, ordering in Spanish. After all, she'd grown up speaking Spanish with her mom. The boys got fish tacos, but since I was vegetarian, I stuck with Chris's choice, a bean and cheese burrito. The food was so good that Chris ordered extra burritos to take with us.

As we sped out of town in Wizard, we sat there just smiling at each other, not wanting to shout over the loud noise of the motor. "Mexican Radio" by Wall of Voodoo played, the perfect song for that moment. Down the desert road of Highway One, we drove through farmland and lots of wide-open space with nothing but nature. When we reached Maneadero, a little town that consisted of some shack-like buildings, men in military uniforms carrying rifles stopped the truck. Nick turned off the stereo and rolled down his window.

"*Adonde va?*" the man asked.

"Punta San Jacinto," Nick replied.

"*De donde viene?*"

"*Nosotros somos de* California," Nick said.

The military man slapped Wizard's fender and another man waved us forward.

"Do you speak Spanish?" I asked Nick.

"No, I only know enough to understand and get by from Spanish class. We don't speak it at home, even though my dad's part Mexican."

"Yeah, my dad was from Poland but he didn't want me to speak Polish, he wanted me to be American," I said. I realized, with a heavy heart, that I'd just used the past tense "was" for Dad.

"Yeah, my parents speak Japanese and I understand it," Toma piped in, "but they don't encourage me and my sister to speak it. You're lucky your mom speaks Spanish with you, Chris."

"It's been a necessary survival tactic," Chris said, "against the heinous craziness that is my dad."

"Heavy," said Toma.

Nick gazed at me. His eyes were filled with compassion, like he sensed what I was feeling.

On we went, down the bumpy, winding road. As we climbed up and down hills, as far as the eye could see were vast vistas of wild desert. Scattered about were ranches. It was the stuff of Clint Eastwood Westerns, which I used to watch with Dad on our tiny black-and-white TV on Sunday afternoons. A road sign read "*Curva Peligrosa.*" I knew from my high school Spanish that *peligrosa* meant "dangerous." We took a sharp turn, swinging me into Nick.

"Sorry," I said.

"No worries," he assured me with a smile as he steadied me with his hand on my back. A tingling went through me as he slid his hand to my shoulder and rested his arm around me.

We were up high on a cliff. A majestic purple mountain range reached for miles to our left, and far below us, a valley with a stream led to a cluster of houses ahead in the distance. Wizard began a steep descent down.

At the bottom of the valley was Santo Tomás, some adobe houses, and nothing else. We continued south, down the dusty road to another small village: Punta Colonet. Nick stopped at a Pemex gas station to fill the car. Toma and Chris went in to buy some beer. I got out to stretch my legs.

I was leaning against Wizard when Nick approached me. I thought he was going to kiss me as his breathtaking eyes met mine, but instead he spoke softly. "Are you okay? How's your head, okay?"

I nodded, my heart in my throat.

"Um," he continued, his tender eyes searching mine, "I heard about your dad and I wanted to say I'm sorry. I . . . I wanted to tell you, but I didn't know—"

I silenced him with a long passionate kiss. He embraced me in his arms and kissed me back gently, making me yearn for more. I held him tight. He met my intensity with his own, pressing against me, his body and his lips eager for me.

"No way—you two are so sprung, legit!" Chris shouted out, walking towards us. Nick and I separated awkwardly, smiling at her.

Chris jumped in the back seat as Toma came out of the

Pemex store carrying a bag. I ducked into the front seat. "Dudes, the ride's gonna get bumpier in a minute," Nick said to me and Chris, leaning in Wizard's window. "It's mostly dirt roads from here."

"No worries," Chris said, looking pleased as she leaned back and put her bare feet up on the back of my seat. "This is *la buena vida*." I must've looked confused, so she explained, "It means 'the good life.'"

"Yeah, sure is," I beamed back at her. My whole being was vibrating with excitement from the adventure we were on—and from Nick.

When Toma got in, Nick jumped into the driver's seat, turned the key, pulled the starter button, and Wizard purred. "It Must Be Love" by Madness was next on the mixtape, an unabashed love song. *Did Nick pick this song for me?* I glanced his way. As if answering my thought, his sea-green eyes sparkled when they met mine and he burst into a grin, slipping his hand in mine. His touch stirred up something wild in me. *He's so hot. And sweet.*

Nick drove a bit more down Highway One, then headed west on a dirt road. There was no one and nothing in sight for about ten minutes until we passed a small farm and an adobe house. A cute stray dog stood to the side of the road, watching us. We passed by a cluster of small adobe houses. Dust scattered in the wind behind us.

We took a left and headed south, crossing through open fields. To our right, a cliff formed an archway over a path down steep terrain to the sea. We were high up on some kind of plateau, a boundless meadow before us. There was something up ahead. I thought maybe it was a tree from a distance, but as we got closer, I saw that it was a horse.

We stopped a few feet from it, and Nick turned off the

engine. The chestnut-colored horse stood still except for its tail, looking at us. It blinked its long, lovely dark lashes. Its dark eyes were trusting, wide-open doors to its noble soul. All the animals I'd met shared this quality in their gaze: Zuzu, Lucy, and the dolphin with the crescent moon scar.

"Is it wild?" I asked.

"Sure looks it," Chris replied.

"That's so rad!" said Nick, sticking his head out the window.

"I've never seen a wild horse before," Toma said.

"Me either," I murmured. It was completely free, roaming the fields. *You're the most beautiful thing I've ever seen*, I said to it in my mind as I leaned out the window. My heart opened as wide as the field we were in. "She's like us, wild, roaming free in Baja."

"Big time," said Nick.

"Totally!" agreed Chris.

After taking in the natural grace of the wild horse grazing, Nick started Wizard and slipped his hand in mine again, causing sparks to go off inside me. We continued south, through the desert countryside to a love song by the Replacements, "Within Your Reach." We soon met with the ocean and approached Punta San Jacinto, known to surfers as Freighters or Shipwrecks. At the end of the road, the Sea of Cortez was waiting for us, sparkling. The ship was huge, a surreal dream image sticking out of the blue sea. Tilted on its side, it looked like a toddler's toy left in a kiddie pool. I could read its name, *Isla del Carmen*, painted in red letters on the white siding.

My heart tightened. Mom's middle name was Carmela. Images of her flashed through my mind: passed out on the burning rug, sleeping in the hospital bed, whimpering in the corner of the loft back home. She was shipwrecked when Dad died. We both were. We'd been through a hurricane, a rough storm at sea. But somehow, I'd learned how to ride it.

There was nothing around for miles besides a couple of panga fishing boats and a beat-up pickup truck. The rugged coast jutted out to the north and west of us, its ochre earth rising up to the distant bluffs—all nature, no houses in sight. Here, there was just a rocky shore and the *Isla del Carmen*, stranded in the surf. The waves were smaller. The right, which looked head high, peeled past the ship and down the beach, where the coastline stretched south.

Nick, Chris, and Toma were getting ready to surf another session, putting wetsuits on and waxing boards. I wanted to get back on the horse and get out there after my scary near-death experience. I needed to shake it off with fun waves that didn't look like they could kill me. This fast, long right was exactly what I needed.

The highlight of the session was when Nick started singing the *Gilligan's Island* theme song and we joked about how crazy it was to surf right next to a half-sunken ship. I was having so much fun taking turns shredding shoulder-high waves with Nick, Toma, and Chris that I forgot all about the bump on my head and how it got there. Life couldn't get any better. Chris was right—it was the good life, *la buena vida*.

When Nick shouted, "Party!" Toma, Chris, or I would join him. Once, all four of us rode the same wave. When Nick was riding at the top of one wave, I was below, and then we crossed; he went down to the trough and I went up to the crest.

"I saw a little left breakin' on the other side of the ship," Nick said to me.

I could never resist a left. They were my favorite, since I was goofy foot, so Nick and I paddled over. Further in towards shore, there it was, about waist-high. We rode a couple of fast lefts and then I surfed one in. My arms were aching, my mouth parched. I turned to watch Nick as another left came. Nick caught it and sped down the line towards me. The sun was low in the sky, a blazing orange orb over the sea. It lit up the shore, patterns of ripples scattered across the ocean to the horizon.

"I think I'm going to head in," I said.

"Me too," he agreed, the sun casting light on his exposed skin, making it glow.

Nick and I changed out of our wetsuits and into warm clothes by wrapping our towels around us, surfer-style. We set up the tent and unrolled our sleeping bags. There was just enough room for all four of us, side by side. *Will I sleep next to Nick?* My heart skipped a beat at the thrill of the thought. I hoped so.

The wind picked up even more, blowing dust, and the chill went right through my sweatshirt to my bones. The ocean was colder here in Baja. Toma and Chris were still surfing as the sun began to set. Nick and I built a campfire with the wood he'd brought, and we placed Jen and Charlie's camp chairs around it and sat close to the fire. The flames flickered, meshing with the neon, peach-streaked sky. Chris and Toma headed in, black silhouettes against the shimmering tangerine highlights of the sea.

"Let's make s'mores," Chris said.

"Oh, yeah!" That sounded perfect.

Nick and I got the s'mores supplies I'd packed from the back of Wizard, while Chris and Toma changed into warm clothes.

The first star appeared, bright and twinkling, like it was smiling at me. *Dad, I'm here in Baja on a surf trip! Thank you for watching over me.* It sparkled back and winked at me. *Always, Misiu,* I imagined Dad replying.

We toasted marshmallows and made s'mores. They tasted so good after surfing.

The dome of the night sky enveloped us, with infinite stars shining bright. Holes to heaven. There were no city lights to screen them out. We saw all of them, shining their brightest, multitudes to infinity. We sat and gazed at their beauty.

Toma offered Chris and I beer, but after seeing what alcohol did to Mom, I wasn't interested. Nick refrained from drinking, too, perhaps out of consideration for my choice not to. Chris accepted a beer, and then Nick said, "Wait, wait," as he ran to Wizard and brought out two sodas and gave me one.

"Slice?" I asked, reading the can's label.

"Guess it's new," he said. He held up his soda. "Let's toast . . . to Ellie's first time in Baja! The raddest, most epic surf trip ever!"

Everyone cheered in agreement. As we sipped the new lemon-lime sodas, Nick and Toma shared stories of their last surf trip at Shipwrecks. Chris spoke about her Baja surfing trips, too, which soon led to all of us sharing our surf adventures.

After lots of stories, Chris announced that she was dead tired and needed to sleep, so we said goodnight and she went into the tent. Toma stayed with us for one more beer before going to bed, too.

Nick and I stayed up by the campfire. I leaned into him and he put his arm around me and squeezed my shoulder. I felt a rush of passion throughout my body, which kind of scared me, but at the same time, it was what I craved. We started kissing and couldn't stop. His tongue lightly brushed against my lips. I parted mine, allowing his tongue to break through and search for mine. Our tongues entangled. *We're French kissing!*

I pulled back, a little shocked by my willingness to receive his tongue. He kissed my neck, and I couldn't help but arch my back against the thrill that shot through me. I pressed my lips and body into his. Again, it was as if all time stopped. The ocean's hum quieted to a whisper. The wind fluttered my hair against our cheeks as we kissed and kissed.

The fire had gone out. I started shivering. "We should get some sleep so we can surf at dawn," I said.

"Sure thing," he said. "It's just . . . you're so beautiful, I can't stop."

I gave him a warm smile. "It's freezing," I said.

"For sure, let's snuggle in the tent and get warm."

We unzipped the tent to find Chris and Toma fast asleep. I quietly got into my sleeping bag next to Chris, and Nick got into his, which was next to mine. It was pitch-black in the tent, but I felt his loving gaze on me. I snuggled into his arms. I didn't think I'd be able to sleep, I was so charged up. But I was so dead tired from surfing that I soon fell fast asleep. We both did. We slept in past dawn. It was so nice to wake up in his arms.

The last day of the trip was just as good as the first, minus the near-death experience. We surfed Salsipuedes, braving the steep dirt road and making it back up. It was well worth it; the left was working. It was my favorite wave of the trip.

The ride home was mostly upbeat as Nick drove along to the tunes of the mixtape—until we reached the border. The streets were lined with people selling things and begging for money—some with missing limbs. A woman came up to the car, holding her baby and two small children close to her, look-ing desperate, her hands open. "Please," she said. Nick gave her some money. "God bless you," she muttered, taking the dollars. A boy who looked about eight years old rushed up to my side of the car shouting, "Chiclets! Chiclets!"

"Oh, I love that gum," Chris said, handing me some

change to give him.

Many more people came up to the car, peddling things: hammocks, tamales, blankets, and pottery. Toma bought us all churros, and we inhaled the warm, delicious cinnamon doughnut sticks as we crossed over the border.

NINETEEN

Impending Doom

Unfortunately, when school resumed, Bonnie's hate club was still in full swing. When word got around that Nick and I were dating, things got worse rather than better. Aisha said the girls were just "crunchy," meaning jealous. And, according to her, lots of girls knew Nick at our high school and liked him. But it didn't matter to me why they acted the way they did. I just wanted them to stop. But it got worse.

I was about to leave the girls bathroom one day when all the preppy girls walked through the doorway, blocking my exit. Caitlyn was with them.

"No way, it's the girl who can't afford tampons, so she bleeds down her leg," said Brooke with a snide grin. They chuckled.

"What should we do with this beach trash?" Bonnie said, planting herself right in my way, hands at her hips.

"It makes me barf, throw it out," answered April smugly, standing next to her. I looked at Caitlyn, who was behind them. She averted her eyes and looked down at the floor. My stomach sunk.

"Get outta my way!" I burst out.

"Bag your face," Bonnie persisted, standing firm. "Like, too bad there's no trash can big enough in here for this butt-ugly bunk."

"*You're* a load of bunk," I retorted. "Move!"

"As if," Tiffany shouted in my face.

Tammy snickered, and a self-satisfied, menacing grin spread across Bonnie's face. "Or we could flush it down the toilet—head first," she said.

"For sure, like, let's dunk her in," said Brooke.

"Yeah, give the poser a swirlie," added April.

I froze stiff in horror, my fists clenched and sweaty. April and Brooke closed in on me, their cruel faces without expression. Tammy poked me in the back.

They had me surrounded. I was trapped. My chest tightened; it was becoming difficult to breathe.

There was loud banging on the door, "Let me in," the voice bellowed. Sheila was pressing her back into the door to keep it shut, but the banging persisted. "Come on, open up!"

"We may let you go now," Bonnie hissed, her eyes stony with hate, "but next time we're going to get you, and what we'll do will be worse. Worse than the black eyes and bruises you get from your whore mom."

"Don't you dare talk about my mom!" I shouted.

"Let me in or I'm gonna tell the principal!" the voice shouted. The door gave way despite Sheila's best efforts, and Caitlyn stepped aside. I hurled myself out the doorway, almost tackling the girl trying to get in, and ran down the hall as fast as I could.

Brooke yelled out after me, "Better watch out, *trash*!"

"Yeah, you're going to get it next time!" April hollered.

At lunch I told Aisha what had happened.

"What do you think they're planning to do?" she asked,

looking concerned.

"I don't know. Whatever it is, it's worse than dunking someone's head in the toilet."

"Ugh . . . you've got to report this." Aisha slammed her hand on the table. "This is going too far. It's warped—mental!"

"I can't. I can't let my mom know what's been going on. She'll move us back East."

Aisha raised an eyebrow. "But aren't you wigging out?"

"Do you think they would have dunked me?"

"They're the worst." She sat back, furrowed her brow, and crossed her hands over her chest. "I think they would've gone totally house on you."

"Caitlyn was with them," I said.

"Traitor," Aisha said bitterly.

"She didn't say anything."

"Of course not. She's chicken."

"But *she* wouldn't dunk someone's head in the toilet," I said. *Would she?*

"But would she stop them?" Aisha said.

"I don't think so."

Aisha shook her head and sighed in exasperation. "Are you surfing after school?"

"Does the Pope wear a funny hat?"

"What?"

"That's something Uncle Charlie says."

"Ha! He's so funny," she said. "I'm coming with you. You shouldn't be alone in case those heinous airheads are planning an ambush after school."

When the bell rang, we darted out the front doors, got our skateboards from the bushes, and were skating down the street in no time. We stopped at Aisha's house so she could grab her jacket and a book. Then we skated together all the way up the strand to my house, where I changed into my wetsuit, grabbed my surfboard, and gave Aisha a blanket so she could wrap herself up in it if she needed to. The wind could come up strong on the beach on winter afternoons.

It felt good to wash the day off in the surf. It was choppy wind swell, but it was nice just being out there with the blue sky above and the ocean horizon before me. I was breathing it all in, the fresh sea air filling my lungs, when suddenly, a dolphin leapt into the air right in front of me. I yelped, shaking with excitement. More dolphins joined in, springing up into the air, over and over, bursting with joyful energy.

As a big set-wave left approached, I thought, *the dolphins brought it!* I paddled out to meet it, turning at the perfect spot—right at the peak—dug deep to get more speed, and popped up. Adrenaline surged through me as I made a thrilling drop that opened into a wide, liquid hillscape. Speeding across its bumpy surface and attacking its steep slope, I went off the top, re-entering the force of the wave, carving up to the curl again and again.

Chris paddled out and joined me, and we split peaks and took turns on waves until the sun went down. When we got out, Aisha ran up to us, jumping up and down. "The dolphins got so close to you—major!"

"It was stellar," I replied, smiling.

"You guys were ripping it up out there," she said.

Chris smiled at her. "You should join us."

"No thanks, that water's too cold. I'll stick to my books."

"I've tried to get her in the water," I said. "She shreds on a skateboard."

"Awesome," said Chris. "I'm not a good skater. I'd rather bike."

"It'd be tiring to skate seven miles to the beach and back

each day," I added.

"No way, you live that far?" Aisha asked Chris.

"Yes way," she replied. "I could surf near where I live, but I'd rather surf here with Ellie."

As we walked through the sand and up to the Strand, the wind howled and the crashing surf echoed. The sky was dark. Pink streaks from the sunset lined the sky, and a lone star shone bright up above.

"So, what are we gonna do about those stupid girls?" Aisha said.

"What girls?" said Chris.

"The airhead a-holes at school. They threatened Ellie today that they'd dunk her head in the toilet or do something worse."

"For real?" Chris stopped walking. "A swirly? Mental . . . that's so mean!"

"They're beyond mean," I said. "They call themselves the No Beach Trash Club."

"Shut up! That's so stupid and lame! Ugh—when did this start?"

"It's been happening since the beginning of the year," Aisha said.

"What are you frickin' going to do about it?" Chris asked, keeping up with me as I continued to walk.

"What can I do?"

"Narc on those narbos. Tell the principal—the teacher."

"I can't risk Mom finding out. She'd make me move back to New York."

"Could you threaten them back?" Chris asked. "With something heinous?"

"Like what?" asked Aisha.

"I don't know . . . getting them expelled?"

"If I did that, Mom would definitely find out." I sighed. "If my dad were here, he'd stop them."

"I'm sorry about your dad," said Chris. "My dad left. He's not dead, but he might as well be."

"When did he leave?" I asked.

"A year ago. It's just been me and my mom. My little sister went with him."

"That sucks," said Aisha.

"Sorry," I said. "I didn't know."

We arrived at the spot on the Strand where Chris's bike was parked. I was getting down on myself for not telling Chris about being bullied. As if she could read my mind, she looked into my eyes and asked, "Why didn't you tell me, Ellie?"

"I . . . I guess I wanted to keep surfing the way it is. All good. I didn't want to mess it up by talking about that stuff."

"Nothing can mess up surfing . . . but we can't let them get away with this bogus bunk. Thanks for the 411, Aisha. We'll figure something out."

"For sure," said Aisha. "Those Barfie-doll jerks are gonna get what's comin'."

Chris got on her bike, holding her board with one hand. "With friends, anything is possible," she said as she rode away.

"Most definitely," said Aisha.

After Chris left, we walked to my house. Aisha handed the blanket back to me. "I had to tell Chris," she said. "You aren't mad, are you?"

"No." I was grateful that she cared. She had my back.

Aisha got her skateboard and headed out the garden gate.

"Thanks," I said.

"For what?"

"For being my friend."

Aisha furrowed her brow. "You don't thank people for

that." She began to do some tic-tacs on her skateboard, swinging the front of her board left and right. Then she pushed off and did a kick-turn—a one-hundred-eighty-degree turn—by kicking the board up.

"Wow!" I blurted out. "That was rad!"

She beamed with satisfaction. "I've been working on that one." As she skated away down the alley, she called out, "See you tomorrow!"

"Okay, see ya." I waved.

As I headed through the garden to the outdoor shower, Mom called out to me, "Ellie!" I was surprised that she was home early. I stepped up to her door. She was sitting in front of the antique art deco vanity with its round mirror, her back to me.

"There you are!" she said to my reflection in the mirror, powdering her nose. "Remember that artist, Mark? He wants to paint you. And me. Would you like to come pose for him at his studio with me?"

"Oh . . . sure. Like, right now?"

"Now would be great. I'll wait for you to get dressed." She shut her compact.

"What should I wear?"

"Oh, it doesn't matter." She opened her red lipstick and began to paint her lips. She was wearing an off-the-shoulder dress. "Wait," she said, pressing her lips together like punctuation. "I think I know just the thing for you. My Norma Kamali top."

As we approached downtown, I started getting the creeps. It was desolate at night, like where we had lived in New York City, but here, the factories were completely abandoned. They were sprawled over so much wide-open space—the concrete barren lands of the homeless, with skid row nearby. It was the American frontier gone apocalyptic.

When Mom parked next to an old industrial building, I wasn't sure it was safe to leave such an expensive, bright-red car on the street. She pointed out a Cessna plane that'd been attached to the side of a building with a giant nail. "It's called *Pinned Butterfly*," she said.

We went into the building across from it. Mom had the key. "They used to manufacture coffee and spices here," Mom said as we got into the elevator and rode up to the fifth floor. Mom also had the key to Mark's door. As we walked in, a beautiful female soprano voice echoed opera throughout the huge loft. At four thousand feet, it was four times the size of ours back home. It had giant windows on all sides. There wasn't any furniture except for a semi-circular vintage sofa from the sixties.

"Hello?" Mom called out. We walked toward the sofa, past giant, haunting floor-to-ceiling portraits of people lining the walls between the windows. Mark was squatting on the floor behind the sofa, furiously drawing a figure with a charcoal stick on a life-size piece of paper. He got up when he saw us, exclaiming "Julia!" He hugged Mom, his hands black from the charcoal.

"Thank you for coming," he said.

"Of course," Mom said, kissing his cheek.

"Thank you," he said, looking intensely into my eyes as he embraced Mom, her back to me.

"No worries." I looked at the floor.

Mom stepped back as he said, "You are saving me, Julia. Look at you. Look at you two; angels descended from heaven to the city of angels. Would you like a drink?"

"Yes," Mom sighed.

He walked over to a table in the corner. "How about you,

Ellie?"

"No thanks."

He lifted a bottle of vodka and poured it into two water glasses. He brought one to Mom, which she swigged while he sipped from the other.

"So, where do you want us?" Mom asked flirtatiously.

"Wherever you can be comfortable for an hour or so." He tilted his head, eating her up with his eyes. "But I'd love for you two to look at each other. To connect."

"How about the couch?" Mom sat down and struck a pose.

He leaned in from behind her and whispered in her ear, "Or the bed."

My stomach began to churn with butterflies. *Does he know I heard that?*

Mom batted her eyes at him. "This is good, yes?"

"Yes," he answered. "Can you sit next to her, Ellie?"

I plunked myself down on the sofa.

"Get comfortable," he said, picking up a big canvas and leaning it against the back of a chair.

I slumped against the back of the couch. Mom did, too.

"Look at each other," he said, as he began to paint.

We looked into each other's eyes. It was awkward. I started to crack up, and then Mom burst out laughing. We couldn't stop giggling.

"Can you two keep still? I can't paint your mouths if they're moving."

I took a deep breath and held it. But then I couldn't help it; the giggles were uncontrollable.

"Shh," Mark scolded, working furiously.

Mom broke into laughter, and then we couldn't stop. It was like we were two kids at school, getting into trouble.

"I'm sorry," I said. "I need to go to the bathroom."

Mom told me it was at the other end of the loft. As I walked to the other side, I passed a big mattress on the floor. The bed was unmade, with messy sheets. The sink was industrial and covered in paint splatters. There wasn't any hot water. I noticed some familiar-looking colorful plastic things on the windowsill. I picked them up. They were Mom's chunky sculpture earrings. Here was proof. *She's sleeping with him!*

When I walked back to the sofa, Mom suggested, "Maybe Ellie will feel more comfortable if she chooses the next record."

"Sure, be my guest," Mark said, gesturing to the turntable on a shelf in the corner. I walked over, took the needle off the record that was playing, and put it back in its case. I thought the woman's voice sounded familiar; it was the soundtrack to the movie *Diva*. Mom, Dad, and I had gone to see it two years ago. I flipped through the records and chose Elvis Costello's *Almost Blue*. Mom loved that album. I played side B.

I sat back down. I needed help to not laugh, so I stupidly asked Mom, "How's Peter?"

Mom's hazel eyes looked like they grew a size. They let loose a tear.

"I'm sorry," I said.

She grasped my hand and squeezed it. Forced to look into her eyes, I was confronted with all of her fear and pain. Mom was shaking her head no. Her eyes were so dark, I thought they'd swallow me up. It was like getting worked and held under in Baja, when I hit my head and thought I was going to die and couldn't see which way was up. *Why is she shaking her head?*

"Is he—?" I started to ask.

"Yes," Mom was grimacing, now nodding her head up and down.

"He's dead?"

"They said it was pneumonia. It was so sudden. He went

into the hospital, and two days later . . ."

"Oh my God, Mom, that's awful." I reached out and hugged her tighter than I ever had. She was shaking. She seemed so fragile in my arms now; mine had grown strong from paddling.

"I didn't know how to tell you. I'm so sorry, darling. I should've told you sooner."

"It's okay, Mom," I lied. I was upset she hadn't told me. *How long has she known?*

"Sorry, Mark," Mom said, patting her eyes with her fingers. It didn't work; her black eye makeup was streaming down her cheeks.

"You've never looked more beautiful," he said. "You're raw, open. Do you mind if I take some pictures of you for reference?"

"Do you mind, Ellie?" Mom asked me.

"No worries," I said.

He took his camera out and took some pictures of us. This time, Mom and I held each other's gaze without giggling. Her hand was shaking. I squeezed it, trying to make it stop.

"I've got it," Mark said finally. "Thank you."

"Our pleasure," said Mom, getting up. "I've just got to fix my face." She went to the bathroom, and I followed.

After Mom washed her face, I asked, "How long have you two been seeing each other?"

"We're just casual," she said, wiping her face with a towel. "Nothing serious." She looked at me in the reflection of the broken piece of mirror on the window ledge. As she put her makeup back on, I noticed that her pupils remained pinpoints under the harsh light bulb above her.

We made our way back to Mark to say goodbye.

"Hey, I'll walk you guys out," he said. "I'm going to get a

coffee at Al's and play a round of pool. Want to come?"

"Maybe later," Mom said. "Ellie and I are going out on the town."

"We are?" I asked.

"Yup. How would you like a bowl of borscht to start?"

"That sounds great!" I said.

I was relieved to see that Mom's car was still parked outside. Mark said goodbye to us and then went into the building with the *Pinned Butterfly* nailed to its side. I noticed that it said "American Hotel" on its black awning.

On the drive over to Gorky's Café, Mom asked, "Do you want to see X at the Roxy?"

"Wow, Mom! Yes!" I jumped up and down in my seat. "You had this planned all along, didn't you?"

She smiled. "The night is young."

It was the best night I'd ever had with my mom. Gorky's reminded me of Veselka's in New York City, where Mom, Dad, and I always went for pierogies and borscht, Dad's favorite. Then Mom drove me to the Roxy on Sunset in West Hollywood, where we saw X, one of my new favorite L.A. bands. I'd heard them on Rodney on the ROQ when I first arrived in L.A. I wasn't sure if Mom would be able to get me into the club, but she put her red lipstick on me in the car and let me wear her vintage leopard-fur jacket. I got in the door with no questions. Mom and I stood in front and jumped up and down for the whole show, sweaty and scrunched together with the crowd. I kept us safe, just far enough away from the slam pit that formed during the faster songs.

When Exene wailed, "Come back to me," the song about her sister who died, Mom put her arm around me, tears streaming down her face. Our sweat mixed with our tears. We bonded that night.

I didn't even mind being tired for my surf session the next morning. But when I came home from school the next day, I heard loud shouting coming from the house. I stopped to listen in the hallway by the surfboards, where I couldn't be seen. Aunt Jen and Mom were having an argument in the kitchen.

"Don't try to tell me what to do! That's what we're doing!"

"Julia, have you seen your daughter?" Jen asked. "She's radiant. She's healthy. She's happy here. And she loves to surf more than anything. It's been her saving grace through all of this. It's helped her, and you're taking that away from her? Please. Let her stay with us! For her sake!"

"*You* are trying to take her away from me. You were always jealous of me, and what I had . . . and now you're trying to take away the only thing I have left. Some sister you are!"

"That's not what's happening here. You need to look at what's best for Ellie. Are you giving her what she needs? Are you able to? You're so busy with the gallery, you hardly have time for anything else."

"Yeah, well, I'm an only parent now. I need to face that, and you need to back off and butt out. Ellie's *my* daughter. *I* decide what's best for her, and we're going back home."

Mom's words hit me like a punch in the stomach.

"What kind of parent passes out from drinking too much, and sets fire to the house?" Jen said.

"Look, I'm sorry. We've been over this. I'm grateful for what you and Charlie have done for us, but for work, I need to go back to New York *for good* this time. And I'm not going to leave my daughter here."

This can't be happening! I felt sick, but I dared not move.

"Julia," my aunt said gently, "there's something you don't

understand."

"Oh, really. What's that?"

"Being a surfer."

Mom let out a huff.

Jen continued, "It's not something you can just *stop* all of a sudden and think you're going to be okay. This is serious. Ellie has worked hard to get where she is; she's made it her sole focus in life. It's her passion, her love. And you're going to take that away from her? She's going to *hate* you for it."

"Of course you think she hates me. That's what you secretly want, isn't it? You want everyone to like *you* more than me. And why wouldn't they? You're always so likable—and I'm the bitch."

"No, Julia, this is about Ellie! Not you! How can you be so selfish?"

"Selfish? For your information, Ellie's father and I had a plan to bring her up in the city, among art and culture, with a good education and everything the city has to offer. Not in some hick town where all people do is hang out at the beach. I've gotten Ellie into one of the best schools, so she might actually have a chance to go to college, instead of being a beach bum all her life."

"I'm only thinking of what's best for her," Jen replied.

I could hear Mom's high heels clicking towards me. I quickly snuck into my room to listen through the door.

"Wait!" Jen screamed like nothing I had ever heard out of her before. "Julia! Wait!"

The footsteps stopped.

"Stay," my aunt pleaded desperately, like she was trying to talk someone out of jumping off a building. "Please stay. Don't do this. If your job here hasn't worked out, it's okay, you can take some time off. We can make it work, the four of us.

Don't do this to Ellie. She's not crying every time she thinks of her dad anymore. She's in a good place now."

Mom raised her voice to a shrill tone. "Excuse me, but she's *my* daughter and *I* decide what's best for her!" I heard her stomp towards the hall. My stomach twisted in knots.

"But what's *really* best for her? Not some idea of what you want her to be!" Jen cried out.

Mom ignored her.

"What's happened to you?" Jen shouted at the top of her lungs.

Mom continued down the hall, cursing under her breath, and went through the back door to the garden. She screeched and yelled out curse words in frustration. Her high heels probably got stuck in the dirt, but it wasn't funny now. I slid down the wall of my room, collapsing onto the floor.

I couldn't believe this was happening. Over a year had gone by, and California had become my home. Aunt Jen and Charlie were like my adopted parents. I had friends now. Mom was always away working. Why, then, would she make me go back with her to New York?

She didn't understand me. She didn't care that surfing was everything to me. Chris was winning competitions. I wanted to join her, or be there to root her on.

That night, as I lay in bed, my head throbbed thinking about it. I'd be forced to say goodbye to Aunt Jen, Charlie, Aisha, Chris, Liam, Wilkies, Zuzu . . . everyone. It would kill me. Poor Zuzu wouldn't understand why. Why did she have to suffer? *I won't be able to say goodbye to Nick without falling apart*, I thought, gazing out the window at the twinkling stars. I touched my lips, remembering his kiss in Baja. I wanted to kiss him again.

Rodney on the ROQ wasn't any help that night. "Institutionalized" by Suicidal Tendencies only increased my aggravation. Back to the rats on the subways and to the sad, worried, hunched-over people who never looked you in the eye. Back to the dirt and trash on the streets. The gray buildings. The cold, empty loft, without Dad. Hot tears blurred the stars into circle shapes. *Dad!* I cried out in my mind and, with all my soul: *Help me!*

To my surprise, when Charlie got back from work the next morning, he had it out with Mom. I could hear it from my room.

"You're not taking Ellie *anywhere*," he said. "Not until you get yourself clean."

"You've got no place telling me what to do," she spat.

"Sure I do."

"What you think doesn't matter in the slightest."

"I'm not going to let you take her," he said in a matter-of-fact tone.

"Legally I can and I will. I'm her mother!" Mom was angry now. I could hear it in how her voice was wavering.

Charlie chuckled. "Ha! Go and try. They'll laugh you out of the courthouse."

"Who are you to tell me what to do?"

"I'm the guy who's been supporting my wife's sister and niece this whole year, that's who! But I'm happy to. Look, have you even asked Ellie what *she* wants to do?"

I took that as my cue to run out to the living room. "I don't want to go," I said. "I want to stay here."

Mom looked shocked to see me. She was sitting at the table. "You don't know what's best, dear. You're too young to know." I was about to protest when she added, "Your father wanted you to have a good education. That's why he chose a college preparatory school for you. They are holding a place for you in the fall."

When she mentioned Dad and what he had wanted for me, I clammed up. I couldn't speak. My head was reeling.

Uncle Charlie paced around the room in a circle, looking at me. Then he stood at the table opposite of Mom. "Whatever you two decide, it's not happening now. Ellie needs to finish junior year. There's no reason to move right now and upset her life, just because you'd rather work in New York."

Mom let out a loud sigh. "I can always go ahead first. And Ellie can fly out this summer, before senior year in the fall."

"That'll give you time to get your act together," said Charlie.

"I'm perfectly capable of handling everything," Mom said, standing up. "I run a very successful gallery, and I don't need you telling me what I can and can't do." She stomped off in her heels.

"You know what I mean," he yelled out. "It's got nothing to do with work. I don't want you going to the hospital again."

I ran back to my bedroom and slammed my head onto my pillow. *Why didn't I say anything? Why did I freeze? Did a part of me feel that she was right? Was this what Dad wanted for me—to finish at the collegiate high school in New York?* That *was* what we had always spoke about. He'd said I'd be a good historian one day, like him. He was proud of me for it. But I loved surfing more than anything, and I needed it. It had become a form of therapy. It was a substitute filler for that empty space in me since Dad died.

My throat tightened at the thought of never seeing Nick again. I was all mixed up. To clear my head, I went out surfing.

On my way back, Wilkies waved and shouted out, "Hey, Charger!"

"Hi," I said as I walked up to him standing next to his old, faded-blue car.

"How's your mom doin'?"

"She's . . . ah, I don't know. She drinks too much, but she doesn't think so."

"Hmm . . ." he grunted. "It's hard to help someone who doesn't think they need help."

"Yeah," I said, "and now she wants to take me back to New York. This summer we leave for good."

"What? What's a surfer girl like you gonna do in New York City? Ha!" He punched the air in frustration. I'd never seen him look so upset.

"I know," I said. "I don't want to go. But she said it's what . . . what Dad wanted for me, to graduate from a good collegiate high school."

"Well, that's the dumbest reason I ever heard. Doesn't your mom know there's some great high schools here? Has she ever heard about Chadwick or Marymount? For Pete's sake!" He slammed his hand down on his car's hood.

"Guess not," I said. I was touched that Wilkies felt so strongly that I should stay. For a moment he looked like he was going to cry.

"Hey, I could try and talk to her if you'd like," he said. "She may listen to me, since I've been there and all . . . I mean, about her drinking problem. And I can tell her about the schools here."

"You'd do that?"

"Course I would," he said.

"Thanks."

Talking to Ol' Man Wilkies gave me a glimmer of hope that I might actually be able to stay in California.

That night, I told Mom that Wilkies wanted to talk to her. She said she was too busy with work right now, and to give her a couple of weeks.

The spring of junior year wasn't so bad, except for Bonnie's group. Now they were spreading a rumor that my mom was a prostitute. They continued to threaten to do something horrible to me, but they hadn't yet. I was worrying about bigger issues now, like having my worst fear realized: having to go back to New York. If that happened, I felt like they'd win; their constant "Go back to New York" would become a reality. I had to think of a way to convince Mom to stay, or at least to let *me* stay. But was that what Dad would've wanted for me?

Aside from this, Aisha, Liam, Danny, and I joked around a lot at school. Nick joined us when he wasn't in the auto shop, along with his fellow senior friends. Our group of friends grew. It also included some junior girls from another homeroom class, Michelle Coleman and Andrea Garcia. Michelle was a tall, whip-smart girl with glasses and brown hair that she tied back in a neat ponytail. She always had something witty and hilarious to say under her breath to combat the meanness of Bonnie's group. Like the time Bonnie and April sneered at me with their noses up in the air as they walked by, and Michelle noted that they must not be able to breathe so well after their "spring-break nose jobs." Andrea, whom we called Drea, had an asymmetrical new wave haircut that was short on one side and chin-length on the other. She wore bright, hip clothes, and when she flashed her friendly smile, it showed off her perfect white teeth. She was full of energy and very social; everyone liked her. When she became a part of our circle, she gave it new life.

Our group seemed to grow larger by the minute. Danny's friends Dave Travers and Mike Adams, who we called Mikey, also joined our crew. They didn't like the preppy girls. They hated everything they stood for. They were local boys whose parents had grown up here and dressed in t-shirts without collars. The preppy girls thought of them as "beach trash," too. But they called the girls names back, like "stuck-up yuppie wannabes," "preppy airheads," "lame preps," "mall-maggots," and "poofers" after their big, blow-dried hair. Dave and Mikey looked rough and tough. You wouldn't want to be on the other side of a fight against them. I was glad they were on our side; they were really sweet to their friends.

Nick and I were getting along great in and out of the water. He insisted on driving me and Aisha to school and back home each day, and we'd go out to the Kettle or to Hermosa with him and our friends. Nick and Toma were making a regular habit of surfing with me and Chris.

Nick talked excitedly about summer break, which was coming up. About how we would surf together all day long and go on surf trips to Baja and Trestles for the south swells. Chris had a contest coming up, and she invited me to join her and compete in it, too. But privately, I knew I wouldn't be able to do any of these things, because I would have to get on a plane and go back to New York that summer. I tried to push it out of my mind. I didn't want to tell anyone and ruin the moment.

Nick and I were crazy for each other. Each night, after surfing till dark, we kissed goodnight at the alley gate to Jen's garden. One kiss turned to many, and it was getting harder and harder to stop kissing and part until we saw each other next, during dawn patrol. But a part of me was holding back, because I knew I'd have to leave and I couldn't tell him.

TWENTY

Lost

I was home one Sunday when the phone rang. I picked it up. "Hello?"

"Hi, I'm looking for Julia. Is she there?" It was a man's voice.

"No, she's at the gallery," I said.

"Uh, no . . . she's not here. This is Richard. I work for Julia here at the gallery, but she hasn't been in today or yesterday. We figured maybe she got the flu or something, but there are some things I need to ask her for some clients."

"I can double-check," I said. I ran through the garden and looked in her room, but it was empty and her car was gone.

I ran back to the phone. "No, she's not here. If she's not at the gallery, then where is she?" I asked, thinking out loud.

"I don't know. I was hoping you could tell me. She's not due to go to New York for another month. Do you have any idea where she might be?"

"No, I'm sorry," I said.

"Okay. Well, if you see her, please tell her to call me."

My throat went dry, but I managed, "Okay." I hung up the phone. My mind raced. *Where could she be?* The only place I could think of was Mark's studio in downtown, or the café she'd taken me to in Venice. I could skate there, but that would take hours. I decided it was best to get Jen and drive up there. But I didn't know where Jen was, or when she'd be back. I called Charlie at the fire station, thinking he might know where Jen was. He was out on a call, so I left a message.

I ran down to the beach, thinking maybe someone I knew would be there. No one was in the beach parking lot, so I bolted to the shore. I couldn't quite make out anyone in their wetsuits. They all looked like the same black figures out there, silhouettes against the afternoon sky. I squinted, trying to catch my breath. A wave was coming in, and a figure hopped up and rode it to shore. *It's Nick!* My heart pounded against my chest.

"Nick!" I shouted out.

He turned and saw me, then took some whitewater in. "Where's your board, Charger?" he asked, smiling, his head tilted sideways.

"I think my mom's lost," I said.

"What?"

"Her work called—they said she hasn't been there for days."

"Where would she go?" he asked, his brow furrowed.

"The only place I can think of is an artist's studio in downtown L.A., or—"

"Let's go," he said.

"Are you sure?"

"We'll take the Morris," he said. "I mean, Wizard."

"I don't want to ruin your surf session."

"Without you it's crap anyway." His sea-glass eyes glistened.

"Not true. Without me you get some waves in."

"That's true," he said with a smile.

When I met his gaze, my knees went weak and I burst into tears. He stepped in and hugged me.

"Sorry to get you wet, I just couldn't bear to see you like that."

"It's okay," I gulped. It felt so good to be in his arms. I didn't care about getting wet. *I need to feel his strong arms around me.* I hugged him tight.

"Are you okay?" he asked.

"Yeah," I said, but the truth was, I was feeling desperate. I didn't want to lose Mom, too. I stepped back, breaking our embrace.

"We'll find her," he assured me. His gaze was so soft and kind, I had to fight to resist the urge to melt in it and embrace him again.

"Okay," I said, wiping the tears from my eyes.

"I'll get Wizard and pick you up," he offered.

"Okay," I repeated.

I focused on putting one foot in front of the other, making my way back to the house. When I got there, Zuzu ran in circles around me, brushing into my leg. I dropped down on my knees and hugged her. She licked my cheek. I went to my room to get the Polaroid of me, Mom, and Dad that I kept there, in case we needed to show someone what Mom looked like.

Nick arrived in a few minutes, and I jumped into the passenger seat. As we drove down Vista Del Mar, a lone hawk soared above us. I thought of Dad and said a private prayer to him, to help us find Mom. Los Angeles was a big city.

As we got on the 10 freeway, Nick said again, "We'll find your mom, don't worry." Side two of the Minutemen's *What Makes a Man Start Fires?* played in his car stereo. "Any exit look familiar?" he asked.

"It's east of skid row, near a bar called Al's. It's in a hotel."

"We'll find it," he said.

I smiled at him. He was so nice, but I wasn't sure that we would find it. When we passed the L.A. river, the spot we were in felt familiar, so we got off at 4th Street, which also rang a bell. We headed down 4th, and things started to look familiar. We took a right at South Hewitt, and I spotted the *Pinned Butterfly* sculpture on the side of the American Hotel building where Al's Bar was. I pointed it out to Nick.

"Radical," he remarked.

We parked and went up to the building across the street, where Mark's studio was. The door was locked, so we went to Al's Bar. I asked the bartender if he'd seen "the artist Mark," but he said he didn't know people's names. I explained to him that Mark lived across the street, but he said grumpily, "Hundreds of artists live here." I pulled out the Polaroid. He recognized Mom, but said, "Sorry, I haven't seen her recently."

We went back to Mark's building and waited to see if anyone would come by. No one did. The streets were empty except for the homeless.

"The gallery might have his phone number," I said. "But they're closed now."

"Could we look him up in the phone book?" asked Nick.

"We could if I knew his last name."

Nick exhaled. "Harsh," he said.

"We could go to the café near here where Mom took me one night. She drove me there, so I can figure out how to get there by car."

"Okay, lead the way," said Nick.

We hopped into Wizard and found our way to Gorky's. But the waitress didn't recognize her and said, "Things don't get hopping here till late."

We had school the next day, so we started to drive home. When we got back on the 10, I remembered the café in Venice. Nick insisted we go there, too, so we took the freeway all the way to the beach, then went south on Pacific Avenue. When I recognized the street, North Venice Avenue, I told Nick to turn right and we pulled up across from the West Beach Café. We hopped out, crossed the street, and went in.

I was relieved to see that the same waiter was there. I showed him the Polaroid and asked if he'd seen Mom. "We were here before," I said. "We ordered . . . Screaming Orgasms."

Nick did a double take, his eyes wide. I'm sure I blushed.

"Yeah, I remember her," the waiter said. "Sorry, I haven't seen her today."

"Do you remember when you last saw her?" I asked.

"Not sure. Maybe last week?"

My heart sank. How were we supposed to find her? Suddenly, it felt so stuffy in there, I thought I would faint. I ran outside to get some air and kept walking toward the beach. A guy loitering in the shadows grabbed my arm. I tried to pull away, but he clung on.

"Hey, get off my girlfriend!" shouted Nick, running up to us. Finally, I was able to break free and ran to Nick. "Are you okay?" he asked.

"Yeah. Thanks." He took my hand in his, and together we walked back to his car. My heart was pounding like crazy; from the fright of being grabbed by some guy, the anxiety of not finding Mom, and the excitement of Nick calling me his girlfriend. That was the first time he'd said it.

On the drive back, neither of us said much. Nick took out the Minutemen cassette and put another one in the deck. The Descendants song "Tonyage" came on.

"Did he just say his girlfriend's a surfer?" I asked.

"Yup," Nick said, "and my girlfriend's a surfer and she's beautiful." He took my hand in his and gave me a warm smile. *He said it again!* I smiled back. A wave of affection took hold of me. At the same time, my hand began to sweat in his, so I pulled it away. Not knowing where Mom was, or how she was doing, was gnawing at my insides. To our right, the ocean was navy-blue, the sky not much lighter.

I asked Nick to pull up to the back of the house so I could check if Mom was back. When he parked, I fought back the urge to jump on top of him. *He's so close—and so hot!* "Thanks," I said.

"No worries. Sorry we didn't find her. I'm sure she'll turn up soon."

I started to open my door to get out, but he popped open his door first and raced around the front of the car and opened my door. I got out and he leaned in towards me, his eyes dancing with mine, and kissed me. For a few minutes I forgot about everything. It was just Nick and me and our hearts beating so close. He started to kiss my neck and, with my lips now free, I whispered, "I have to go," though my entire body wanted more.

"Okay," he said, backing off. "Call me if you need me."

"Kay," I said, unlatching the gate.

"Or any time," he added. "Want to meet up to surf first light?"

"Yeah," I said. My knees went weak when I met his gaze.

I raced to Mom's room to check if she was back, though something was telling me she wouldn't be. She wasn't.

When I opened the back door to the house, it was such a relief to find Aunt Jen that I ran into her arms and burst into tears. Zuzu ran in circles around us, brushing into my leg.

"Mom's missing," I said, squeezing my aunt.

"Oh God. Okay. Don't worry, we'll find her." She held me close. She didn't seem too shocked. I explained the phone call and told her how Nick and I had checked for her at both cafés and at Mark's studio in downtown. I told her I planned to call the gallery when it opened in the morning so I could get Mark's number.

Jen called Charlie, and he told Jen he would handle it. He would file a missing person report at the Manhattan Beach police station right away; he had friends there. He said not to worry, that we should both get some sleep. He also said he would personally set out to find Mom first thing in the morning, when he was off duty, if she wasn't back by then.

Jen tried to comfort me as best she could. She made macaroni and cheese for dinner, with fresh-baked peanut butter cookies and hot chocolate with marshmallows for dessert. I couldn't eat much, though. She lit a fire in the fireplace, and we sat gazing at it as it blazed, its blue and orange flames flickering. Zuzu leaned into me. As I pet her, I finally started to relax.

"Nick called me his girlfriend today," I said.

"He did?" Jen's mouth was agape. "Wow, you guys are so cute together. That's great. Isn't it?" She beamed her radiant smile.

"Yeah, it's just that with everything that's happened today . . . I feel too much. Like I'm going to explode."

"It's a lot," said Jen. "Let's get some sleep, huh? I bet Julia will be back home sleeping in her bed like usual when we wake up."

"Yeah," I said, but I didn't think so. I said it just to comfort Jen and myself. My stomach knots were forming, telling me that something wasn't right.

Before falling asleep, I put my Walkman on, relieved that Rodney on the ROQ was on the radio. Black Flag's "Nervous Breakdown" summed up my frustration. I looked up at the stars and, with all my heart, asked Dad to please help Mom find her way home. When Nena's "99 Luftballons" came on, my spirits lifted a bit and I drifted off into dreamland.

That morning, before surfing, I peeked into Mom's room and turned on the light. The empty room stared back at me, and the gnawing in my stomach intensified.

I paddled out at first light alone. The water froze my face when I duck-dove. It was coldest here in the spring. After duck-diving three waves, I was relieved to make it outside, so that I didn't have to go under again. I sat on my board and breathed in the ocean air, but the gnawing wouldn't leave my stomach. *If Mom is gone, too, I'll be an orphan.*

I rubbed the rail of my board, calling the dolphins. In a few minutes, there she was—the dolphin with the crescent moon scar! She surfaced six feet from me. It was her for sure; the scar was clear, but I could hardly believe it. She studied me with her dark, intelligent eye. All at once, I experienced communion with her. I felt that she had empathy for me. Floating on the surface, half out of the water, she stayed for a few minutes, which felt like a really long time. Then she disappeared underwater.

I took some deep breaths, taking in all the nature around me. Above the light-blue horizon, the clouds became pink as the sun rose behind me. Suddenly, the dolphin breached, bursting her whole body and tail into the air. It took my breath away. She plunged back underwater, leaving me with my heart beating frantically. Then, from behind me, she leapt into the air over me, spraying water everywhere. Exhilarated, I felt lucky to experience this, to be alive, to have Jen and Charlie, and to be Nick's girlfriend. Even school was okay, because I had friends there now.

A wave was surging on the horizon. I lay on my board, turned around, and paddled for it. We met and it took me, leading me with it as I rode its liquid slope. I soared, flying down the line toward its crumbling end, where it gushed and sprayed iridescent foam.

The moon was still bright in the sky, and some stars twinkled. It was a thrill to see Nick paddle out, even though I knew he would come like he said he would. *My boyfriend!* I glowed. He asked if Mom had shown up, and I shook my head.

The waves were chest-high and steep. Nick said to go when a juicy right was rolling through, so I went for it and got a backside barrel while crouching low, grabbing my rail. Chris cheered me on as she paddled out; she'd seen me get cover and was stoked for me. A little while later, Toma and his friend, John, showed up, and then Liam and Danny.

There was offshore wind, and as a green, crystal-clear wave broke north of us, its back spray formed a rainbow. I gasped, it was so beautiful. Behind it, the red-and-white-striped stacks of the steam plant reached sky-high to their smoky ends. An oil tanker sat out in the distance, and beyond it, the purple Santa Monica Mountains. To the south, I could see the pier in the distance, and beyond that, the lilac cliffs of Palos Verdes and the blue outline of Catalina Island.

It was a good morning. I didn't want to get out of the water to go to school. No one did. Chris had to get out first because she had the long bike ride back to Torrance. I got out with her and told her about my mom.

"I'm so sorry, Ellie. I hope she comes back soon." She put her board down to give me a hug before getting on her bike. "I'll be back after school," she said.

I ran up to the house, hoping Mom was back. I opened the garden gate and the door to her room, but she wasn't there. I rushed across the garden, opened the back door to the cottage, and set my board down in the rack in the hallway. Charlie was back home, and Nick's dad, Bob, was there too, sitting at the kitchen table. Jen was baking muffins.

"Charger—how was it?" asked Charlie when he saw me.

"Good," I said. "Barrels."

"Nice!" said Bob.

"You guys should get out there," I said.

"Ah, surfing's overrated," said my uncle with a side grin, making a motion with his arm like "forget that."

Just then Nick walked in through the back door. "What are you doing here, Dad?" he asked.

"Wha—I was going to ask you the same question," said Bob.

"I wanted to see if Ellie's all right," he said.

I turned to Nick and smiled.

"Get to school, kid!" said his dad.

"For sure," Nick said. He smiled at me, his green eyes twinkling, and backed out past the surfboards in the hall. I followed him to the garden.

"Thanks for checking on me," I said. "I felt like I was going to explode earlier. It's all too much. Everything is crazy." Suddenly I had to pour my heart out and tell him everything. "I don't want to go back to school, because those mean girls want to do something horrible to me."

"What?" he asked, looking confused.

"Something worse than dunking my head in the toilet," I said.

"They did that to you?"

"No, they were going to, but I got away—but they said they're going to do something worse now."

"Want me to scare them so they leave you alone?" He made a fist and punched his hand.

I shook my head. "No, they're not worth it."

"Who is it? Is it those same jerks with the tacks who said this?"

"Yeah," I said. "Bonnie Bradford's the leader, but there's

also Brooke, April, Tammy . . . basically all the girls in my homeroom except for Aisha."

"What a buncha bogus losers!" The way Nick looked at me with his gray-green eyes made my heart skip. I felt hot. I was sure I was blushing.

"Well, I'd say let's cut school today and just surf, but I know my dad would kill me," he said.

"No, it's okay. School's only a couple of hours, and I'll be with Aisha."

"Well then, let me at least give you a ride," he said. "I'll give you both a ride, and I'll pick you up right after I change."

"Okay, thanks," I said, smiling. He stepped in towards me. My heart started pounding as he gave me a hug. It felt good to be in his arms. I let him hold me.

"It's gonna be okay," he said gently in my ear. "You're okay. And they'll find your mom."

"I hope so," I said, backing away out of his embrace.

"They will," he said. He picked up his board and headed out the gate. "And we'll have a rad afternoon surf sesh! See ya in a bit!"

"Okay," I called back.

When I went back inside the house, there were two policemen sitting at the table with Bob and Charlie. I must have looked like I'd seen a ghost, because Charlie got up and assured me that there wasn't any bad news. These were his friends, and they were going to help us find Mom.

"Ellie, I can take you to school," Jen said.

"No, I'm okay. Nick's gonna take me."

"Oh. Well, would you like a muffin? I made blueberry."

"Sure," I said. I went to my room to change, and when

I came back out everyone was gone except for Jen, who was cleaning up in the kitchen. I took a muffin from the bowl.

"Hey there," she said as she turned to me. "Give me a hug." I pressed into her, my head next to her heart. She held me for a few moments. I didn't feel annoyed, like when Mom squeezed me too tight. A pang of guilt struck me for feeling that way about Mom now. *Where is she? Is she okay?* Why did she always make everything about herself? I resented her for that.

Guilt tore at me with the thought that I didn't really need her anymore. Jen and Charlie were such great substitute parents. I wanted to stay here with them and never go back to New York.

"You should get out there," I said to Jen, squeezing her tight. "There are barrels."

"Okay," she said, choking up. "Maybe later." She was trying not to cry.

"You should go now before the onshore wind picks up," I said, releasing my embrace and backing up in order to meet her gaze.

She broke into a smile, her eyes shining with pride and brimming with tears.

"I'll call the gallery at lunch," I said. "That's when they open. I'm sure she's at that guy Mark's house or something."

"Okay," Jen said. "Or I can call?"

"I got it," I said.

TWENTY-ONE

The Truth

During lunch, I went to the school office to call Mom's gallery when it opened. The same guy who had called me, Richard, answered.

"It's Ellie, Julia's daughter."

"Oh hi, have you seen her?"

"No. I was hoping you could give me her friend's number, the artist. Mark is his name."

There was silence on the other end of the line.

"Hello?" I asked.

"Mark Santiago? She didn't tell you? He's dead."

"What? But I just saw him! Is there another artist named Mark?"

"No. Only one Mark. He OD-ed. Overdosed. It's just awful. I'm so sorry. You're welcome to contact the other artists, but I already have and no one has seen her."

In a state of shock, I left the office and went to sit with Aisha on the stairs by the parking lot. I was just about to tell her about Mom and Mark when the No Beach Trash Club rushed up behind us. I turned around just in time to see that Bonnie was holding up a pink spray can.

"Pegged!" she shouted, aiming it at my head.

I jumped up, raising both of my arms to block her. I

grabbed her arm that was holding the spray can and pushed it down. Bonnie struggled, trying to get out of my grasp, but I was so much stronger from surfing that I forced her down to the ground. I pried the spray can loose from her grip. Aisha picked it up.

"Nair?" Aisha said. "Really? You're sick in the head."

"Get off me!" Bonnie squealed, wriggling as I pinned her down.

"What were you trying to do?" I demanded, adrenaline pumping through me.

"Make all your grody hair fall out," Brooke smirked.

"Better step off, or I'm gonna spray *you* with it," Aisha said, raising the spray can threateningly. "All of you!" Brooke and the others stepped back.

"No, Aisha—don't stoop to their level," I said, releasing Bonnie. As I stood up, my heart raced.

"Most definitely," Aisha fumed. "They're mental."

"Bite me!" said April.

Bonnie, muddied from the ground, grimaced as she got up on her hands and knees and spat, "This trash thinks she's above us." She slowly rose, glaring at me with hate. "Your mom's a whore!"

Someone was running toward me. *It's Nick!*

"You think I don't know how she looks?" I shouted, louder than my pounding heart, and despite the stabbing knot in my stomach. "She's heartbroken! My dad died, and she can't deal with it! Then her best friend died, and now Mark is dead! But if Mom's alive, I'm going to tell her to keep trying."

Aisha's eyes were locked on mine, full of compassion. It gave me strength. And Nick was here, by my side. He reached for my hand and squeezed it. I turned to Bonnie, who was now standing. "Nothing you ever say or do will hurt me, because I know it's not true," I told her.

"What's true is you have friends because you're a good person, Ellie," Aisha said. "Not like you jerks!"

Just then, Liam, Danny, Drea, and Michelle came over. They'd probably heard my outburst.

"Ellie can get barreled by a double overhead wave," said Nick. "What can you lamebrains do?"

"Lame loser preps," Liam added.

"You're just beach trash," Bonnie hissed under her breath, only loud enough for me to hear. She scrunched up her nose like she smelled something bad, her hands planted on her hips.

"No duh," Tammy echoed, by her side. "Like, bag your face."

"You stuck-up bimbettes better step off!" Drea exclaimed with a dismissive wave of her hand.

"Yeah, you'll need another nose job after you get decked," Michelle piped in.

Dave and Mikey showed up to see what all the commotion was about.

I stepped right in front of Bonnie's face. "My dad taught me it's what's inside a person that counts. And you're ugly inside."

Bonnie sneered, backing away.

"And a total bitch," Aisha said.

"Moded!" shouted Dave.

"Scratch!" added Danny.

"You better leave my girlfriend alone," Nick said, stepping up next to me.

"Yeah, get bent, poofers!" Mikey made a fist.

Bonnie and her group had shocked expressions on their faces. They weren't going to go up against bruisers like Mikey and Dave.

I couldn't believe it. I'd stood up for myself. And so had my friends. *I have friends!* I realized. *Nick called me his girlfriend in front of everyone!*

Suddenly, the school security guard walked up to us. "What's going on here?" he asked.

"She tried to spray Ellie's head with Nair," Aisha said, pointing at Bonnie. She handed the spray can to the security guard.

"What?" Nick said, utterly shocked.

"I blocked it just in time," I said.

"Both of you—to the principal!" spouted the security guard.

"But Ellie didn't do anything," Aisha protested.

"You too," the man said to Aisha. "The three of you. Follow me."

"Hey, Mr. Farren, these two didn't do anything," Nick said in our defense.

"Sorry, but I have to take them all to the principal," he said. He obviously knew Nick.

"I'll wait outside the office," Nick said to me.

"No you won't, Nick, you're going straight back to class. All of you." The security guard waved his arm. "Unless you all want to come with me to the office."

When Aisha and I explained to the principal what had happened, she suspended Bonnie for a week but let us go back to class. It may have helped that Aisha was an honor student. Bonnie argued that I pushed her into the mud, but the principal said I'd acted in self-defense.

When the bell rang after school, a crowd of friends gathered outside my homeroom.

"Oh my God, are you okay?" said Drea, turning to me.

"Yeah," I said, "thanks."

"Like, I can't believe what they tried to do to you—that's crazy," said Michelle.

"Finally, Bonnie got what she deserved," Aisha said.

"Did you see her big hair get flattened in the mud?" Danny said, cracking up.

"Thanks for having my back, guys," I said, "but there's much better things to think about. Like how the waves are right now."

"Yeah, Charger, let's go," said Liam.

"I'm down for the beach," Aisha agreed.

"For sure," said Michelle.

Just then, Nick arrived. Like magnets, we rushed to hug each other. At his touch, I felt a spark which ran throughout my body. My heart radiated waves of gratitude.

It turned out to be a good day. I'd faced Bonnie's group at their worst. And beat them. I didn't feel scared anymore. They seemed childish to me now, like middle-schoolers. *I'm stronger than them*, I realized. They were all threats and hardly any action.

All of us went to the beach after school. Danny took Michelle and Drea in his car, and Nick drove me, Aisha, and Liam. Some of us surfed, some of us hung out. When I'd stopped in to grab my board from the house, Jen hadn't heard any news about Mom yet, but she told me not to worry and to go get some waves. I couldn't tell Jen about Mark. Not yet. I told myself I'd tell her after surfing.

I did catch waves, which was the best remedy for any worry in the world. Saltwater, the magic elixir. The minute I dove in, I was refreshed. Renewed. Surfing not only demanded my full attention and awareness, it required a connection with the power of the ocean as it moved me. In harmony, I sensed what spot to paddle to, and when. It took perfect timing to catch a wave. Tuning into the ever-changing shape of the water, bending myself to match its form. Being in the present moment, in communion with the ocean, there was no space for worry. At one with the waves, the past or future didn't exist.

Chris showed up, and my heart nearly leapt out of my chest at the sight of Nick, paddling up to me, beaming a smile, with Toma just behind him. All of us took turns and split peaks. We were stoked just to be out there, though it was only shoulder-high and mostly close-outs.

When we got out, Aisha told Chris how I'd stood up to Bonnie's group. Chris said, "Most triumphant! Way to kick ass, Charger!"

"Legit, she told them kooks what's up," said Nick.

"No way," said Toma.

"Way!" Liam piped in. "She set 'em straight, all right—big time! This one almost got 'em back with their own poison," he added, putting his arm around Aisha. "I kid you not."

"Dude, I didn't know Ellie had mad skills," Aisha blurted out. "She fights as well as she surfs!"

"For real?" Nick raised an eyebrow at me. I beamed at him, and we both cracked up.

"Chee-uh!" added Danny. "She told 'em to kick rocks."

"Righteous!" said Toma.

"I'm stoked Bonnie got suspended," Chris said.

"Totally," Drea agreed.

"Like, trying to spray her with Nair?" said Michelle. "Smooth move, Ex-Lax!"

"Yeah, nice play, Shakespeare!" added Chris.

As the sun set over the ocean, we all walked to the Strand together, where we said our goodbyes. "I'm so amped for you,"

Chris beamed, "for standing up to those warped narbos." She gave me a hug before she got on her bike and headed home. Nick, Aisha, and Liam stayed and walked me back to my house. At the back gate to the garden, we paused awkwardly. Aisha glanced at me and Nick. She said she had to go, then Liam said he had to go, too. Aisha gave me a big hug. "I hope you find your mom soon."

"Thanks, I hope so."

She and Liam skated off down the street together.

"I . . . I think I want to go in alone, in case Jen's heard any bad news," I said to Nick.

"You sure?" Nick's tender eyes searched mine.

I smiled. "I'm okay," I said, though I was a mess, my insides churning. "Nick, there's something I haven't told you. I haven't told anyone."

"Huh?"

"Well, if they find her . . . my mom wants to take me back to New York this summer."

"What? For the summer?"

"For good," I said.

Nick's jaw dropped in surprise.

"I'm sorry I didn't tell you sooner. I just couldn't."

"Is that what you want?" he asked.

"No—no it's not. It's been my worst fear all year. I've been hiding what's been going on at school from my mom 'cause I didn't want to give her any reason to go back."

"Then stay." His eyes pleaded with me, shining with affection. He was so close to me. My heartbeat quickened.

"I can't," I said, mentally pushing aside the longing in my heart. "She said it's what my dad would've wanted for me, and I think she's right."

"It can't be," said Nick. "Your dad would've wanted you to

be happy. Surfing makes you happy."

"Yes," I said, my heart wrestling with my head. A wet tear rolled down my cheek. Nick stepped in towards me, held me in his arms, and kissed my cheek where the tear wet it. I nudged into him and our lips met. We stayed pressed against each other, my knees weak and my head woozy. I leaned into him. He tilted his head and kissed me more firmly. I opened my eyes. His eyes, shining like sea glass, took me in and caressed me as his gentle smile touched my core. Stunned, I stepped back and smiled, my heart melting.

"Dawn patrol?" he asked softly, his sweet eyes twinkling.

"Sure," I said.

"Okay, see you soon, then," he said and turned away to head home. Then he whipped back around. "But call me or come get me any time you need me, day or night. Sunshine or rain!"

"Okay!"

He almost walked into a tree when he turned back around, jumping back with exaggerated surprise and exclaiming, "Whoa—I didn't see that!" I giggled, watching him walk away.

I opened the garden gate with renewed energy, ready to face whatever news there was.

"They found Julia," said Jen as soon as I walked into the living room. "She's okay."

"Oh, thank God!" I let out a huge breath and slumped forward. "Where is she?" I rushed up to Jen, who was sitting upright on the edge of the sofa, her brow furrowed.

"Sit down, Ellie. There's more."

I fell back into the armchair.

"The good news is . . . you're going to be able to stay here with us this summer."

"Really? Mom said it's okay?"

"She doesn't have a choice," said Jen.

"She's staying? For real?"

"Your mom needs help. She's in a rehab facility. She's been on drugs, Ellie . . . strong ones."

"What?" I bolted upright, clenching the chair as my free hand flew over my mouth.

"I didn't know," she said in a quivering voice, trying not to cry. "I'm so sorry, I didn't know." She burst into tears.

"I didn't know, either," I said, springing up to sit next to her. I put my hand on her back and hugged her as she sobbed. I'd never seen her break down. She'd been the one who was solid and strong, the whole time I'd known her. She shook as she bawled her eyes out. Then she sniffled and squeezed me tight.

"I'm so glad you're staying here this summer," she said. "I never want you to leave."

"Me too," I said. Jen wiped the tears off her face. Her smile wasn't any less radiant with tears in her eyes. It was even more so.

"That guy," I said, "Mom's friend, the artist Mark . . . he died of an overdose."

"Oh my God. Oh my God! That could've been Julia!" Aunt Jen burst into tears again.

"But she's okay," I said.

"She's okay," she echoed.

I held her tight until she stopped crying. I patted her back, assuring her that Mom was okay.

Wiping her nose, she said, "She's my big sister. She took care of me when we were little. Grandma Ellie was always working. It was just us."

"How about we celebrate finding Mom?" I suggested. "We

could bake some brownies."

Jen smiled, choking back her tears. "I think that's an awesome idea."

Later, I learned that Charlie, Bob, and their policeman friends had found Mom in downtown L.A., east of skid row. She was in a dilapidated building with missing windows and no furniture—a drug house. People were squatting there, meaning they were living there illegally. They'd found Mom on a mattress on the floor, with a needle in her arm. She'd been high on heroin for days, almost to the point of being in a coma. They rushed her to the hospital. The doctors gave her fluids and said she was okay. She hadn't overdosed, so she wasn't in danger of dying. I learned that it happens all the time with heroin. People die. Like Mark.

When the police find drugs and paraphernalia on someone, they arrest them for possession. But since they were friends of my uncle and Bob, they'd given Mom the option of going into a rehabilitation facility. She took the rehab option. They brought her to Cri-Help in North Hollywood, where they held daily meetings for alcoholics and drug addicts and had grief counseling. She would be there for a month.

Two weeks later, I had to pee into a cup to be allowed to see my mom. Aunt Jen had to, too. They tested our urine to see if we were on drugs.

We were the only ones allowed to see her. The friends she'd made here either didn't show up or couldn't pass the pee test. That included everyone at the gallery. Mark's praises about Mom being "the darling of the art scene" rang through my brain. I couldn't believe no one visited her.

We walked through a metal detector doorway. I wore the

silver heart necklace Mom had given me for my birthday. I thought I'd have to take it off, but it didn't make the machine beep. Jen had to take her keys out of her bag and hand them to the guard.

Jen stayed in the hall while I went into the room first. Mom looked less pale than usual, but weak. Her bleached blonde hair had grown out, showing dark roots. She hugged me too tight, with what strength she had.

"Mom, are you okay?"

"I'm feeling better," she said. "How are you?"

"I'm okay. I brought you my Walkman so you can listen to music. It's in Jen's bag."

"Oh, you didn't have to do that! Thank you, my darling." She bit her lip. "Ellie, when I came to . . ." Her voice started to crack as she spoke, fighting to hold back sobs, gasping before each word. "The only thing I thought about was you." The sobbing overcame her.

"Mom . . ."

Just then, Jen walked into the room and put her arms around Mom. "It's okay, Julia," she said, comforting her.

"I'm so sorry Jen, I . . ." Mom started to curse, but changed her word. "I messed up. I really messed up. I'm so sorry."

"It's okay," Jen said. "Just say that to Ellie. She's the one who was depending on you. She's your child, even though she might not look or act like a kid."

"I know. I guess I deserve to be talked to like an idiot, because I have been one. I thought I was doing okay—as long as I got my shot, I could deal. I just needed it to get through the day, and then I thought I could run the gallery and do it all, and no one would know. I didn't think anyone would get hurt by it. But I have hurt you. My girl . . . I'm so sorry." Her eyes searched mine for a shred of forgiveness.

"It's okay, Mom," I said.

"But it's *not* okay! You deserve better. I had some conversations with your dad when I was going through withdrawal. I swear I saw him. It was more real than a vivid dream. He told me to let you stay in California . . . so you can surf."

I hugged Mom tightly and didn't let go, a gut reaction. Wet tears ran down my cheeks, my heart deeply touched at the thought that Dad's spirit had appeared to Mom on my behalf. Mom let out a big sigh and slumped into me. "I want you to be happy."

"Really?" I asked. "You're okay with me surfing?"

She nodded, her eyes brimming with tears.

I relaxed into her, hugging her, a wave of relief washing over me. Mom had looked down on me for surfing this whole time, but now she'd changed her mind. *Dad changed her mind!*

"Thanks, Mom," I sighed. "Thank you, oh, thank you!" I squeezed her again, and when I let her go, I beamed a big smile at her. Her eyes lit up, her eyebrows raised, but then she looked down.

"I'm sorry I'm a mess," Mom said.

"I'm sorry about Mark," I said.

She exhaled and swallowed. "When I found out . . . that pushed a button. First your father, then Peter, then Mark. It pushed me over the edge, it sent me into a tailspin." I reached for her hand and held it.

"Julia, we can do this together," said Jen, putting her hand on Mom's shoulder. "You, me, Charlie, and Ellie."

A nurse walked into the room to say that visiting time was over.

"Now, you just get better," Jen said with a warm smile. "And we'll see you soon."

She handed me my Walkman, and I gave it to Mom.

"There's a mixtape I made for you in the deck," I told her, getting up.

Then Mom actually smiled back at us. I couldn't remember the last time I'd seen her smile like that. Her smile lit up the room, just like her sister's did. She stood up to say goodbye, hugging us both.

I turned to walk out, but Mom called to me before I got to the door. "Ellie!"

I stopped and turned around.

"Ride some waves for me."

"I will!" I rushed back and hugged her again.

"I love you, Misiu," she said softly, squeezing me tight.

I was surprised. Mom had never called me that. It was nice to hear it spoken out loud after so long. Mom's hazel eyes were brimming with love for me—so much, that I felt Dad's love for me too.

"I love you too, Mom."

TWENTY-TWO

Your Star Shines Above Me

I awoke the next morning with the thought: *I'm staying here—it's real!*

I jumped out of bed and over Zuzu, who started wagging her tail in excitement. After petting her, I put on my wetsuit, grabbed my board, and headed down to the beach. The patch of blue widened as I ran, engulfing me. Blue-green lines on the horizon were moving towards me. *Corduroy!* My mind was already in it as I shot across the sand, soft and cool, pushing between my toes. I stopped at the water's edge. As I bent down to strap my leash onto my left ankle, cute snowy plovers and sanderlings nipped at the wet sand.

After paddling out, I sat up on my board and took it all in with a deep breath. Infinite ocean, waves incoming. The pelicans soared overhead, gracefully surfing the wind. I turned to face the small beach houses in rows. This was my home now, this little seaside town. The moon shone above, and the sun was rising.

Out of the corner of my eye I saw movement. Gray, wave-shaped fins among the waves. *The dolphins are here!* My heartbeat quickened as I watched a fin getting closer, heading straight for me. The dolphin surfaced and leapt into the air over me, as another one appeared in front of me. *They're celebrating that I can stay!* Another dolphin jumped high into the air and, with a jerking motion, shot its tail up, diving straight down and creating a big splash. Water sprayed, raining down on me.

"Woo-hoo!" I shouted. I communicated to the dolphins in my mind, thanking them for visiting me as they passed by, towards the lavender Santa Monica Mountains in the distance.

My eyes feasted on a wave that was forming, growing, rising up, and rushing towards me. I paddled towards the peak. At that hollow spot of glassy green, I joined with it, girl in the curl. Together we soared, flying down the line, my heart uplifted. I played in the open space in front of me. Carving across turquoise liquid hills, from bottom to top, crest to trough, again and again. The swell continuously rolled on, the effect of a thunderous storm from across the sea, finally reaching land. As it exploded into whitewash whirls, I kicked out, lay on my board, and paddled back out.

After surfing lots of waves, I was in the whitewash when Nick appeared. My heart beat so wildly I thought it would explode.

"Ellie—it *is* you!" he exclaimed with a big smile, his sea-glass eyes sparkling in the sun.

I beamed back at him. "Hi, Nick!" I let my board go, floating next to me. "Guess what?"

"What?" He tilted his head, leaning in closer.

"I'm staying here for good. In California!" I threw my arms up in the air and jumped.

Nick dropped his board in the water and, to my surprise, embraced me, planting an ardent kiss right on my lips. He was on fire. When my frozen lips met his, they began to melt. My wet body shook in his arms.

He pulled back to look at me with concern, strands of hair flying across his forehead in the breeze. His hair was still dry. "Sorry, I . . . was that okay?" He ducked his head, smiling sheepishly, a playful glint in his eye. "I don't know what happened, I just had to do that."

"It's okay," I said, beaming back at him. "I liked it."

"Yeah?" Before I knew it, he leaned in and kissed me again. This time I kissed him back, his soft lips warming mine. I clung to him, steadying myself in the surf. I pressed into him, my heart and body warmed by his, my soul on fire. All my longing and love for being in the wild ocean surf was met and responded to in Nick.

With a gust of fresh ocean air, a group of pelicans soared just above us.

"Woo-hoo! Radical!" Nick shouted up at them. I fell backwards into the oncoming foam, giggling as I surfaced. He bent down and reached a hand out to pull me up, but I pulled him down with me. He fell into the water next to me, and we both came up laughing.

"I'm going to get some more waves," I said, getting up and grabbing my board.

"I'm gonna get me some too. Woo-hoo!" Nick cheered.

I paddled out, Nick just behind me, and we split the next peak. He went right and I went left. *I'm never going to stop surfing! I'm staying here!*

That surf session—beginning with corduroy, and then dolphins, and then Nick—was the best way to celebrate my staying in California. It was pure magic.

Nick and I often went out for pizza together, or had root beer floats at the Kettle. Most of the time we went with Aisha, Liam, Danny, Toma, Chris, and her girlfriend, Trini. Sometimes Michelle and Drea joined us, or Dave and Mikey. Liam had a crush on Aisha, and she was finally beginning to like him back. Toma and Danny both seemed to like Chris. They didn't yet know she was gay, and that Trini was more than a friend. But it didn't really matter who liked who that way. The most important thing was that we were all good friends.

Since Mom was in rehab, we talked a lot over the phone. She said she was working through the Twelve Steps in Alcoholics Anonymous and Narcotics Anonymous, and that she was sorry for not being there for me when I needed her most. I told her it was okay, but she insisted she needed to apologize to me. She hoped I could forgive her. So, I told her I forgave her, but still she said she needed to make it up to me. She said she was doing grief counseling about Dad, and that I should do it, too. I told her I would, and so Aunt Jen arranged for me to meet with a therapist.

I confided in the therapist how much I missed Dad. About feeling alone and sad over the past year and a half. Then, about how happy I was to stay with my aunt and Charlie and friends, especially so I could keep surfing. It felt good to talk about stuff. I realized that it would be good for me to talk more with people I trusted. When I opened up about Mom to Aisha, she told me her oldest brother was in A.A., too.

Aunt Jen and I went to some Al-Anon meetings, for the family of alcoholics and drug users. It was surprising to see that so many people had the same issues in their families. I began to realize that how Mom was acting, and what she did, wasn't my fault. There was nothing I could do or could've done to help her. That was hard for Jen, too; she wanted to help her sister. But we learned that the best thing we could do was to let go and trust that Mom was helping herself.

That June, I was relieved when school finally let out. Though I wasn't scared of Bonnie's group anymore, I didn't want to have to run into them every day at school. Now it was summer vacation, and I could leave all of that behind me.

Nick, Toma, and Chris graduated high school. Thankfully, they all were going to stick around. Nick and Toma planned to attend El Camino, the local community college. Chris got a job waitressing at Good Stuff restaurant in Hermosa and continued surfing in competitions. Aisha got a summer job at Beach Books in downtown Manhattan. We planned on going on lots of surf trips together that summer, up and down the coast, from Big Sur to Baja.

Mom called from rehab to tell me that Wilkies had visited her and offered to go with her to A.A. meetings when she got out. She said she would.

"I'm so impressed that an old surfer who doesn't even *know* me would go out of his way to visit me," she said, her voice quavering. "So many people care about you here. You've made some good friends, Ellie."

"Thanks," I said. "They care about you, too."

"Ellie," she began with a quick sob and a sniffle, "you've grown up . . . in this past year, you've grown up. Your father would be so proud."

"Mom," I said. "I'll go to Chadwick or something next year if you really want me to."

"Really? Oh."

"It's just, I don't really want to 'cause I heard you have to get on the bus by seven in the morning to get up the hill on time, so I'd miss surfing when it's best, and—"

"Listen," Mom interrupted. "How about we apply to some good universities instead. That's what your dad wanted most for you."

"That sounds great, Mom. I think I'd like to go to school for writing. Like Peter did."

"Oh, that would be . . ." Mom choked up again. "That would be so great. Your father would be so proud."

That summer, I finally got to watch Chris compete in a surfing competition, and she won! Aisha, Nick, Toma, Liam, Danny, Michelle, Drea, and I rushed down to meet her at the water's edge after her heat. We were all jumping up and down, surrounding her, cheering. She did so well, and she got so many good waves! Aunt Jen put a flower lei around her neck that she'd made for her. Chris won a trophy that day. We celebrated back at the house with bean and cheese burritos that Charlie brought.

Though I was happy for Chris, I decided that I never wanted to do a surfing competition. It just wasn't what surfing was about to me. I didn't want to mess up the most enjoyable thing in the world. Surfing was sacred, and I wanted to keep it that way.

That night, I went back down to the beach alone for a surf at dusk. A star shone brightly, high up above. A streak of pink cloud looked like a brush stroke across the darkening sky. During intervals between sets, I sat gazing out at the horizon until there was no distinction between sky and sea. It all became cobalt, and then darkened to midnight blue. The moon shone bright.

Walking back up to the cottage, I looked up at the bright, twinkling stars beaming at me, my heart open. As one star sparkled, I felt Dad's love for me. It was so much love, it was overwhelming, too much to take in. I smiled through happy tears, and my soul answered: *It's me, Misiu. Everything's going to be okay, Misiek. I love you more than the moon.*

One with the Waves

A PLAYLIST

1. The Beach Boys, "The Girl from New York City"
2. U2, "New Year's Day"
3. The Clash, "Ghetto Defendant"
4. Elvis Costello, "Alison"
5. X, "Some Other Time"
6. Blondie, "Dreaming"
7. The Mamas and the Papas, "California Dreamin'"
8. The Beach Boys, "Surfer Girl"
9. The Police, "Every Breath You Take"
10. David Bowie, "Let's Dance"
11. Eurythmics, "Sweet Dreams (Are Made of This)"
12. Grand Master Flash & the Furious Five, "The Message"
13. Dick Dale & His Del-Tones, "Misirlou"
14. The Beach Boys, "Surfin' U.S.A."
15. Jan & Dean, "Surf City"
16. The Surfaris, "Wipe Out"
17. The Beach Boys, "Surfin' Safari"
18. A Flock of Seagulls, "Wishing (If I Had a Photograph of You)"
19. The Descendents, "Marriage"
20. The Plugz, "El Clavo Y La Cruz"
21. Modern English, "I Melt with You"
22. Bad Brains, "Attitude"
23. Bob Marley, "Three Little Birds"
24. Wall of Voodoo, "Mexican Radio"
25. Madness, "It Must Be Love"
26. The Replacements, "Within Your Reach"

27. *Diva* Soundtrack; Cynthia Hawkins, "Aria from *La Wally*"
28. Elvis Costello, "Good Year for the Roses"
29. X, "Come Back to Me"
30. Suicidal Tendencies, "Institutionalized"
31. The Minutemen, *What Makes A Man Start Fires?* Entire side two: "Sell or Be Sold," "The Only Minority," "Split Red," "Colors," "Plight," "The Tin Roof," "Life as a Rehearsal," "This Road," and "Polarity"
32. The Descendents, "Tonyage"
33. Black Flag, "Nervous Breakdown"
34. Nena, "99 Luftballons"

ACKNOWLEDGMENTS

Thank you to Jeffrey Goldman at Santa Monica Press for believing in this book. To my son, Jack, thank you for believing in me. To my husband, Toby, thank you for patiently putting up with me throughout the many years I worked on this book, and for sharing memories of your awesome surfer dad, Charlie.

Thank you to my grandmothers for being brilliant, creative, radical thinkers: Olenka, for encouraging me to write from my heart and teaching me about Anton Chekov, and Grandma Ellie, for showing me how everything we do can be an art form.

Thank you to my father, Janusz, for being the first to see the writer in me, and to my mother, Laura, for cultivating an appreciation for music, art, and literature in our home.

I'm grateful to my brother, Lukasz, for always being there for me, and I can't thank my entire family enough, especially: my aunt Karin, Jessica, Tatiana, Toni, Uncle Dan, and Denise. My brilliant friend, Saskia Jell—I'm grateful for your writing feedback and insights.

Thank you to my editor, Kate Murray, for fine-tuning the book to become its strongest version. Thank you to Barbara Jones for your guidance, and Lesley Wells for editing my first draft and teaching me so much in the process.

For reading early drafts of my manuscript and giving me helpful notes, thank you to: Pat Bailey, Regina Don, Amy Gorbey, Mary Holden, Sarah Weissman, Sophia Wesolik, and the wonderful women of my book club, Rikki Balk, Erin Cassaday, Michelle Cimmarusti, Laura Jordan, Valerie Minor Johnson, Dani McMillon, Jennefer Moseley, Paige Parker, and Chelsea Rothert.

Thank you to my friends and mentors for your support

and encouragement: Patty Brown, Maureen Chianese, Chris Davidson, Denise and Susie Donahoe, Elizabeth Freund, Raghubir Kintisch, and Melainie Mansfield.

Thank you for contributing to my research: Liz and Mike Benavidez, Wendy Irwin Barrett-Gilley, Ben Horton, Don Kadowaki, Liz Lopresti, Miles Ono, Ken Saylor, and Pam Sousa.

Tony Gold, thank you for your totally awesome title design.

Thank you Jan Tyniec and Christyne Forti, for your help with Polish translations, and Victor Diaz, for your help with Spanish.

To everyone at ET Surf, the 26th Street Ohana, my fellow pier rats, surf buddies, and the South Bay surfing community, a big thank you for continually inspiring me in and out of the water.

Mother Ocean and the dolphins, thank you for calling out to me when I needed you most. It's an honor to play in the surf with you.